BLOOD, SWEAT & TEARS

A POSTAPOCALYPTIC NOVEL

BOOK 5

THE NEW WORLD SERIES

G. MICHAEL HOPF

Copyright © 2015 G. Michael Hopf
No part of this book may be reproduced in any manner whatsoever without permission except in the case of brief quotations embodied in critical articles or reviews.
For information contact:
geoff@gmichaelhopf.com
www.gmichaelhopf.com
All rights reserved.
ISBN: 10: 1515357562
ISBN-13: 978-1515357568

DEDICATION

TO ALL THE VETERANS WHO HAVE SERVED THIS
GREAT REPUBLIC OF OURS
'ALL GAVE SOME, SOME GAVE ALL'

"I would say to the House as I said to those who have joined this government: **I have nothing to offer but blood, toil, tears and sweat**. We have before us an ordeal of the most grievous kind. We have before us many, many long months of struggle and of suffering.."

- Winston Churchill

PROLOGUE

October 19, 2066

McCall, Idaho, Republic of Cascadia

Haley looked over the rolling fields with pockets of towering aspen trees towards Jughandle Mountain, its granite cap white with fresh snow. She loved the long vistas and majestic scenery the house provided. It had been years since she had sat on the gray weathered deck and appreciated it, but more notably it had been many more years since she had sat there with her father. Haley's unexpected arrival at the old Van Zandt cabin in McCall shocked her sons, Hunter and Sebastian, but for Gordon it was the most pleasant of surprises but not entirely unexpected.

After Sebastian's arrival weeks ago, then Hunter's earlier that morning, he suspected that Haley wouldn't be too far behind. She was an astute woman who didn't let many things get by her. This made him proud, as he had instilled that skill at an early age, and apparently it stuck.

Haley and Gordon shared laughs and tears as she detailed her life by filling in the blanks since the last time they had seen each other.

Gordon withheld the fact that he knew all the information she divulged through loyal contacts within the government.

Hunter and Sebastian sat in the comfort and

protection of the house, watching their mother and grandfather reconnect.

"It has been one crazy day," Hunter exclaimed, his reflection prominent in the massive window that overlooked the back deck where Haley and Gordon sat, hands embraced.

The combination of laughter and sobbing came and went like the tide ebbed and flowed. Years had separated them, but Hunter could see the deep father-daughter bond they had just by their interaction.

Haley kept petting Gordon on the head and hadn't let go of his ever-shaking hand since she had sat down by his side over an hour before.

"I'm getting hungry and Granddad doesn't have anything good to eat here," Sebastian commented, his eyes scanning the limited variety of food that sat on the shelves in the pantry. "It's like he's still *surviving*. Let's see here, there's tuna, oh, and tuna and, wait a minute, we have tuna in oil," Sebastian said, now holding up a can.

"Oh, what will you do?" Hunter mockingly said.

"Listen, I've been here for over a week, but I keep thinking I'll find a gem in this dusty old pantry," Sebastian lamented and closed the door. "Let's run into town. The restaurant at the Hotel McCall is great."

Hunter couldn't stop watching the two outside. In fact, watching wasn't the word for it, he was studying them. It was like he was in a dream, like he had been transported to a place where only miracles happen.

"Brother, you do realize how special this is, don't you?" Hunter asked.

Sebastian, defeated by his inability to find anything to eat, exited the kitchen and walked up to his brother. "I do; hence why I called you."

"Seeing Granddad is amazing. It's like getting a chance to meet George Washington."

"But without the bad teeth," Sebastian joked.

"Is everything a joke to you?"

"I've been here for a bit, not that I don't feel the moment, believe me I do, it's just that I'm starving, and you know how I get when I don't eat."

"Here they come," Hunter said, excited when he saw Haley and Gordon rise and head towards the sliding glass door. He raced over and slid it open. A crisp breeze swept in and reminded him the mountains were much colder than his new home in central Texas.

"Your grandfather needs to eat," Haley said, escorting Gordon inside.

"That's what I'm talking about!" Sebastian cheerfully shouted.

"Sure, what can I get started?" Hunter asked, eager to help.

Inside, Haley closed the door and asked Gordon, "What do you want, Dad?"

"A steak, medium rare," Gordon replied.

"Steaks? You don't have steaks. Trust me, I'd know, I've dug through that chest freezer in the garage," Sebastian declared.

Gordon held up his index finger and said, "Give me a minute. Why don't you all go sit down while I prepare dinner."

"No, Dad, we can do it. You look tired. Maybe you should get some rest," Haley insisted, not letting go of his arm.

Gordon looked into her light eyes and with a reassuring tone said, "I'm fine. Now go sit down and relax."

"Should I fire up a grill or something?" Hunter asked.

"Just sit down, get yourself a drink," Gordon said. Walking towards his office, he paused and turned. "In the closet below the stairs you'll find an old wooden crate. I hope you like scotch," he said and continued towards his office, disappearing in the shadows.

"Mom, I can't, um, this is just too much."

"You're still angry with me?" Haley asked.

Hunter approached her and said, "No, I'm just in awe. How is this even possible?"

"Things are possible if you make sure they are," Haley replied.

"What does that even mean?" Hunter asked.

"Don't you know anything?" Sebastian asked Hunter.

"How do you keep something like this quiet?" Hunter asked, his eyes wide with anticipation for an answer that would satiate his curiosity.

Haley stepped up to Hunter and caressed his stubbled face. "Make sure you know who your friends are is the first thing."

"And?"

"And I'm thirsty, how about finding that scotch?"

Haley said as she walked around Hunter towards the great room to find a comfortable seat.

"On it, Mom," Sebastian said, making his way to the closet.

Hunter followed Haley and sat next to her on the couch. "I can't stop saying it, but it's amazing."

"And sad," Haley softly said.

Hunter looked at her face; he could see the strain. "What's wrong?"

She took his hand and squeezed it.

"Holy shit, this scotch is over ninety years old," Sebastian squealed with excitement, holding up a bottle of Macallan thirty-year-old scotch that had been bottled in 2014.

Appearing from the dark hallway, Gordon laughed. "That's the last bottle from my old buddy Jimmy. He gave me three. I gave one to Colonel Barone, I opened one the day I was inaugurated, and that one there shall be opened today to celebrate family coming together."

Sebastian happily walked over and sat the bottle on the table with four glasses.

Gordon shuffled over and sat down. He melted into the couch and sighed.

"Everything all right?" Haley asked.

"Life couldn't be better, I just wish your mother was here is all," Gordon lamented.

"Me too," Haley replied.

"Here you go," Sebastian said, handing each one a glass of scotch.

"What should we toast to?" Hunter asked.

"Family," Gordon answered and held his glass high.

In unison the others said, "To family."

They tapped their glasses and all took a sip.

"When can we get the steaks fired up?" Sebastian asked, his stomach tightening from hunger.

"Soon," Gordon said as he swirled his glass, admiring the scotch with its rich caramel color.

"I'm sorry, but I want you to continue telling us what happened. How did you eventually become president?" Hunter asked, sitting on the edge of his seat while the others were sitting fully back, relaxed and enjoying the soft cradle of the couch.

Gordon looked at his watch and said, "We have a little time. Um, where did I leave off?"

"The Battle of Rainbow Bridge," Hunter blurted out.

"Yeah, that's right. We had just defeated Major Schmidt," Gordon replied, then looked down at his glass. His hand shook as he lifted it to his lips and took another sip. "I brought Sebastian's body home and we buried him right out back that day. He was the first Van Zandt to go in the ground back there."

"I still miss him," Haley quietly said.

"Me too," Gordon said. His blue eyes were still as radiant as when he was in his prime, but when Haley looked into them, she could see the pain. He had seen so much death and tragedy. From his early years he had known loss. In that room sat the only remaining blood relatives he had. The name was gone, but his blood flowed through the boys' veins.

Gordon shook his somber feeling and said, "So, yes,

the Battle of Rainbow Bridge. Well, not much happened after that. Like most wars, there are battles then days or weeks where nothing happens. It was the same for us. We were fortunate by spring boarding from that victory into smaller ones; we also had early success at recruitment. Gunny was able to track down Master Sergeant Simpson and convince him to head our way. At first he was reluctant to join our cause, but after what Colonel Barone had put them through, he thought it best to ask his Marines what they wanted. Overwhelmingly they voted to join Cascadia."

"How? How did Gunny convince him?" Hunter asked, interrupting Gordon.

"Simple, everyone needs a place to call home," Gordon replied.

"Makes sense," Hunter said.

"With Top's Marines and many local recruits, we had a decent-sized army. Most, and I mean most, I'd guess seventy-five percent of the recruits were just average joes with no experience, training or military knowledge. We acted fast after our victory. I knew I couldn't sit around and let the people get lazy or complacent. With no help from Chenoweth, me and a few others worked quickly to train and outfit our new army."

"Chenoweth, Chenoweth, that name sounds familiar. Who was he?" Hunter asked.

"I'd rather not talk about him," Gordon answered.

Haley grumbled something unintelligible.

"What? Who was he?" Hunter asked, leaning further over the massive coffee table in anticipation of hearing something that few others had ever known.

"He was a—" Haley spat, but Gordon cut her off.

"Haley, honey, don't get your blood pressure up," Gordon said.

"Wait, you have to tell me," Hunter urged.

"You'll soon find out who Mr. Chenoweth was," Gordon said.

"I'll wait, then, but you've definitely piqued my curiosity. So tell me, how did the attack go on Mountain Home?" Hunter asked.

Gordon looked over at Sebastian, who was slowly sipping his scotch. He wasn't ignoring Hunter, he just was curious why the two boys were polar opposites. "You really don't talk much, do you?"

Surprised that Gordon asked him a question, he sat up straight and replied, "Nah, I kinda lay low unless there's something really important."

"You don't think any of this is important?" Gordon asked him.

"I'm not saying that, I'm enjoying knowing how it all started. I just don't batter people with endless questions like someone I know," Sebastian said, giving a jab at Hunter.

"He's just lazy, that's all," Hunter fired back.

"Well, at least I don't work for—"

"Not again," Hunter snapped, interrupting Sebastian.

"Boys, enough, you both need to learn how important family is and realize that the only person you can really trust is sitting across from you," Gordon lectured.

"He just infuriates me," Hunter said.

"Don't let petty issues get in the way of the big picture. You two need one another," Gordon said.

"Sorry," Sebastian said.

Gordon looked at Hunter and waited for his response.

Hunter nervously looked at Gordon then turned his gaze to Sebastian. "Sorry."

"Good. Let me continue. We had just defeated Schmidt and had spent the next eight weeks training recruits for our new army. We had small skirmishes against US troops here and there, primarily old Idaho National Guard units sent up, but no major engagements until Mountain Home. I knew the only way to win the war was to go on the offensive. We had an advantage, but we couldn't allow Conner to field another force, so I needed to strike at a major installation."

Hunter couldn't control himself; he had another question nagging. "Why there and not go for Fort Lewis, it's close to Olympia?"

"We sent some forces into Washington but they had gotten as far as Yakima. I believed the best way to win the war quickly was to defeat Conner on his turf and take Cheyenne and Mountain Home was on the way to Cheyenne. If we could march on his capital, we could then sue for peace and end it quickly. So against Charles's wishes, I moved my army south. I also had the weather to consider and didn't want to get stuck in the valley during winter."

"But you still risked a lot moving them towards

Cheyenne with winter approaching," Hunter interjected.

"That may be, but at the time I needed a major victory, one to show Conner, Olympia and the people that we could win and win big. You see, Hunter, not all missions are conducted solely for strategic military reasons but also for politics and morale. Taking Mountain Home would accomplish all of our objectives; one was to remove any doubt that our early victories were an anomaly. I also had hopes that if we won at Mountain Home, Conner might just want to talk. Of course, that was proven wrong." Gordon paused and took a sip of scotch.

"Tell them why, Dad," Haley requested.

Hunter looked at Haley then to Gordon.

Even Sebastian perked up after Haley spoke.

Gordon shook his head, clearly frustrated.

"I don't see why you're still mad about it. We all know the eventual outcome," Haley said.

"I was just a fool. I let my anger control me too much when I was younger," Gordon said. He looked up and fixed his gaze on Hunter. "Don't let that Van Zandt anger control you. Channel it, control it; don't let it control you."

Hunter nodded.

Sebastian also nodded, knowing that he had some of that quick temper in him too.

"What happened?" Hunter asked, too impatient to allow Gordon an extended pause.

Gordon leaned back and looked at the large painting that hung above the mantel. He could still hear Samantha convincing him that it belonged there instead of the musket or deer head he had wanted. He eventually relented and allowed her to do what she wanted. Life was too short, he thought then, to quibble. If letting her favorite artist hang in a prominent spot gave her happiness, how could he deny that? He now reflected on that decision and was happy he had agreed with her. Seeing it, like other things, reminded him of her and how wonderful she was. He wished his temperament outside the home could have been similar, but it wasn't and it got him in trouble a few times.

"Dad?" Haley asked, touching Gordon on the knee.

Jerked back to the present, Gordon apologized, "Sorry, I drifted away there. That painting there was your grandmother's favorite."

"It looks out of place," Sebastian said, looking at the painting. "Who is it?"

"Anastasia, a czarina of Russia, it's painted in the iconic style often found in Orthodox churches," Gordon explained.

"Now it makes sense," Sebastian said as he cocked his head, admiring the painting more now that he had a tidbit of information on it.

"It's an original, by the way. Cost me a few bucks back in the day," Gordon said.

"Worthless now," Hunter said.

"On the contrary, it's priceless to me and I'm sure someone would pay top money for that now. Smirnov was an acclaimed artist of the late twentieth century," Gordon said, defending the art.

"Anyway, please continue with what happened at Mountain Home," Hunter pressed.

"Before I do, I want to stress the importance of not allowing your emotions to run your lives. People will redefine it to make it sound sexy by calling it passion, and let me tell you, too much passion can get you in a heap of trouble. I'm not saying you can't have fun or be adventurous, I'm just saying to use all your faculties, one being your mind. Let your heart speak, but give your head equal footing."

"Think before you leap, so to speak," Sebastian said.

"Exactly, but train your mind to do it quickly, it's important. Take, for instance, when your grandmother and I debated having that painting there. I really wanted to put a stuffed head up there or an antique musket. You see, I wanted this old house to feel like a cabin in the mountains, but for my Sam, she always envisioned that painting there, that along with the other items like the stain color, drapes, rugs, etcetera; that was her vision not mine. She had always wanted a mountain home to look a bit more *mountain chic,* as she called it. I say we debated it, but we really argued. I looked at the mantel as my last refuge to win, but I relented, and now I'm glad I did. I look around this place and everywhere I turn I see her. I could have put my foot down, got angry and let my pride and desire to win take over, but I didn't. I can't express enough how happy I am that I thought before I went stupid and blathered nonsense. If only I had that wisdom at other times."

Both Hunter and Sebastian nodded as they intently

listened.

A smile broke out on Haley's face and grew wider the more Gordon mentioned Samantha, her mother.

Gordon lifted the glass and tossed the rest of the scotch back. He leaned forward, placed the glass on the table, and stretched. "The morning was cold that day. It was the first frost, actually. Over a period of three weeks we had sent people into Mountain Home, pretending to be refugees. The plan was to have people on the inside to get a little rebellion going with the civilians camped there. I just never expected to find what we found. It was horrible; the FEMA camps could be better described as death camps. The neglect and utter disregard for the people surviving there was astonishing. How it's portrayed in the history books is quite different than what really happened that day."

"Like what?"

"It was a great victory, but it wasn't a glorious battle. The US forces that were there were haggard and their morale was low. Anyway, our people on the inside did exactly as we had planned and started a revolt in the camps; this was the perfect distraction. With everyone focused on the riots, we advanced on the base," Gordon said and paused. His hands shook as he rubbed his eyes and forehead. He turned his head and looked outside.

Hunter looked at Haley then to Sebastian, who shrugged, indicating he wasn't sure what was wrong with Gordon.

After an awkward pause, Gordon continued, "I can still see the children, those poor children." He reached out and grabbed the bottle of scotch and poured. With a quivering hand he lifted it and gulped. After wiping his mouth, he said, "I was already angry over what had happened to Sebastian, but it was seeing those poor children gunned down that sent me over the edge, and when I say over the edge, I went head first."

OCTOBER 28, 2015

"You will not be punished for your anger, you will be punished by your anger." – Buddha

Mountain Home Air Force Base, Idaho

A welcome cool wind swept over Gordon, chilling him slightly but providing a respite from the heat his body was giving off. Sweat mixed with blood streamed down his face and soaked the top of his shirt. The blood was not his but those who had fallen at his hands. Around him the last vestiges of the opposing forces were being cleaned up and finished off with the exception of the command element. With nowhere to go and reeling from the surprise attack by Gordon and his Cascadian army, they found refuge in the two-story headquarters building.

The building bore the scars of the battle. Many of its windows were shattered and the concrete exterior walls were riddled with bullet holes. A small fire had started on the far right end of the second story; its smoke poured out and rose into the gray skies.

Gordon knew this fire would spread and soon he'd be face to face with his enemy. Just thinking or saying that word still seemed odd to him. It wasn't that long ago he'd considered these people fellow countrymen, but with Sebastian's murder at the hands of Conner, he had lost all connection.

Even though his army of thirty-five hundred was

formidable, it was always tough for any army to attack a fortified position and be successful. With this knowledge, he'd decided to create a ruse, a distraction that would throw the forces on the inside off guard. Over the past few weeks he had sent over a hundred of his people into the base, camouflaged as refugees seeking shelter.

Mountain Home had been designated by the federal government and the state of Idaho as a refugee center. Using what one commodity it had, protected land, it opened its gates to all that came seeking shelter and safety. What many didn't know was after several months the camps transformed from safe havens to collections of humanity all trying to survive with what few resources the base had. The only hope for those there was the monthly shipment of MREs and medicine that would flow in from Cheyenne. With limited supplies, corruption was rampant, as a few opportunists took advantage and thrived under the blind eye of the military.

At first the reports Gordon received sickened him, but he saw an opportunity. Under any tyranny there were always those who resisted. He directed his people to find them, connect and begin the stages of the ruse that would be the prelude to his full-scale attack.

Like a well-oiled machine, the plan worked. The revolt in the camps took off like a flame to gasoline. Soon the thousands of starving refugees rioted and overwhelmed the few guards who had the unfortunate responsibility of being on watch. Within an hour the riot turned to an all-out revolt and spread across the base.

When Gordon and the main force arrived, they

found the gates unguarded. They moved in to find a situation that was chaotic and bloody.

Fearing for their lives, those military units that had once sworn to protect Americans turned on them. With ferocity and ruthlessness, Gordon watched as dozens of children were gunned down. These weren't victims of collateral damage, they were targeted and murdered. Their pleas for mercy fell on deaf ears as he heard the commanders order the troops to shoot them.

A deep-seated anger resided in Gordon, one that went back to his treatment at the hands of an over-politicized military after his altercation in Iraq. Seeing these defenseless children slaughtered was too much, and if they were not shown quarter or mercy, he would show the same disregard to those he was fighting.

Gordon wiped his brow with his hand and smeared the bloody sweat on his trousers. His AR-15 hung from a two-point sling in front of him. A thick tactical vest protected his vitals, and holstered on the front of that was a Sig Sauer P220, a .45-caliber semiautomatic pistol. Also clinging to his vest were several HE hand grenades, two smoke grenades and three magazine pouches containing thirty-round magazines for his AR-15. He saw the smoke from the second-story fire growing, and now visible flames could be seen licking the exterior of the building through the gaping windows.

"Should we storm the building?" a voice boomed from behind Gordon.

"No, they'll come to us," Gordon replied.

The man who asked the question stepped next to

Gordon and turned. "If you say so."

Gordon didn't return the look; his eyes were fixed on the building and the ever-growing fire.

"We kicked ass today," the man said.

Not wanting to chitchat, Gordon ordered, "John, radio the company commanders. Instruct them to gather the refugees up and calm them down. It's time we show them we're the good guys."

"Roger that," John replied. "Um, what about the agitators and camp thugs?"

Finally breaking his gaze, he looked into John's brown eyes and flatly said, "Kill them."

"Roger that," John said and walked away. John Steele was Gordon's executive officer and over the past two months had grown to become a trusted friend. John was a native of Idaho but left shortly after high school. He was highly intelligent with an intense intellectual curiosity and drive to succeed. The combination of these characteristics led him to become the founder and managing partner of one of the largest contract law firms in San Francisco. He was married and had a young son named William, but everyone called him Bill. Like everyone else, John's story included tragedy. His wife had been murdered and his journey back to Idaho was filled with similar altercations and harrowing tales of survival all known too well by many who had lived on the roads following the initial super-EMP attack.

Gordon found him capable, smart and only willing to give advice when his advice could be used. Just after meeting John following the Battle of Rainbow Bridge,

Gordon felt like he'd known him for longer. There was a bond or connection the two had that Gordon couldn't quite explain but knew he couldn't ignore. With Nelson in McCall, Michael in Olympia and Gunny Smith moving with the smaller towards western Washington, having someone he could trust was important.

Another familiar face came up behind Gordon. "Sir, I've got a call from Chairman Chenoweth."

Charles Chenoweth had gone from being the leader of the western Cascadian movement to the chairman of an elected committee that would oversee the formation of a formal government for the republic. In a nutshell, he was the political leader of Cascadia while Gordon was the military leader. The committee was comprised of twelve members, with Charles being the thirteenth, so his vote would ensure no vote ended in a tie.

Michael Rutledge, Gordon's friend from McCall, was a member of the committee and had moved his family to Olympia after his election.

"Jones, tell the esteemed Mr. Chenoweth now is not a good time," Gordon barked. His tone and response told everyone within earshot that Gordon and Charles no longer got along nor pretended to. Shortly after Gordon's successful victory at Rainbow Bridge and subsequent speech upon the tank, Charles had begun working against Gordon. This information found its way to Gordon, who didn't take it well.

Charles was envious of Gordon's quick rise and influence, and let it be known to whomever would listen that he didn't want someone like Gordon having any say over how their country was formed.

Fortunately for Gordon, actions spoke louder than hateful words and his military successes bred confidence in the newly elected committee, and with victory essential, they voted Gordon to be the supreme military commander for Cascadia, a position he happily accepted.

"Sir, he says it's urgent," Jones said, holding out the satellite phone.

"It's always urgent with him; tell him I'm fighting a war for them and that I'll call back later."

"Sir, he says he needs you," Jones pressed.

Gordon cocked his head and looked at Jones. He smiled and said, "Tell him to go back to his committee meetings and spreadsheets; I'll be in touch soon."

Screams and yelling from the building rang out.

"Looks like we'll get to meet the hosts of the party soon."

"Sir, he says—"

Gordon grabbed the phone and quickly said, "Charles, I'll call you back soon, bye." He clicked the red button and hung up on Charles. Gordon handed the phone back to Jones.

Jones took it and pocketed the phone. He wasn't too surprised by Gordon's behavior, but he could tell Charles was clearly upset.

Gordon stepped towards the building and hollered, "Whoever is in the building, you have three choices: burn alive, come out guns blazing and die, or surrender. It's up to you, I personally don't care!"

More screams echoed from the building. The smoke

and flames had grown and now covered two-thirds of the second story. Thick black smoke billowed out of all the open windows, trailed by long bright orange flames.

"Once again, you have three choices! What will it be?" Gordon yelled.

The front doors opened slowly.

A line of armed men in front of Gordon took aim.

A hand appeared waving a white cloth.

"Good, they're surrendering," Jones said.

"Hmm," Gordon grunted as he stepped up behind his men and waited to see who came out.

One by one uniformed people came out, their arms high above their heads.

"Go gather them up, process them, and bring me the commanding officer," Gordon ordered.

Jones watched Gordon and saw a distinct difference in the man he had met months ago in Oregon. He was harder, more distant.

A squad of men ran up to those surrendering and began the rigorous process of separation and prisoner processing.

Gordon watched intently but soon found it boring. He turned his attention towards the activity all around and beyond where he was. The base was alive with activity. Chattering, cries, moans, screams and cheering were coming from all corners. He had won, but he wasn't proud. The victory was great and would show Conner and those leaders in Cheyenne that Cascadia was a force to reckon with. The goal was to show such force that Conner would want to talk and end the war, but something ached in him. There was something about being back in combat that he missed. He couldn't quite pinpoint it, but in some deep dark crevice he didn't want it to end just yet. He wanted revenge, and if they won their freedom and peace came, he would feel cheated.

"Gordon, Gordon, we have the commanding officer over here!" one of his men called out.

Gordon didn't give himself a rank or title. He was beyond that, he was just a man fighting for his family like all the others. He didn't look at himself as a general or officer. He was their leader, but he was just Gordon.

He turned and marched towards the disheveled uniformed man kneeling on the ground. Gordon stopped just inches from him and towered over the man.

A trickle of blood came from the man's nostril and dripped down his upper lip. Soot and fresh abrasions covered his face.

"Look at me," Gordon ordered calmly.

The man lifted his head, meeting Gordon's hard stare.

"Who are you?" Gordon asked.

"Who are you? This is a government facility, a refugee camp. You've attacked a sanctuary, you savage!" the man spat.

"Who are you?" Gordon again asked.

"I'm General Warren, United States Air Force. Who are you?"

"Who's your second in command?"

"I am," a man blurted out several feet away.

"Good, you're going to travel back to Cheyenne and

deliver a message for us," Gordon said.

"Cheyenne already knows about this heinous attack. They're sending reinforcements," Warren snapped.

"No, they aren't. We've been monitoring your communications. I know you've contacted them, but I know they're not sending anyone just yet."

Warren's face turned ashen when confronted with the fact that Gordon knew what was happening.

Gordon stepped over to the other man and said, "We're going to give you a vehicle. Drive as fast as you can and give President Conner this message," Gordon said, handing the man an envelope. "Tell him that we can end all of this now. Tell him that we can meet in a neutral place and sort this out."

The man took the envelope, pocketed it and stood up. "Who do I say it's from?"

Gordon ignored his question and walked back to Warren. He looked down at him and asked, "Did you order those civilians be shot down? Did you? Were you the one who did that?"

"No, absolutely not!" Warren blasted.

Gordon was tired and didn't want to play games. He pulled his Sig and placed it against the head of the man who was directly to the right of Warren. "Tell me or he dies."

"No!"

Gordon looked at the man he held the gun to and asked, "Do you want to die?"

The man's eyes were full of fear. He mumbled, "No."

"Did General Warren order civilians be gunned down? Did he order the slaughter of those children? I saw it with my own eyes right over there!" Gordon bellowed and pointed in the direction he'd seen the gruesome incident occur.

The man looked out of the corner of his eyes; he was terrified and didn't know what to do.

"I'm going to count to three. One, two…"

"Yes, he did. He ordered that the riot be suppressed; he ordered that they kill them all. Those were his words!" the man cried out.

"I did not!" Warren huffed.

Gordon turned his pistol on another man. "One, two…"

"Yes, he did!" that man declared.

"Lies!" Warren yelled.

Gordon holstered his pistol and said, "Also tell Conner that we don't play games, and if he's thinking about fighting a bitter and bloody war, that we will resist. We will fight like him, we won't give quarter, and we won't show mercy. We will conduct this war like his Major Schmidt conducted himself as he plowed through one town after another. Tell him that in Cascadia we serve justice to butchers no matter their rank," Gordon said. He looked down at Warren, squinted and in the next second punched him squarely in the face.

Warren reeled backwards from the punch and fell hard onto his back.

Gordon jumped on him and began to level one punch after another. With each punch his anger grew.

"You like to have little children killed, huh?" he barked as he laid a succession of closed-fist punches to Warren's face.

Jones watched Gordon's fierce attack and was in awe.

Gordon stopped punching. He flexed his fist and was concerned he might break it. Not yet finished with his brand of justice, he removed his pistol, grabbed it by the barrel and continued beating Warren. This time the butt of the pistol grip was smashing into his face. After a half-dozen blows, the sounds of bones crunching could be heard. Gordon stopped, looked at Warren's unrecognizable face, and determined he was dead. Just before getting up, Gordon spit in his face. He stood up, took a deep breath and said, "You tell Conner what happened here, and if he doesn't want peace, we'll come to Cheyenne and we'll take it just like we took Mountain Home."

"Yes, sir. Can I tell him who you are?" the young officer asked.

"Yeah, tell him Gordon Van Zandt sent you," Gordon replied. He turned to one of his men and ordered, "Get this man a vehicle."

"What about the others?" another man asked.

"First things first, take Warren's body, strip it naked and post it at the entrance to the base with a sign tied around his neck that says 'Child Killer'."

"You're horrible!" an officer yelled.

Gordon pulled a rag from his pocket and started wiping the fresh blood from his aching hands. "Kill them, kill them all."

"What? No. That's not us," Jones interrupted upon hearing Gordon's order.

"You have a problem with taking out the trash, Jones?" Gordon asked.

"I don't have a problem killing, but this is murder. They've surrendered to us. There are rules."

"Not anymore."

"Gordon, you're angry after what they did to your brother. This isn't right."

Gordon rubbed the blood from his knuckles onto his shirt and breathed deeply. Battering Warren had winded him. "You're right, I'm angry at what they did to my brother. I don't know what happened to my sister-in-law, she's missing, could be dead for all I know. Then we come here and what do I see, them essentially executing little kids. These people here are animals, but you're telling me I shouldn't just take them out because we're better than they are. What's up with this insane moral equivalence? We're not the same, we don't murder little children. We don't just execute people for no reason."

"Not true, you're about to kill them just like Major Schmidt killed your brother," Jones reminded him.

Gordon grunted and replied, "Would you like it if I had a trial? If we found them guilty, could I then kill them?"

Jones thought for a moment and decided that was the best compromise. "Yes, that would work."

"Well, when we have time and the resources to spare, we'll do that for the next group, but not these guys.

They allowed the people in those camps over there to suffer at the hands of thugs, and they did nothing when their commander ordered little kids shot down. They're just as guilty as if they did it. They turned away fully knowing what was happening and chose to do zero, squat. I know the story that they were just following orders. I'm here to tell you now, Jones, that's bullshit and a cop-out."

"Please don't kill them. There has to be a better way," Jones pleaded.

Gordon turned to find everyone was watching the back and forth he was having with Jones.

"Gordon, don't do this, find a better way, please. I lived through Colonel Barone; I saw what happens to men when they believe they're judge, jury and executioner."

The mention of Barone hit home and made him pause. "And what about what I did to the general there?"

"I understand that; you're sending a clear message. There was purpose in that, but executing the others doesn't make sense."

Gordon lowered his voice, leaned closer and asked, "So what do we do with them?"

"We hold them, maybe use them to barter later with the president."

"Hmm, interesting," Gordon replied. He folded his arms and pondered for only a few seconds. "You know, Jones, I'll take what you suggest into consideration."

"Thank you, sir."

"But in the meantime I'm going to have these

officers shot. The enlisted prisoners I'll find something for them to do," Gordon said and turned back towards his men, who still stood frozen waiting anxiously for their orders. "Kill them!"

Jones shook his head and exhaled heavily. He knew this was sending a message, but it was the wrong message.

The officers all began to beg and whimper.

Gordon's soldiers stepped back, took aim and fired in unison.

The officers fell to the ground dead, each one shot through the head.

Gordon stepped over to the firing squad and said, "Good job."

They all nodded.

"You know, come to think of it, this entire place was just a fucking hellhole brought to you by the United States government," Gordon said and hesitated. He looked at his hand and could see it was swelling slightly. "John, get over here."

John ran over and asked, "What's up?"

"How many prisoners do we have?"

"Um, right now we have collected about sixty."

"Hold a court for these people, have the refugees preside over it, and let them choose who lives or dies," Gordon said, then turned to look at Jones. "How does that sound?"

Jones shook his head but didn't respond.

"I take that as a yes," Gordon said smartly. "Go make it happen."

John took off.

Satisfied with the outcome, Gordon looked back at Jones and asked, "Any other criticism for me today?"

"No," Jones said. He was disgusted. He looked at the men lying dead and wished it could have gone a different way. He didn't have any problems with killing the enemy, but just executing people without a trial didn't feel right. His phone began to ring. He pulled it from his trouser side pocket and turned it on. "Jones here." It was Charles again and this time he was in a panic.

"Gordon, it's Charles again. He needs to speak with you."

"I'm too busy to give him an update and too busy to chat about policy. Tell him I'll call back."

"Gordon, you need to take his call, it's critical," Jones urged.

"What could be so urgent?"

"Olympia is under attack," Jones conveyed.

Gordon stopped and turned. "By who?"

"By a brigade of Marines."

McCall, Idaho, Republic of Cascadia

"Mommy, when is Daddy coming home?" Haley softly said, walking into the kitchen.

Samantha was busy preparing dinner and paused for a brief moment to reply, "I'm not sure, sweetie, but he won't be gone for too long." Of course, this was a lie and Samantha hated having to say it, but one of her jobs as a parent was to make Haley feel safe.

The rich smell of meat and vegetables stewing filled the kitchen.

Haley took a sniff and asked, "Are we having deer stew again?"

"Yes."

"Yuck."

"Yuck? I thought you enjoyed my venison stew," Samantha said, astonished by Haley's comment.

"I love it," Luke hollered from down the hall.

"Thank you, deserving child," Samantha hollered back.

"We just have it so much, I'm tired of it," Haley whined.

"You'll get what you get and you won't get upset," Samantha joked, quoting from one of Haley's favorite children's books.

"Are there any more cookies left?" Haley asked.

Samantha completely stopped what she was doing, wiped off her hands and took Haley by the hand. She led her to the large couch in the great room and took a seat, placing Haley on her lap. "I know you're missing Daddy, I am too, but he'll be fine, and soon this whole thing will be over and he'll be back here."

"I miss him so much," Haley whimpered.

Samantha saw Haley's lip quiver. She embraced her tightly, kissing her on top of the head. "Oh, sweetie, your heart is so big."

"I just don't want him to die like Uncle Sebastian."

Hearing Haley say that made her cringe. "He won't,

honey. Your daddy is big and strong; he'll be fine." Again Samantha peppered her with lies.

"Luke told me they were fighting a war, is that true?"

Samantha bit her tongue as she thought about how she'd answer the question. "Um, it is true that Daddy is off fighting, but he's only doing so to keep us safe. He will be fine, you'll see."

"I heard a lot of people die in war."

Haley's questions were like punches to her gut. "It's true, people do die in wars, but your daddy won't."

"Mommy?"

"Yes."

"You don't have to lie to me."

Samantha opened her mouth to respond, but nothing came out.

"I know you're scared, and I hear you talking to Uncle Nelson. I'm scared too. I just want Daddy to come home."

Samantha petted her head and squeezed her. "I want him home too."

A loud banging on the door caused Samantha to jump. "I wonder who that might be."

"I'll get it!" Luke hollered as he ran down the hall towards the front door.

"Luke, where's your gun?"

Luke stopped just shy of opening the door. He opened a drawer of a small table next to the front door and pulled out a small revolver. "Sorry, forgot." He held it and remembered the brief time Sebastian had tried to train him with a firearm. That was months ago and since he hadn't handled a gun all that often. He had a general understanding of how to use one but really wanted to learn more. He looked to the door and called out, "Who's there?"

"It's Nelson."

Luke unlocked several deadbolts and opened the door. He shoved the small framed pistol into his trousers and greeted Nelson, "Hi."

"Hi," Nelson replied. He looked past Luke and saw Samantha sitting on the couch with Haley. "Oh good, you're here."

"Come in," Samantha said.

Nelson stepped across the threshold and into the foyer.

Luke slyly put the revolver back and stood just to the side of Nelson.

Nelson removed his frayed ball cap and combed his long hair back with his fingers. "I came over as soon as I got the word."

Samantha's heart dropped when he uttered those words.

Seeing her expression change, he immediately corrected his tone and said, "It's nothing to do with Gordon, he's fine. Um, can we speak in private?"

"Sure. Ah, Haley, go with Luke back to his bedroom and read a book."

"But I want to hear what Uncle Nelson has to say," Haley insisted.

"No, now go. I'll be in shortly to read one too with you," Samantha said, pushing Haley off her lap.

"Fine, but it's not fair." Haley scrunched her nose and stomped off with Luke just behind her.

"How about we go out back?" Nelson suggested.

The two stepped onto the deck.

Samantha motioned for him to sit, but he pointed to an open space further back behind the large garden.

"Really private," Samantha said.

Quietly he said, "I just don't want the kids eavesdropping."

They cut through the garden and took a seat on a large granite boulder near a grove of aspens.

"So what is so urgent and private?" Samantha asked.

"I apologize for acting weird, but Gordon gave me specific instructions not to alarm the kids or make them worry."

"Like telling me it's so urgent we have to hide to tell me? That won't make them worried at all," Samantha joked, rubbing her arms against the cool air.

"You know your man, he's a stickler, and I don't want to be the guy that upsets the kids."

"Oh, he wouldn't get too mad."

"Are you kidding me? He's changed somewhat, he's…" Nelson said then stopped. He looked out towards the east.

"He's what?"

"Ever since Sebastian was killed, he's been withdrawn, bitter, angry, more than he was after Hunter's death."

Samantha sighed because she knew he was right.

"He's a bit unhinged is the word I'm hearing from

the field," Nelson said.

"Who's saying he's unhinged?"

"People."

"Who?"

Nelson cocked his head and said, "People, I don't want to get into this."

"Nelson Wagner, you're one of his oldest and dearest friends. You don't want to tell me because you're protecting others? Is it because you believe it too?"

Nelson grunted and replied, "I believe it a little. Heck, I've seen how he's been since poor Sebastian was murdered."

Needing to defend Gordon, Samantha said, "He has a right to be angry. He's lost friends, a son and now a brother. I say he has every right to be pissed off."

"I'm not saying that, it's just that he's done some things."

"Like what?"

"Listen, I didn't come here to argue much less discuss this. I wanted to tell you something else."

"What has Gordon done that's so bad? Answer."

"There was a battle today…Gordon and the army were successful. They took Mountain Home Air Force Base, but he did something that upset some."

"What? Dammit, stop beating around the bush!"

"He executed some American officers who had surrendered peacefully."

Samantha thought for a moment. She shrugged and said, "So what, it's war."

"You can't say so what. Actions have consequences,

and he has to look at this politically now. I hate to say it, but he really has to," Nelson stressed.

"No, he doesn't, all he needs to do is win," Samantha said and stood up. She walked over and looked towards the eastern mountain range.

"Sam, it is important. Gordon shouldn't be executing people for no reason. He needs to show he can be a leader that has compassion and will administer justice. He also killed an unarmed man with his bare hands; he beat him to death."

"I'm not listening anymore. He had a good reason, I'm sure of it. Whoever that man was probably did something wrong."

Nelson stood and approached her. "He did, but there should have been some sort of trial. We can't have a new country if the leader of our military is acting like the tyrants we're trying to free ourselves from."

Samantha turned around quickly and barked, "Don't you dare compare Gordon to Conner and especially not to that animal Schmidt!"

Nelson looked down. He hated conflict, and here he was, right in the middle of it. He couldn't be surprised by Samantha's response; after all, she was Gordon's wife. "I'm not saying they're the same, but those who dislike Gordon—and you know the politics began the day he stood on that tank and he had already created political enemies—will use this as a wedge issue. All I am saying is when you speak to him next, ask him to think more before acting out."

"You really piss me off; I thought you were his

friend."

Nelson stepped around and stood in front of her. "I am, his best friend, and I'm being a friend by looking out for his interests here and in Olympia."

"Then show it."

He shook his head, frustrated that she refused to listen. Knowing he wasn't getting anywhere, he went to the next major topic. "Samantha, I know you don't want to hear what I have to say about Gordon, but we need to be prepared for some dustups especially after what happened today in Olympia."

"Now what?"

"Olympia was attacked today; it's been taken over by US forces. The council and committee were able to escape. They're headed here, but the grumblings are already beginning, and like anything political, they want to blame someone, and it's Gordon they're laying this on."

Samantha rubbed her temples to soothe the migraine that was coming on. "Of course they will, that's what politicians do. They point fingers and blame someone else from the seats they never leave; hence why their asses are so wide."

"We need to prepare ourselves and rally support for Gordon. Michael is already taking heat and is disregarding the calls from Charles to divert Smith's forces from Yakima and attack Olympia."

Confused by it all, Samantha found herself back on the granite boulder. "And no word from Gordon?"

"No, Gordon has ordered Smith's forces to return to McCall and defend it just in case Conner's army moves east."

In disbelief from the endless bad news, Samantha chuckled and said, "Do you know what Haley told me today?"

"What?"

"She told me to stop lying to her. I keep telling her everything will be okay, but she sees right through the bullshit. She's so young but so wise beyond her years."

"She doesn't need to know the gritty details, but maybe it's becoming time to tell her it's not so safe."

"I can't do that. You see, it's my job as a parent to make sure my children feel safe. That's not to say I can't warn them of dangers, but telling her *everything* won't help her understand better or prepare her."

Nelson nodded.

"For a while I was beginning to believe my own bullshit."

"And now?"

"I'm not so sure everything will be okay; I'm not so sure we'll survive this."

Cheyenne, Wyoming, United States

"So today you're telling me we're batting five hundred?" Conner asked, looking through the memo concerning Mountain Home.

"Yes, sir," Baxter replied.

"Let them have Mountain Home; we have his

capital," Conner said and stood up from his desk, clearly excited about the news from Olympia. He spun around and looked out the window but hesitated when he saw his own reflection. The stress of the endless fighting had gotten to him. His once pudgy face was replaced with a lean and weathered one. Deep wrinkles now resided across his skin, and the dark circles he had always had were deeper and darker than ever before. Gone was the soft and chubby man who had been the Speaker of the House of Representatives. Not wanting to get lost in why his complexion had transformed, he turned and faced Baxter. "It's a day to celebrate. We have their capital, and soon we'll move on McCall and end this."

"Sir, when can we begin bombing operations?" Schmidt asked. He too looked like a different man since his encounter with Gordon. The muscular frame had been reduced and replaced with a lean and almost frail body. His appearance had changed so drastically that Conner began to wonder if he was sick.

"Major, I know you want nothing more but to bomb McCall back to the Stone Age, but I don't want that. We can defeat these rebels without collateral damage and killing innocents. The approach you had before did nothing but enrage the civilian population, which then led to them rising up against you."

"Why aren't we hammering his forces in Mountain Home, then?" Schmidt asked.

"Major, do I have to repeat myself? There are thousands of refugees there; the risk of collateral damage is too high. I can't risk another public relations scandal.

Plus he doesn't have a lot of armor. He has trucks, old cars and only a few thousand men. Not enough to worry about just yet, and believe me, if he gets close to us, we'll light him up," Conner said.

Conner was burning with a desire to use what limited air power he had against Gordon, but he didn't want to waste it if he could just take care of Gordon and his army with traditional ground forces. General Baxter along with the men and woman at Warren Air Force Base had managed to get jets, helicopters and drones functioning again, but this force was severely limited and required raping other aircraft to get one working. What support he had from other nations was diminished and reduced to mainly humanitarian aid. The two Marine battalions that had sailed from the East Coast were now engaged in an occupation of Olympia, and with the other large standing army, he was left with a force that was similar in size to Gordon's along with an equal number of militia he had activated. The temptation to use his air force was strong, but he had to also play politician, and his harsh responses to the other secessionist movements had backfired, causing an uproar in Cheyenne. It was mainly the unintended injuries or civilian fatalities that caused the opposition to his military campaigns. So in an attempt to provide balance, he had reduced his use of aerial attacks.

"Sir, in defense of my actions before, you gave me carte blanche to do what I needed to do."

"Not murder people and burn everything down," Conner fired back.

"But, sir, you did," Schmidt insisted.

With Baxter sitting there, Conner didn't want to admit he *had* all but given Schmidt the orders to do what he needed to do to crush the secessionists. "Major, you're lucky I didn't have you up on court-martial. Now just sit there and shut up."

Schmidt shuffled in his seat, clearly disturbed by the ass chewing he had just received.

Baxter too shifted, feeling uncomfortable because he knew Conner was lying and some of the harsh tactics were still being used, just not as often and done so he could have plausible deniability.

"It took those Marines forever to finally make a difference," Conner said, referring to the Marine battalions that had sailed from the East Coast. Their original mission had been to deal with Colonel Barone, but with that situation taken care of, they marched north and took Olympia with hardly a fight."

"And can I say how proud I am of them," Baxter glowed.

"Any news on when I Corps can mobilize from Fort Lewis and support the Marines in Olympia?" Conner asked, referring to the US Army's corps of soldiers stationed at Fort Lewis outside of Tacoma, not too far from Olympia.

"That has been a tough situation for us. They have lost over eighty-five percent of their men and with those deserters went valuable equipment. We will have a small unit that will be able to effectively deploy in two weeks," Baxter answered.

"And how are we doing with the conscription of

locals for the militia?" Conner asked, referring to a law he'd passed requiring all able-bodied men between eighteen and thirty-five to register for the militia and get physicals.

"Slow, we're not getting everyone's support," Baxter replied.

"We have to be able to enforce the law, sir," Schmidt said. His forehead was gleaming with sweat.

"You don't look good, Major," Conner said.

Sitting up in his chair, Schmidt said, "I'm fine, sir."

"If you need to take some R&R, please do. You've been working around the clock."

A tap on the office door drew their attention towards it.

The door opened and Wilbur appeared. She was out of breath as she rushed into the office and grabbed a seat next to Schmidt. "So sorry I'm late."

"Late? Hell, you almost missed the entire meeting," Conner said.

"I'm sorry, couldn't be helped," she said. Wilbur's role of secretary of state had grown to include handling all the refugees. What once was only a side issue for Cheyenne and Conner's government had grown into a full-blown humanitarian issue as more poured in by the thousands each day.

"Baxter will brief you on what we've covered so far after the meeting. I understand you have something you'd like to present to me," Conner said.

"Um, yes, sir, I do," she answered, removing a small stack of papers and a binder from her leather messenger bag.

Conner sat on the edge of his desk and crossed his arms. "I'm all ears."

"You had us put together a team to conduct testing on what might be ailing the refugees. Well, we've narrowed it down."

Conner nodded and asked, "Is it NARS?"

"No, no, it's not."

"Then what is it?" Baxter asked.

Schmidt coughed loudly and the sweat on his brow grew.

Wilbur was sitting next to him and recoiled when he began to cough more heavily.

Conner looked at his watch and was growing impatient. "Please continue."

With one eye on Schmidt and the other on Conner, she answered somberly, "They're dying from severe radiation poisoning."

"Radiation? From where?" Conner asked, but he already suspected its origin.

"The refugees who are getting sick originated back east. They must have come into contact with contaminated areas around the nuke plants that melted down."

"Just as we feared early on," Conner said.

"It was only a matter of time," Baxter said.

"Here are my suggestions," Wilbur said, taking out a notepad and handing it to Conner.

Conner flipped through the pages of notes quickly. "Too much to read, what's your recommendation?"

"Quarantine in a separate camp," Wilbur offered.

"Can't be that simple. What about their families?" Baxter asked.

"They go with them if they choose, but the sick mixed in with the healthy is causing problems and disrupting the healthier population," Wilbur stated.

Conner rocked in his chair, thinking about a solution. "Do it. Set up a quarantine camp and get it done ASAP. We don't need the animals in the zoo any more riled up than they are."

Wilbur leered at Conner briefly then said, "I'll get right on it."

"Ah, sir, the conscription issue," Baxter said, reminding Conner of an issue they skimmed over.

"Yes, how's that going?"

"Like I mentioned, slow. Your old friend from the coffee shop has organized against it, and his group is growing," Baxter said.

The old friend was Pat, the owner of Pat's Coffee Shop in downtown Cheyenne. Conner and he had forged a relationship in Conner's early days in Cheyenne, but tension grew as Conner began to implement is harsh policies against secessionists and those he deemed enemies of the state. Martial law had been implemented on and off in Cheyenne to disrupt raucous protests that had sprung up against Conner and his government. The crescendo of descent for many in Cheyenne and the camps surrounding followed Conner's decree that ended Project Congress. This also was the last straw for Pat.

"First Dylan now Pat." Conner lamented his loss of

trusted friends.

"Want me to arrest him?" Schmidt asked.

"No, God no, that would only play into the narrative that I've become a dictator. In fact, I've been thinking I want to rescind my executive order concerning protests. Let's have the people take to the streets. Let's give them space to speak their minds."

"But what happens if they get violent?" Schmidt asked.

"Of course we're not going to tolerate violence. If anyone acts out, we'll take them down. Just make sure it doesn't get too out of hand," Conner warned.

Schmidt shifted in his seat, growing a bit taller with the news he might have a chance to engage the rowdy protestors.

Baxter scrunched his face and asked, "Sorry, Major, but do you think you're the best one to handle this?"

Schmidt cocked his head and replied, "What does that mean?"

"Only that you don't look well. I really hate to call you out, but, Major, you are sick and I don't think it's the flu."

"You really do look bad," Conner said.

"I'm fine and I'm quite capable of overseeing security for any protest," Schmidt countered, his anger flaring.

"No one is challenging your ability to handle a situation, Major, we're just worried about you. I want you to go see my doc at the air base later today."

"But, sir," Schmidt protested.

"No buts, go. It's an order," Conner demanded.

"Yes, sir," Schmidt replied sheepishly.

"If that's it, let's close this meeting. We all have important issues to tackle," Conner said.

"Sir, I have one more item I'd like to discuss," Wilbur said.

"Go ahead."

She nervously looked at Schmidt and Baxter before putting her eyes back on Conner, who sat patiently waiting. "It has something to do with the protestors. In fact, it has something to do with the various secessionist movements around the country."

"There aren't that many left. We put down the leaders of the Dixie Federation, Mr. Faye in Arizona lost, so did the Lakotas and Colonel Barone, and we wiped the Pan American Empire off the map. All we have left is Mr. Van Zandt and his Cascadians."

Interrupting, Baxter asked, "So you've completely written off Texas and Oklahoma?" His question referred to the deal Conner struck with them to allow access to the port in Houston: autonomy for unfettered access.

"Yes and no. I will deal with those traitors once we're stronger. And before you ask, Hawaii and Alaska—they're too far to deal with for the foreseeable future and might be gone from us forever, unfortunately."

"Hmm," Baxter mumbled as his only response.

"Sir, the thing is, and Major Schmidt will agree if he dared tell you the facts, but we might have squashed the leaders of the movement, but we haven't changed any of the hearts and minds in those states. The rebellious spirit still thrives, and soon a new leader will rise up and take the mantle and push their agenda forward. I fear we're in for a long fight."

"What are you saying, Wilbur? Just get to your point," Conner said.

"I think we need to seriously consider giving these people what they want, independence."

Conner sat up and barked, "Not while I'm alive."

"But, sir, the only way to truly win is to hold these places, and that takes boots on the ground. We've done our best to incorporate those civilians still loyal, but it's not enough, and the no-holds-barred tactics deployed has only made matters worse."

"So surrender, that's your answer to these rebels, these goddamn traitors?" Schmidt barked.

"It's not surrender. We have to understand what's really happening, Major. We don't have the people, resources and equipment to hold these states, and the state governments are struggling to maintain order. Some have all but collapsed; mobs and gangs are having their way in many major cities. It's like we're playing whack-a-mole."

"Fucking coward!" Schmidt yelled.

"I'm not a coward. I don't want to let them go, but it's inevitable, I fear. Let's make the situation work for us by allowing them to go but remaining allies."

"You are a coward, ready to surrender what is left of the United States," Schmidt continued.

"Stop!" Conner ordered. "Listen, we're not going to surrender, nor are we going to negotiate a truce with these rebels that cedes one inch of the United States. We aren't in the best shape, but we're not desperate," Conner declared. He took a deep breath and continued, "We have our troubles in other parts of the country, which we'll fix. Here in Cheyenne and the surrounding area we have relative peace. We will stabilize any discontent here while simultaneously dealing with the secessionists. These things take time, but in the end we will prevail."

"Sir, when my people were conducting the health inspections of the camps, they reported back a high level of frustration and anger, mostly directed at us," Wilbur said.

"I know the people are frustrated and impatient, but we have to make this work. Giving up is not the solution. These are tough times, but we can make it, I know we can," Conner said, trying his best to motivate his staff. He looked at them but could see it hadn't worked. The long months and slow progress towards reestablishing something that resembled the past had tapped their positive outlooks. Even he found it hard to believe his own bullshit. "Now, I need you to go out there and work. Get with your people and tell them that we will make it, we will persevere."

"Sir, I have an idea," Schmidt said.

"And what's that?" Conner asked.

"I think you should give a speech to the city. Show them you care. You make the announcement that the protest restriction and martial law is being suspended and—" Schmidt said but was interrupted.

"And announce that you're restoring Project

Congress," Wilbur blurted.

Baxter's eyes widened when Wilbur mentioned the now defunct and controversial project.

Schmidt glared at her for talking over him.

Conner rubbed his chin and thought. He stepped over to a side table. Scattered on it was a map of the United States; the red and green lines he had drawn from a meeting months ago showed the reality of what they were dealing with. He lifted it up and studied the lines. As he went to put it back on the table, he saw a stack of papers attached to a clipboard. It was Dylan's clipboard. He didn't realize it was there after all these months, sitting underneath the map. It showed him how long it had been since he'd focused on such things. A realization suddenly came to him. He was waging a war against multiple secessionist movements, but he was also waging a war with those who still showed loyalty to the United States. He needed to show them he wasn't the monster he was being painted as by the likes of Pat, but a benevolent leader who cared and was willing to make the tough decisions to keep them safe. He spun around and said, "You're both right. I need to give a major speech. I'll announce an end to martial law, and the icing on the cake will be that Project Congress is back on. I'll set an election six months from then. This will give the people hope and something to focus on."

Wilbur and Schmidt both nodded.

Baxter exhaled, heavily relieved that Conner wasn't overreacting to Wilbur's request.

"When should we make these announcements?"

Wilbur asked.

"I don't want to wait, set the date for two days from now," Conner said.

"What about the vice president, do you want him present?" Wilbur asked.

"Not a good idea, sir," Schmidt said.

"I agree, not a good idea," Baxter added.

"Agreed, keep him bunkered down in Cheyenne Mountain. It's not necessary to have him there," Conner replied.

Cruz and Conner hadn't seen each other for months now. Wanting to ensure continuity of government, Conner kept Cruz secure in the massive underground facility.

Conner looked at his three top advisors and waited for any other response. Upon seeing they had none, he dismissed them except Wilbur. "Secretary Wilbur, please stay for a moment."

"Yes, sir," she replied.

When the door closed, Conner squinted, cocked his head slightly and sternly said, "I know you've had a soft heart for the secessionists from the start. I can forgive that to a point. I've kept you around because you're capable and because it's always a good idea for a leader to get opposing or contradictory views. But never mention surrender again."

"But, sir—"

He held his index finger up in her face and barked, "Never!"

"Yes, sir," she said, her eyes focused on the floor.

"Now get the hell out of here," Conner ordered.

She sheepishly exited the office.

Conner made his way back to the desk and picked up the phone receiver. A female voice suddenly spoke. *"Yes, Mr. President."*

"Send my doctor to Major Schmidt's quarters immediately, and tell him I need a full physical done on him."

"Yes, sir."

"And when he's done, have him touch base with me personally. He has my number and can call me at anytime."

"Yes, sir."

Conner hung up the phone and walked back to the table. He looked at the map again but tossed it aside. He picked up Dylan's old papers and notes on Project Congress and began to read through them. A smile began to crease his face as he looked at Dylan's doodles and handwritten notes. He missed his old aide and wished things could have turned out differently. Having someone he could trust completely was the most difficult thing to find. He walked back towards his desk, papers still in his hand. He sat down, opened a desk drawer and fumbled through the contents until he found what he was looking for, a lighter. He flicked it until an orange flame appeared.

"Sorry, old buddy," he said out loud as he waved the flame underneath the papers. Quickly they caught fire. He watched as the flame ran up the page, destroying the doodles, notes and detailed plan for Project Congress. He grabbed his trash can, emptied it and tossed in the papers.

He watched with a wider grin as the fire devoured the remaining pages and destroyed Dylan's last effort to recreate the country he had lost.

Sandy, Utah

Shortly after returning to Sandy, Annaliese received word via a ham radio operator that a war had erupted between the United States and a group of secessionists in Idaho. She knew exactly who they were talking about. The war became the topic of discussion at many dinners, and Annaliese couldn't stop wondering what was happening and if Sebastian was safe, much less alive.

Determined to find him, she convinced Samuel to let her and her savior, Eli Bennett, return to Cheyenne and search for Sebastian. He agreed and set them up with plenty of fuel, food, water and weapons to go looking, but her hopes were dashed the morning they were set to leave.

A ham operator in Idaho reported to Samuel that the war between Cascadia and the United States was being fought hard and that Cascadia was winning. The name Van Zandt was mentioned in the conversation, with Sebastian named as being dead, executed by an American army officer.

Samuel and Sebastian had a difficult relationship, but when he heard of Sebastian's demise, he felt horrible but knew the news would destroy Annaliese, which it did.

For a couple weeks she locked herself up, not talking or seeing anyone. She had fallen into a state of depression, lost and confused by how a God she had grown to revere and love could take away the man she loved so much. With her emotional state shattered, it would take something to snap her out of it, and one day that something happened when Hector was brought to the gates of the ranch.

Annaliese had many talents; one of those was her ability to nurse and care for people. Though she would never consider it a talent, it took someone special to have the patience, attention and tenderness to take care of the sick and needy.

Hector had been found in the desert northwest of them by a former ranch hand of Samuel's. Unable to care for him, he took Hector to Samuel's ranch in hopes they could help the man.

Samuel brought Hector in, but his skills were lacking, so he convinced Annaliese to help. Putting aside her pain, she went to ease Hector of his.

Hector had been the survivor of a horrible crash. One-third of his body was burned, with over half of his face receiving second-degree burns. Both his legs, one arm and countless other bones were broken or shattered. She had never encountered much less cared for anyone in this condition. It would be challenging, but Hector needed her. What she didn't realize was she would also need him.

Weeks went by and Hector showed improvement. She tried her best to set his breaks, but without an X-ray and proper medical training, it was hard to determine if she had done a good job. As the weeks turned to months, his condition improved and there was no doubt he'd survive but would be disfigured and maybe unable to walk for the rest of his life.

She didn't know much about him except his name. Apparently when Samuel's ranch hand found him, he'd muttered Hector in a scratchy voice when asked his name. His lower jaw had been shattered, which reduced his ability to speak but didn't mean he couldn't. Samuel questioned if his throat had been scarred from severe smoke or fume inhalation from the fire he had been in. His communications primarily consisted of nods and head shakes. When he did speak, he gave garbled grunts that sounded like yeses and nos. She could see his effort to talk was painful. She did get some answers from him, like he was Mexican and had a family. When pressed, he just stopped responding. Annaliese knew how painful it was to discuss or talk about the past, so she eventually stopped her questions.

Annaliese didn't mind Hector's limited communication, she thought most people talked too much anyway. She also took advantage of his condition for selfish reasons; when she needed to talk and express her emotions over the loss of Sebastian, she'd break down to him. He never responded or moved but did look at her with his brown eyes showing her he was listening. She started thinking of him as her therapist; he was a safe place to go and talk.

After two and a half months, Hector was able to get

around using a wheelchair.

She often would find him sitting out on the deck, looking towards the horizon. He would just do that for hours and it didn't seem to bore him.

With Hector healed, she had time on her hands and discovered in the process that it gave her purpose. She convinced her Uncle Samuel to use one part of the barn on his ranch as a makeshift hospital for any person they encountered that required medical attention.

In a month's time her hospital grew from a one-woman show to four people, one being a medically trained doctor and two registered nurses.

Her powers of persuasion extended beyond that, as she convinced Samuel to open up parts of his large ranch to refugees. Annaliese came to believe that in order for them to survive long term, they would have to create a community of like-minded people, but instead of seeking it out, why not create it.

It took some time, but Samuel relented, and soon they opened the old metal gates to those in need and looking for a home. Samuel was not blind to the fact that all those who came looking were not in need. The world was still violent and not void of bandits and marauders. Keeping that in mind, Samuel established an interview process. Slowly the community grew from them to thirty-three hardworking survivors, all giving and sharing. Gardens popped up and new structures were built to house everyone. Samuel had several wells on site, with each having their own separate twenty-thousand-gallon holding tanks. There was enough land and water, and at the rate they were growing food and with the livestock he had, the community began to flourish.

Word spread around the area to his neighbors, who thought them crazy for inviting in so many people and highlighting their location. Samuel began to worry about their security while Annaliese was not about to sit back and merely survive. Having lost Sebastian so easily changed her. At any moment they could fall victim to someone or something, so why not live, truly live, and create something great out of the chaos. The vision was bold but risky.

"Hector, are you hungry?" Annaliese asked, coming out to find him sitting in his typical spot on the porch, looking towards the western hills.

He craned his head and nodded.

"Great, I made a surprise for you," she said, excited, and went back inside.

Hector turned his head back towards the hills and sat. His right eye had lost most of its vision due to the second-degree burns that side of his face had suffered. The black hair on the right side of his head had been burned off, with only patches growing back. Scars now covered that side of his head. The scars extended past his face to his neck and his shoulder, side and arm. Self-conscious, he wore long-sleeve shirts and baseball caps.

Annaliese opened the door and asked, "You want to eat out here? It's getting chilly?"

"Yes."

"I figured," she said and fully came outside with a tray. On it was a plate of a Mexican specialty, chicken chilaquiles. Corn tortillas were cut into quarters then lightly fried, with a green salsa, pulled chicken and seasonings. Excited to present him with the meal, she placed it on a round glass table behind him.

The aroma of the rice and chicken hit his nostrils. His mouth watered and his stomach churned. He spun the wheelchair around and pulled it up to the table. With his eyes closed, he inhaled the steam coming off the hot food.

She was nervous, she guessed he was Mexican and had wanted to make him a meal he might find familiar. She had her arms crossed and bit her lip, waiting to see his response.

Hector didn't need any explanation; he knew what she had done for him and found it special. He looked at her and said in his raspy voice, "Thank you."

Her eyes widened hearing him say something more than yes or no. "I know it doesn't have fresh onions or queso fresco, um, and it's from a Betty Crocker recipe, so I don't know if it will be hot enough; hence why I put some jalapenos on the side there," she said, pointing to his plate. "They were canned and pickled, so again, probably not authentic."

He again said, "Thank you." He meant it and felt touched that she had done something so nice and random for him. He was impressed with her and her family. Never in his life had he seen such love. They had no reason to take him in, but they had. They asked for nothing in return and expected nothing from him. He looked back at the steaming food and swore that he'd pay them back; he would find a way to reward them for their unsolicited generosity.

"Go ahead, try it," Annaliese said.

He picked up a fork but stopped. He pointed at the food then her.

"Oh no, I know how you like your privacy, and I already chatter away too much," she replied.

He again pointed at the food then her and nodded firmly, signaling that he demanded she sit with him.

"You sure?" she asked.

He nodded.

"Okay," she said and went to get a plate.

He sat and patiently waited.

She returned with a full plate and sat next to him. Still looking nervous, she said, "Please try it first. Let me know."

He lifted his fork and dug in. With a heaping of the chilaquiles on the fork, he took a bite.

She watched him, anxious for his response.

He chewed several times and nodded. He then said, "Yes."

"You like it?"

"Yes."

"Is it kinda authentic?"

"Yes."

"Yay," she said, clapping. She quickly took her fork and began eating.

The two sat in silence, enjoying the food.

Annaliese was on top of the world, knowing that he liked it.

They finished their plates and sat without her saying a word. The happy look on her face suddenly changed.

He could see this shift and wondered what it was that plagued her mind.

"I know I bore you with my stories and babbling, but I'm going to bore you again."

He didn't speak; he just looked at her.

"I miss my husband. Sebastian was a good man. I feel cheated. We only had a short time together compared to so many other couples, but I don't want to live in a place of regret. I appreciate my time with him and will forever cherish that. You know, I want to thank you."

He pointed his index finger at himself.

"Yes, you, um, I saw you that day, the day you were brought here, and I thought this man needs help. He needs someone to care for him. I remember at first dismissing you and chalking you up as a casualty of this new world we live in, but I made a huge shift that day. I thought of Sebastian and if someone had stepped up to help him, he may not have been killed. That someone would have looked at him as a human being who had a family, a wife, and thought, 'Hey, I'm going to help him find his way home.' If someone had said that, then acted, he might be here today. I saw you, and let me tell you, you were in bad shape. But I told myself then that you might have a family somewhere, a wife maybe, a child, parents who love you, and I said I will help you, I will do my best to ensure you can see them again. You know, if more people acted this way, things probably wouldn't have fallen apart. If we all came together, we wouldn't have had a collapse. We would have worked together and made things come back much faster, but a lot of people aren't built that way, and it's sad. So you saved me as much as I saved you. You gave me hope, Hector; you made me not depressed. I'm still sad that I've lost so much, but having known those special people in my life like Sebastian makes my life that much better. We're building a great thing here, and I hope it continues to flourish."

All the words she said hit him hard. He thought about saying something but resisted just at the point of talking. He appreciated her words, and one day he might find the courage to speak and tell her how her kindness had changed him too.

A tear streamed down her cheek. She brushed it away and finished, "Sorry, I can get emotional easy. But I want to just say thank you, or *gracias*."

He nodded.

Wishing to change the topic, she said, "I'll take these plates inside. I wish I had some Mexican dessert to offer, but I don't."

He smiled.

She gathered the plates, put them on the tray and disappeared into the house.

Hector wheeled back from the table and assumed his usual spot. His family came to mind; he missed them and prayed they were safe. Maybe one day he'd see them again, maybe.

OCTOBER 29, 2015

"Only free men can negotiate. A prisoner cannot enter into contracts." – Nelson Mandela

Mountain Home, Idaho, Republic of Cascadia

Gordon looked at his watch and grunted when he saw the time.

"The northern checkpoint just reported their chopper landed," Jones reported.

"About damn time, I guess being fashionably late is still fashionable," John quipped.

"You look antsy, Gordon, this must be someone important," Jones said.

"I don't like waiting, even if the person is important," Gordon grumbled, deliberately not disclosing the secret arrival.

"Gordon, have you given more thought to Chenoweth's request?" John asked.

"No," Gordon quickly answered.

"Very well," John replied.

"I received a communication from Top. His forces are pulling back; they expect to be back in defensive positions near McCall in a week," Jones informed him.

"Good," Gordon said. Impatient, he stood up from the vinyl office chair and began pacing the large conference room.

"Oh, the company commanders are asking what our next move will be," John said.

Gordon stopped and said, "We press forward to the next objective."

Jones looked at John and raised his eyebrows and said, "And what is that? Because I haven't heard you mention it before. We put so much into this operation that we didn't think past this."

"You didn't, but I did," Gordon said, reminding him that he was the visionary.

"So what is it?" Jones asked.

"Cheyenne," Gordon replied.

"We'll never make it within a hundred miles of Cheyenne. Their air assets will destroy us. It's their trump card, the eight-hundred-pound gorilla in the room that we haven't factored in," Jones challenged.

"You let me handle that. Just have the company commanders ready for new orders tomorrow," Gordon said.

"Gordon, you're a military man, you know our small army will get ravaged by his aircraft. To be quite honest, I don't know why he hasn't moved on us yet," Jones confessed.

"It's because they're weak. They're pulled in several directions with limited assets. The reason you're confused is because you still think the world is somewhat the same, but it's not."

"That's kinda harsh to say," Jones complained.

Gordon walked over and patted Jones on the

shoulder. "I don't mean it like that. You still remember fighting wars and having everything at your disposal, you imagine a battlefield similar to that, but it's changed. Conner is swamped with fighting on several fronts, and he has a worsening problem with refugees. This is not adding in the staggering death toll that's occurred. The population is not what we're used to. He lacks manpower, equipment, fuel, ammunition, food, you name it. He's suffering like we are and doesn't want to waste it until he believes he has to."

"Then that brings me back to my point, how are we going to get within a hundred miles of Cheyenne?"

"Even with Conner's issues, we are the ones at a disadvantage, it's clear to anyone. So when you're the underdog, you have to fight differently. Take, for instance, how we took this," Gordon said, motioning his arms around the room. "You see, Jones, we have to fight creatively, and we may not be able to win just going at him. Yeah, I'll talk shit and say we are, but I'm not a fool. We need to fight him using non-kinetic warfare."

John looked up and asked, "I'm just a lawyer, what the hell is non-kinetic warfare?"

"I didn't tell you?" Gordon asked, surprised he hadn't shared his thoughts with John.

"You may have, but unless I was stone-cold drunk, I would remember."

Gordon began to pace but kept talking. "We're going to exploit the problems he has within Cheyenne by fostering discontent. Similar to what we did here, but we're not going to move in and take it because, like you said, we won't be able to get within a hundred miles. We're going to keep sending teams masquerading as refugees. We're going to get in there and stir the pot so much that all hell breaks loose. He'll be so overwhelmed with that and the victories we do make from one city to another, he'll realize he can't win and sue for peace."

"That's a big gamble," Jones said.

"War is a gamble. There are no guarantees except the fact that if we aren't successful, we'll most certainly die."

"By the way, why is this meeting so hush-hush? Who exactly are we waiting for?" John asked.

"Soon," Gordon said.

As if on cue, someone knocked loudly on the door.

"Come in!" Jones hollered.

The door opened and in stepped four men. The man who led the way was a short and thin man. He wore faded tan cargo pants and a black sweater. He removed a black beanie from his head, exposing his balding scalp. "Which one of you is Gordon Van Zandt?" the man asked, his voice raspy with the tinge of an accent.

Gordon stepped over with his hand outstretched and replied, "That would be me."

The man took Gordon's hand and they shook firmly. "Nice to meet you finally."

"Same here," Gordon said, thinking that the man's deep voice didn't fit with his physique.

The man turned to Jones and put his hand out. "Nice to meet you."

Jones took it and shook.

The man pivoted to John and did the same.

"Please take a seat," Gordon said, motioning towards a chair.

The other three men found chairs and sat down.

"Thank you for coming. How was the flight?" Gordon asked.

"Boring, but I agreed with you. We needed to meet," the man said.

An awkward silence filled the room as both parties sat not saying a word.

Jones got Gordon's attention, raised his eyebrows and nodded his head to the men.

Breaking the silence, Gordon said, "You being here tells me you're ready to make a deal."

"I've been interested in discussing diplomatic ties since you contacted me two months ago, but I have to admit I was doubtful it was wise for our two parties to do so, and quite frankly, we weren't getting anywhere with your counterparts in Olympia," the man said.

Jones scratched his head, wondering who these men were.

"Well, you and I are similar—we're not cut from political cloth; we are average men who want to make sure our new countries survive," Gordon said.

"I agree," the man said.

"So it's settled?" Gordon asked.

Jones and John were both befuddled and felt like they were eavesdropping on a conversation but came into it in the middle.

"So the terms we discussed over the phone will be it, correct?" the man asked.

"Yes."

John's instinct as an attorney kicked in. "Hold on, um, Gordon, can we speak for a minute?"

"Why?"

"This, what is this? What are you agreeing to?" John asked, motioning with his hands.

"My head is just in the clouds. John, Corporal Jones, this is Jacques Marceau, the prime minister of Western Canada."

"Gordon, we need to talk right now," John said, an urgent tone in his voice.

Jacques looked at John and asked, "Is something wrong?"

"No, not at all. The thing is my men here weren't aware of the deal I struck with you, but there's no need to be concerned. They don't have a say in how things are run," Gordon reassured Jacques.

Gordon's response didn't reassure Jacques, who said, "I know these things can be difficult, and if you're not ready to make a treaty, then we can discuss it later when there's more consensus."

"Not necessary, did you bring the agreement?" Gordon asked.

"Of course, like you requested," Jacques said.

"Stop!" John snapped. "Gordon, you can't sign anything unless I look at it. I'm a contract lawyer, for Christ's sake, this is what I made millions doing."

One of Jacques's men removed a packet and handed it to Jacques, who in turn handed it to Gordon.

Seeing the desperate look in John's eyes, Gordon

relented and said, "I will need tonight to go over this. It looks thick, you know, the fine print."

"Then we'll finalize, say, tomorrow morning," Jacques said.

"Tomorrow morning it is," Gordon said as he reached across the table with his hand open.

Jacques took Gordon's hand and shook it. "I look forward to our mutually beneficial relationship."

"Me too. What's the saying, the enemy of my enemy is my friend?" Gordon said.

"Correct," Jacques said and stood.

"Jones, take them to the officers' quarters and find them accommodations," Gordon ordered.

Jones sneered but did as Gordon instructed.

As soon as the door closed, John snatched the packet and tore it open. "Good God, man, you don't sign contracts much less fucking binding treaties unless a lawyer looks at them."

"This is a good thing," Gordon stressed.

John whipped through one page after another, quickly reading.

"This assures we'll have an ally to the north and disrupts Conner."

"Exactly how does this help us? I don't understand," John asked, his head still in the papers.

"Jacques and his people are not unlike us. They've carved out the western provinces of Canada and declared it independent from the eastern half. They're not recognized by Ottawa nor the United States…"

Jones burst into the room unexpectedly. "What the

hell are you doing?"

"I was just explaining to John."

"Gordon, might I remind you Jacques is a renegade, a murderer; he's best known for blowing up the legislature in Edmonton. I distinctly remember Charles talking about this guy and how he was the one obstacle to gaining the territory of southwestern British Columbia for Cascadia. If you sign this, you will, pardon the pun, blow up all the work that Charles and the others have accomplished in Olympia. They have been working hard and are close to getting the legitimate Canadian government to the table."

"The Canadian government, or what's left of it, has no power and can't do anything about Jacques or promise us we'll get that territory in BC," Gordon said, defending his actions.

"You don't know that, but regardless, you need to follow protocol."

John kept his head down and kept reading, ignoring Jones's emotional outburst.

"By striking this deal, we give up a small chunk of Cascadia, but in return we get a strong ally," Gordon fired back.

"Who's to say Jacques won't turn his ambitions south?" Jones asked.

"I don't know that, but I think he's only concerned with maintaining the traditional boundaries. If he has other designs, we'll deal with him then. This secures an alliance with the strongest player north of us."

"How do you know he won't make a deal with

Conner?" Jones asked.

"He won't and Conner would never entertain it; he needs to stay true to the leaders in Ottawa. According to Jacques, the Canadian government in Ottawa was in talks with Conner to assist militarily against him after the United States had stabilized everything."

Jones plopped into his chair and grunted. "Gordon, Gordon, Gordon," he lamented.

"It will be fine," Gordon said, his tone more subdued. "Jones, you know and I know that there was never going to be a deal with Ottawa—never—and Jacques was defiant in his standing that we had no legitimate claim on any part of Canada. And you know something, I agree with him. He is the biggest player up north; he has a small force and is willing to use it against us. The last thing we need is another front to fight and defend."

"Let me go through this with a fine-tooth comb tonight," John said, holding up the small stack of papers and all but ignoring the debate between Jones and Gordon.

"Sure," Gordon replied to John.

"Yesterday, now this, Charles is going to go ballistic," Jones said.

"Let him, I'm doing what is best to win this war."

"Did you ever bring this up to him? Did you ever discuss it?" Jones asked.

"Yes, but he shot it down right away. He has his heart set on getting those parts of BC. Going after that land complicates what we're doing. It's enough to make us independent from the United States, but trying to seize land from another country? Too much," Gordon stressed.

Jones chuckled and said, "Gordon, I already knew you had big balls, but I seriously think you have the biggest balls of anyone I've ever met."

Warren Air Force Base, Wyoming, United States

It didn't matter how many times Conner snuck away from his security detail, every time made him feel like a mischievous teenager sneaking away from his house while his parents were home.

As he approached Schmidt's quarters, he could hear him coughing loudly. He stopped in front of his door and paused before knocking. In many ways he felt sorry for the one man who was willing to do whatever was necessary for his country. If there was anyone he could trust, it was Schmidt. Yes, he had made some mistakes, but his unshakeable duty to country made his errors forgivable.

Conner's doctor had called after visiting Schmidt and the report wasn't entirely surprising. Yes, Schmidt was sick and it appeared to be something serious, but further tests would have to be done, but those would have to wait because Conner had what might be Schmidt's final mission.

Waiting until his last bout of coughing ended,

Conner knocked.

"Who the hell is it?" Schmidt hollered from behind the door.

"It's your boss," Conner barked halfheartedly, sounding like he was angry.

Sounds of fumbling could be heard followed by more coughing. "One second, sir."

The door flew open and there stood Schmidt looking worse than he had the day before. He hadn't shaved and his eyes looked sunken in. Only wearing a robe, he quickly apologized for his attire, "Sorry, sir, had I known you'd stop by, I would have cleaned up and been in uniform."

"Don't worry about it," Conner replied, standing there waiting to be invited in.

"Is everything okay?" Schmidt asked.

"Can I come in?"

"Yes, sir, sorry, yes, please come in, sir," Schmidt said, stepping out of the way to allow Conner in. He jogged around his quarters, gathering loose items that were out of place. "Had I known, sir, I would have made my space less messy."

Conner shut the door and said, "Major, I don't care." He walked over to a bar stool in the kitchen and took a seat. Schmidt's quarters were better described as a one-bedroom condo. It had a small kitchen with bar, living room, powder bathroom and one bedroom with a full bathroom. A stale smell was the first thing that hit Conner as he stepped across the threshold. It reminded him of the smell he'd encountered when he visited his great-grandfather years ago at his house just before he died.

"Can I get you something to drink?" Schmidt asked then coughed.

"Major, just sit down, rest."

"I have some good bottled water," Schmidt said, shuffling over to the refrigerator.

"Major, sit down. That's an order," Conner scolded.

Schmidt stopped what he was doing and took a seat next to Conner.

Conner looked around and said, "These officer's quarters are quite nice. We've done a lot since we got here. The power is back up; things are working again. You have power, a refrigerator that works."

"No TV yet," Schmidt joked.

"We're working on that, but who really needs the brain rot anyway?" Conner quipped.

Schmidt chuckled but kept his head down. An intense feeling of vertigo came over him, so he closed his eyes and breathed slowly.

Conner saw this and commented, "I spoke to the doctor."

"Sir, I'm fine to do whatever it is you need me to do. Please don't relieve me of duty. This is all I have, if you take this away from me, I, um, I don't know what I'll do," Schmidt pleaded, believing Conner was there to take away his responsibilities.

"Major, calm down. I'm not here to relieve you; I'm here to give you another secret mission," Conner said, reaching out and touching Schmidt on the shoulder.

"Sure, whatever I can do, I'll do," Schmidt said, sitting up erect in an attempt to look healthy, but it was no use; the unidentified sickness was too far along to be masked.

"I'm giving my speech tomorrow afternoon, and I'm expecting a large crowd. Now I know you're going to provide the best security a president can ask for, but…"

Schmidt's eyes widened and he asked, "Where's your team, sir?"

"You just noticed?"

"Sir, you can't do that, it's too dangerous. There are many people who would see you dead."

"I'm fine. Let me get back to what I need you for."

"Sorry, sir."

"I need you to plant a good number of agitators, some people that will cause mayhem and trouble. Hell, even plant a bomb. I want things to go very badly tomorrow." Conner could see the excitement build in Schmidt as he talked.

"Great idea, sir, this will give us the pretext to hammer those traitors. We can lay the blame right at the feet of Pat and his group," Schmidt said, glowing.

"I feel terrible having to do it, but it has to happen. If America is to survive, we need to remove those people, and showing that they're no better than any terrorist we've encountered will give us exactly what we need. I need it to be very bad, do you understand?"

"That means a high body count. Yes, sir, I understand."

"And, Major, no one can know except those men

you pick. It is imperative that you don't tell anyone."

"Of course, sir, I don't trust General Baxter or Secretary Wilbur anyway," Schmidt confided.

Conner raised an eyebrow. "What do you mean?"

"I just don't trust them, especially Wilbur."

"Don't trust her because she's a bit more liberal in her views?"

"No, sir, I don't think her loyalties are completely there. I've had some of my men tail her—"

"You've been watching her? This must be serious for you to do that," Conner asked, concerned.

"They've seen her coming from Pat's Coffee Shop a couple times."

Conner shrugged and said, "That could be anything. I know Pat is against my policies, but I don't see why someone shouldn't be able to get a coffee or drink somewhere."

"More than that, sir, and it was only after I started to get truly suspicious that I started to piece things together, but when I sent my men to go arrest Van Zandt at the hospital, we found them fleeing like they had been tipped off."

"Maybe they were just walking and saw guys with guns coming for them."

"It was something that was glossed over, but in the report my men stated that the vehicle she got in was waiting for them."

Conner hesitated from replying as he took in the conspiratorial information.

"I went and had the phone records pulled up, and

their hospital had received calls from Wilbur's office a couple times, and there was a call to their room from a phone in an empty office two floors below yours, sir. Unfortunately it happened before we installed any security systems that could record."

Hearing this made Conner feel uncomfortable. It was one thing to know Wilbur disagreed with some of his policies, but utterly something else if she was actively working against him. This thought brought him back to Dylan. At the time he had wondered if he acted alone but never could get an answer from him, and before he could press him further, he was dead. "Major, what you're telling me would mean that Secretary Wilbur is a traitor."

Schmidt hesitated, and when he spoke, he stuttered. "I-I can't say for sure. It's more circumstantial than conclusive."

"I can't do anything without conclusive, but circumstantial is enough for me to be wary. While you're at it, assign a two-man team to keep tabs on her."

"Already doing that."

"Keep close tabs on her tomorrow after everything happens."

"Yes, sir."

Conner stood and patted Schmidt on the shoulder again. "I knew I could count on you."

"Yes, sir," Schmidt replied, standing up quickly.

"I'll show myself out," Conner said. Walking to the door, he paused and turned back. "Major, I will need you to go see the doctor for further tests tomorrow at noon, though."

"But, sir, I have to plan this operation," Schmidt replied, a look of concern stretching across his face.

"You'll have plenty of time. Work on it now, get on it, just make that appointment tomorrow. And please make sure your men don't get caught, so think this through a bit."

"Sir, can I please skip the appointment tomorrow?"

"Major, you're my best and most trusted officer; I need you healthy, so go get those tests."

Confused but loyal to a tee, Schmidt nodded and said, "I'll be there, sir, and you can be assured the mission will go exactly as needed."

Conner arrived back at his offices, and like before, his security detail hadn't missed him nor noticed he had been gone. He found this both convenient and disturbing. Walking from the elevator to the large lobby just outside his office, he found Wilbur sitting.

"Madam Secretary, you're a bit early," he said.

"I was close by and thought I'd just wait here," she said, standing up as he approached.

"Let's go into my office and discuss what I called you about," Conner said, walking past her and into his office. He beelined it for a shelving unit in the corner and poured himself a glass of scotch. "Can I offer you a glass too?"

Wilbur slipped in and sat down in the same chair she had sat in the day before. "No, I'm fine."

"More for me, then," he joked as he walked back to

his large leather chair and fell into it. "Thanks for coming. I'm worried about Major Schmidt."

"How so?"

"Major Schmidt is without a doubt sick, but I'm concerned about his mental state too. I believe he may crack down too hard on the protestors, which I'm sure will show up tomorrow in full force for my speech. I want you to field a detail of plainclothes security to keep tabs and help keep the peace if things do get a little crazy tomorrow."

"You think he may do something?" Wilbur asked, genuinely concerned.

"Not like start something, just that he may come down too hard on the protestors. I want to have a fresh start with the people of Cheyenne, and I can't do that with my security forces cracking too many skulls, so to speak."

"I'll put together a detail. Should I be monitoring the major as well?" Wilbur asked.

"No, I don't want him to get suspicious that we're watching him too closely. He has a tendency to be a bit paranoid as it is," Conner said, then chuckled. "I heard him saying something about my old friend Pat just before the meeting yesterday."

"Like what?"

"That he had it coming, something along those lines."

"What does that mean?" Wilbur asked, almost seeming concerned.

"Maybe he said something about paying him back, I

really can't remember, he was mumbling under his breath."

"Hmm, interesting."

"Speaking of Pat, I really miss the coffee and the friendship; I'm so saddened that we've had a falling out. Maybe he'll appreciate my mea culpa tomorrow. Say, do you go there for coffee or drinks?"

"Um, no, not a big coffee drinker."

"Not even for a drink, you know, the hard stuff," Conner said, holding up his glass.

"Nope, that's not me."

Conner laughed and said, "Well, you should, he has some good booze there."

"I try to stay away from troublemakers," Wilbur said, her eyes losing contact with his.

The subtle shift in her gaze told him she was lying. Was Schmidt correct in his suspicions? "So that's it, just keep an extra eye out for any dangers and make sure his people don't go crazy if anything happens."

"I think things will be just fine tomorrow. I believe the people of Cheyenne are reasonable and willing to listen. I think tomorrow will be a great day for the city and our country," Wilbur said, smiling.

"Well, I'm glad you feel so confident."

"If that's it, I'm going to head back to my office and start putting together that detail," she said, standing up and heading towards the door.

"Ah, one more thing, but keep this quiet, just between you and me."

She stood waiting for the second item, but it didn't

come. She watched him move towards the window and look out. The afternoon sun beamed through the window and cast his shadow long in the room. "Was there something else?"

"Um, yes, sorry, forgot. Your offices, where are they exactly?"

"Two floors below here," she replied.

"Huh," he said and took a drink.

"Why?"

"Oh, no reason, it just dawned on me that I don't know where everyone's office is, that's all."

"Thank you for trusting in me, sir," Wilbur said then quickly left.

When the door shut, Conner drank the remaining scotch, turned and threw the glass. It smashed against the far wall. He looked at the shattered glass and grumbled, "You wouldn't know trust if it smacked you in the face."

Mountain Home, Idaho, Republic of Cascadia

Gordon hung up the satellite phone and instantly felt sad. Hearing Samantha's and Haley's voices made him long for home. All he wanted was to be there, in their arms, safe and sound, but none of that would matter if he didn't win this war, a war he didn't choose but was thrust on him.

Samantha took Nelson's advice and discussed the sensitive and controversial items concerning Gordon.

Hearing her explain things always soothed him. She seemed to be one of the few people whose voice could get through his thick skull. He promised before hanging up that he'd heed her advice and think before acting or opening his mouth.

Samantha told him about the increasing number of people who were expressing their displeasure with independence and the war. Gordon dismissed them and felt they were a small but vocal crowd. He'd discovered long ago that he couldn't make everyone happy, and he chalked this up as one of those situations. Gordon knew the war must be fought, he knew that tyrants like Conner and their henchmen wouldn't stop until they had crushed all opposition, and in this age that meant wiping them off the map. As Gordon's influence and tales of his victories spread, so did the threat to his personal safety and his family. Before he left for his campaign, he instructed his oldest and dearest friend, Nelson, to care for them. Nelson was the best person for the job and took it seriously.

The attention he was getting also brought deals like he had struck with Jacques. He had also received communications from his counterparts in Arizona and Georgia. Unfortunately any alliances with them were short lived, as word trickled down that Conner had snuffed them out.

A single filament bulb suddenly turned off without notice, then flickered back on. He looked up at the single bulb suspended from the ceiling of his quarters and felt grateful. The base had been running off of a spotty system of generators sent from Cheyenne, and when they became overloaded, the entire system would go black. Just having power was a luxury he didn't take for granted, and one that, when he had it, made him appreciate the days not so long ago when power was so available. He sometimes thought of how the world would look if they succeeded in their pursuits of independence. Things like getting the power back on and returning life to a state of pre-attack normalcy would be a priority, and if not done quickly enough, could also spell doom for them. Winning the war of independence against the United States was but one war they'd have to fight; the second would be providing a sound government. It was critical to be successful with the second as much as the first.

Jones had reported not long before that the company commanders were anxious to know what their next objective was.

Gordon couldn't agree more that keeping the army moving was necessary to morale both in his army and at home. But exactly where would they go next? This vexed him as the earlier conversation with Jones replayed in his mind.

A map of the Pacific Northwest lay unfolded on a table behind him. After spending hours going over new objectives, he still wasn't any closer to making a decision.

A light tap at the door gave him a much-needed reprieve from his thoughts. "Yes," he called out.

The door opened and in stepped a beleaguered-looking John Steele. "Hi, Gordon."

Gordon looked at John's weary face and bloodshot

eyes, then saw he was holding the treaty in his hand. "So is it solid?"

John closed the door behind him and walked to a folding chair next to the table and sat down with a huff. He tossed the treaty on the table and finally answered, "It looks good; I don't see anything that could pose us a problem. It doesn't bind us to do anything; all it spells out is that both parties mutually recognize the other and respect the boundaries referenced. I double-checked what those were with the coordinates listed, and it all checks out. They get all of BC with no further claims by us."

"So it's a good deal?"

"Yeah, good for them, of course, but for us, I'm not so sure," John confessed.

Curious as to John's comment, Gordon took a seat across from John and asked, "Please clarify."

"The deal doesn't reference a military alliance. I think it should, I think we should add something that one pledges to help the other if they are attacked. You know sorta similar to what NATO was."

"Okay."

"And the biggest threat is what kind of political shit storm this is going to cause with Charles and the committee. Jones was right; they're going to go berserk. Do you want that trouble?"

"I can deal with them," Gordon replied confidently.

"What if they don't take the military alliance?" John asked, going back to his first point.

"I gave the man my word verbally the deal I was looking for. They had all but threatened to attack us for

BC. We don't need another front opened up against us."

"I understand, but all this treaty does without the military alliance is give us their promise they won't wage war over those lands, nothing more. You see, you're showing that we're weak in some ways," John said.

"We're not weak; we're vulnerable if they come for us too," Gordon declared, his voice rising slightly.

"You don't know this Jacques. Jones is right; he's not a good guy but a shrewd politician. He sees this is better for him than you and could exploit it."

"In my defense, Jacques didn't want to deal until he saw we had some successes. Now he's willing to get into bed with us," Gordon said.

"Then he may be open to it. The weakness he has is he may need us down the road if the Canadians ever get their shit together and go after him," John surmised.

"That's what I'm betting on," Gordon said.

"Then tell him that, tell him Cascadia will come and help if he's attacked," John said then yawned. "Sorry, I'm exhausted."

"You'll be there tomorrow too and can help present our case."

"I have your back if you need it," John said, grinning.

Gordon returned John's grin. He could see John was waning and didn't want to hold him longer but needed to make sure his closest confidant was good on the home front. "So how's the family, did you get a chance to call them?" Gordon asked.

"Yeah, I did, they're good. You know, having these sat phones makes life almost seem normal."

"They're a bit spotty, but they do work well, and it beats not having any comms."

"Listen, I'm whooped and my eyes hurt. I'm calling it a night," John said, rubbing his eyes.

"Thanks for doing this, and please don't ever stop being you." Gordon smiled.

"Being me?"

"You held me accountable but in a good way. You're a smart guy and I needed you to step in and make sure the deal was right. And your advice on adding a clause about military support is brilliant."

Nodding his head and with a great sense of pride in his tone, John replied, "You don't become one of the most successful law firms on the West Coast by luck."

Gordon extended his hand and said, "Thanks."

John took it and shook it firmly. "You're welcome." He stood up but stopped just short of walking away. "So where to next?" John asked, looking at the map on the table.

Gordon placed his head between his hands and sighed. "Between you and me, I don't know. I'm going to sleep on it and hopefully I'll have an answer in the morning."

OCTOBER 30, 2015

"A lie told often enough becomes the truth." – Vladimir Lenin

Mountain Home, Idaho, Republic of Cascadia

Gordon stood quickly from the table, a grin stretched across his scarred face, and one final time offered his hand to Jacques. This time the handshake sealed a treaty that would bring both new nations closer while creating a chasm in his own. "I look forward to a long and prosperous relationship between our two countries," Gordon declared.

"Me too," Jacques replied. He had agreed to the change in terms, which created a military alliance between both nations. This would be a huge step for Gordon and he planned on using this soon.

Each party gave platitudes and said their farewells.

Gordon escorted Jacques and his delegation to their helicopter and saw them off.

No sooner had the helicopter disappeared over the horizon than Jones stepped forward, a frown on his face and the satellite phone in his hand. "Your timing is impeccable."

Gordon gave him a devilish grin and said, "Let me guess, Charles?"

"Yeah."

A chilly wind swept over them. Gordon didn't know if it was coincidence or it portended the conversation he was about to have. He grabbed the phone and placed it to his ear. "Van Zandt here."

"I've just arrived in McCall, thanks to Master Sergeant Simpson, but I hear you have no plans of sending him to Olympia," Charles bellowed over the phone.

Gordon held the phone away from his ear only to bring it back to answer, "No, I need them to fall back and get into defensive positions in case Conner's forces head east."

"Might I remind you that Olympia is our capital?"

"Olympia is the capital of the west; McCall is the capital of the east."

"We're one now, and as one, we have one capital. Without a capital, we don't have a country!"

"Charles, calm down. The country is alive and well as long as I'm out taking territory and you're there representing the people."

"The committee is calling you back. You need to come to McCall right away and tell them face-to-face why you're refusing the demands of the duly elected leaders," Charles snapped.

"You must be confusing me with someone else, but I'm the supreme leader of all the Cascadian forces. I feel it best to keep my troops driving towards Cheyenne, and Simpson's falling back to defend McCall. By the way, the governor of Idaho has fled and Boise has fallen too. That comes as no surprise, but we are making progress, and I'm not about to leave the field to come back and talk,"

Gordon said, a slight irritated tone in his voice. He could hear Samantha's voice echoing in his head and he'd promised he'd keep his cool, but if Charles kept coming at him, he wasn't sure how long he'd be able to keep that promise.

"Gordon, you have an obligation to follow the laws of our new country. You're being summoned and you need to come," Charles demanded.

"Not going to happen."

"Then you leave me no choice but to call for your formal dismissal as commander of all Cascadian forces."

"Go ahead and try it," Gordon dared him.

"I have the votes, especially after your inhumane behavior following the surrender of the US forces in Mountain Home."

Jones's jaw had dropped and his eyes were glued on Gordon as he heard the defiant tone he was giving Charles.

"Like I said, go ahead and try it."

"I will."

"And who will lead this army, huh?"

"We have capable people," Charles said but was unable to name one person. Charles took a deep breath and paused; he could see how the conversation was going sideways. *"Gordon, come back, talk to the committee. Put John Steele in charge until we can get through this,"* Charles said, his tone shifting in an attempt to reconcile.

"Charles, do me a favor and relay this to the committee: I don't apologize for not sending Simpson's forces into a battle they'll most surely lose. I'm fighting this war to win, and winning means I have to do things that aren't popular or politically expedient. If my decisions lead to us losing this war, then my punishment will be more severe than anything you or the committee could ever deal out. I'm pressing forward and taking advantage of my successes, and will see you and the committee when I return victorious against the United States."

Jones could only hear one side of the conversation and, upon hearing Gordon's speech, raised his thumb and nodded.

No reply came from Charles.

"Charles, you there?" Gordon asked.

A few voices burst over the phone. There were too many people talking for Gordon to make out who it was or what they were saying. Suddenly the voices disappeared and Charles came on. *"I put the phone on speaker so the entire committee and the McCall council could hear. All I can say is they are not happy. Your insolence and disregard for the civilian command are noted and will be dealt with,"* Charles threatened.

Gordon's blood began to boil. If there was one thing he hated, it was being threatened. "Put the phone back on speaker," he snapped. That was it, the promise of keeping his cool was gone.

Charles obliged.

"Whoever is there listening, it's easy for you to sit and pass judgment. You're not here on the ground fighting; you're sitting comfortably back there trying to dictate how a war should be conducted. I witnessed for myself how that is folly. The wars this republic will fight will be led from the battlefield, not a conference room. Like I said earlier, if I fail, then you can pass judgment and do what you will, but if I succeed, and I plan on doing just that, I want to have each one of you who opposes my efforts to publically apologize then step down from your positions."

The phone erupted with chatter and yelling.

"And one more thing you can chew on while you're sitting on your asses. I have signed a treaty with Jacques Marceau, the prime minister of Western Canada."

Charles clicked the phone off speaker and yelled into the receiver, *"You did what?"*

"He just left not two minutes before you called. I forged a mutually binding agreement between our two countries that will benefit us both."

"You don't have the authority!" Charles blasted.

The behind-closed-doors rivalry between Charles and Gordon had now erupted into an open feud, only Charles had one advantage, that being he had been able to convince the political forces to side with him. What Charles miscalculated was Gordon's strength, that being he had the allegiance of the army.

"This treaty will hasten the end of the war and help us secure our victory sooner," Gordon informed him.

Side chatter over the phone was confusing for Gordon.

Charles emerged again and declared, *"You misplayed your hand, Gordon. Your days are numbered. You see, I have the votes—"*

Gordon's blood was boiling. He had heard enough

from the people he considered political hacks. Not letting Charles finish, Gordon fired back, "You may have the votes, but I have the soldiers."

Sandy, Utah

Annaliese exited the house, expecting to find Hector, but he wasn't there in his typical spot on the porch. She stood and placed her hands on her hips and thought it strange. Ever since he could wheel himself around, he had come out there daily. It didn't matter the weather, she'd always find him there. So where was he?

Back inside the house, Annaliese called out, "Hector?"

No reply.

Her mother exited the mudroom, holding a basket of rags. "Off to do some cleaning."

"Have you seen Hector?"

"Not since breakfast."

"Hmm."

She put on a heather gray sweater, pulled her long blonde hair into a ponytail, and went looking for him outside. A bit of concern crossed her mind only because he was always in his spot.

Samuel had built a ramp off the deck, but he had only used it once right after it was completed. Nope, Hector was a homebody if anyone ever was.

The property was huge, so if he left the house, he'd

have many places to get lost.

Her first stop was the gardens, not there. Every one she came upon she'd ask his whereabouts, but got the same response, no one had seen Hector.

From the back gardens to the corral to the storage facilities, she looked for him but nothing. Her concern turned to a tinge of fear. He couldn't get too far and he couldn't walk, or at least not that she was aware of. She had attempted physical therapy with him, but he refused to really try.

Flustered as to his location, she stood in the wide open yard in between the main house and the barn that operated as their clinic. She hadn't looked in there, and it was the last place to go.

She hurried there, opened the front door and immediately spotted him.

Hector was sitting next to a patient who had been brought in not unlike him. She was covered in third-degree burns over most of her body. The difference for this patient was her prognosis was not good, so they had stopped giving her critical medicines that were in short supply and put her on a stream of morphine.

She walked towards him but stopped when she saw he was holding the woman's hand.

He had left his comfortable spot on the porch to give love and comfort to a patient.

She was in awe at the sight of him petting her hand.

He bent over and whispered into the unresponsive woman's ear.

Annaliese couldn't make out what he said, but he had

talked more than yes, no or thank you.

Done, he lifted his head but spotted Annaliese and nodded.

This was her signal to approach. She came forward and said, "You're so sweet to come sit with her."

He nodded.

"She won't live long."

He nodded again.

"So you just decided to come and pay a visit? This isn't like you. What's gotten into you?" she asked him.

He pointed at her.

"Me."

"Yes."

"You came and visited her because of me?"

"Yes," he said and pointed at her again then himself.

"Because I cared for you, you're returning the favor and caring for her?"

"Yes."

"So you were listening last night; you can understand me. Sometimes I wondered if you don't talk because you don't understand English that good."

He pulled his wheelchair back and started for the door.

"Where you off to now?" she asked.

He wheeled to the door and pushed against it.

She rushed over to help.

He shook his head, telling her to stop.

He used all his strength until he had the door open, and wheeled outside.

She followed him into the late morning sun.

Like a man with a purpose, he crossed the yard and into the backyard. He pulled out a pad of paper and drew what looked like parallel bars, then pointed to an area next to the swing set.

"You want those things right there?" she asked.

He nodded.

"For what?" she asked.

With his left palm open, he took two fingers on his right and mimicked walking.

She lit up. "You want to try to walk, you want to do some physical therapy?"

He nodded.

She touched his shoulder and exclaimed, "Absolutely, I'll let Samuel know. We'll get someone on that immediately."

For the third time in two days he said, "Thank you."

McCall, Idaho, Republic of Cascadia

Samantha had mixed feelings concerning the extra security that was placed around her. She appreciated the protection but missed the privacy a life of anonymity brought.

Gordon had handpicked the men, all Marines from Simpson's forces, to stay back and provide close protection, and put Nelson in charge of making sure things ran smoothly.

For Nelson to be in charge of Marines made him feel

uneasy, but Gordon wouldn't have it any other way.

"Here you go, ma'am," a young Marine lance corporal said, opening the door of the Humvee for her.

"Thank you, Lance Corporal Sanchez," Samantha said, stepping out into the brisk cold air. She steadied her step on the icy ground, ensuring she didn't slip. A few inches of snow had fallen overnight with more coming down lightly.

With Haley and Luke going to school now, it gave Samantha time for herself. She missed the kids but also enjoyed her me time.

Reopening the schools was an important step in returning to normalcy. Everyone got behind it and supported it as best they could. There were some logical issues like no power, but the teachers and staff improvised and did the best they could with what they had.

Halloween represented the beginning of what Samantha called the extended holiday season. She enjoyed this time of year and was hoping she could make the most of it in McCall, especially for Haley and Luke. That night they planned on attending a costume party at the Shore Lodge in lieu of trick-or-treating on Halloween night. Even in the relative safety of McCall, she didn't want Haley going door to door. Not having easily available stores or up-to-date merchandise to buy, she had to get creative in order to make a costume for Haley.

Last year Haley had dressed up as Rarity from *My Little Pony*, but this year her choice was vastly different. Knowing her father was off fighting, Haley wanted to be a Marine. This was a stretch from years before, as Haley tended to be a very girlie girl.

Samantha had first suggested she be a princess, fairy or even a cuddly animal, but Haley wouldn't change her mind. When asked why, her answer couldn't be disputed. She told Samantha that she was dressing up like Daddy. How could any parent object to that? Other children went for their favorite characters or superheroes, but Haley considered Gordon to be her hero.

Fortunately, Samantha was surrounded by Marines, so getting a uniform to use as material was easy; now she just need to have one made that actually fit Haley's tiny six-year-old frame.

Phyllis, a local and confidante and friend of Samantha's, was a master at everything homesteading. She had contributed greatly to the community and specifically to Samantha by teaching her skills that had been lost on the modern woman, one of those being sewing and clothes making.

"I'll be right back," Samantha said to Sanchez and carefully shuffled towards Phyllis's house, a small log-sided home within the city limits of town.

When she stepped on the front steps, the door opened quickly. The strong aroma of pumpkin spice wafted over Samantha, giving her a warm and fuzzy feeling. "Good morning, Phyllis."

"Good morning to you, my dear," Phyllis replied. She was not an elderly woman, in her late fifties, but the many years of living in the harsher conditions up north and spending countless time outside had weathered her face, giving her the appearance she was older than she was. "It's a beautiful morning, isn't it? I just love the first snows and crisp air," Phyllis happily said.

Phyllis's jovial attitude always made Samantha feel welcome and helped to brighten the gloomiest days.

"Is it okay if I say I miss San Diego weather?" Samantha joked as she stepped inside the foyer.

"You're already fed up with the weather and winter hasn't even started yet. Dear, you're in for a shocker," Phyllis quipped, taking Samantha's coat.

Samantha slipped off her Sorels and slipped on a pair of Uggs that Phyllis provided for her guests. With her eyes pressed closed, she inhaled deeply. "Smells so good in here."

"I'm making some pumpkin spice muffins for the party tonight," Phyllis said, walking into the small kitchen.

Samantha followed her in and said, "I've said it before, but how do you do so much in a kitchen so small?"

"It's not the size that matters," Phyllis joked.

Feeling giddy, Samantha joked, "Depends on what it is."

"Missing your man?" Phyllis asked.

"I just want him here. I want to feel him next to me in bed. I wish this whole mess was done and over," Samantha lamented.

Phyllis began pulling muffins from a tin and replied, "I don't think it will be over for some time. All we can do is pray."

"Prayer is something I haven't done in a while,"

Samantha confessed.

"I don't like to pressure people, but you're always welcome at my church. I know it does me good."

"Thank you, I'll keep that in mind."

"How's your little princess?" Phyllis asked.

"Princess Marine now."

"Oh, yeah, back in the second bedroom, her costume is lying on the bed," Phyllis said.

Samantha headed back, excited to see Haley's costume. She refused to call it a uniform because doing so would make it seem too real for her, and the thought of Haley in a warrior's outfit seemed distressing. In the bedroom, she found the tan pixilated uniform lying on the bed. It looked perfect, right down to the name tags with VAN ZANDT above the left chest pocket.

"What do you think?" Phyllis asked from the doorway. She had walked up without Samantha knowing.

Samantha jumped and answered, "It's perfect, thank you. What do I owe you?"

"Nothing, my pleasure."

"No, we agreed you'd take payment of some sort."

"Fine, fine."

"So what shall it be, some canned food, a box of ammo, batteries?" Samantha said, going through a short list of what had become the currency of the time.

"Follow me," Phyllis said, motioning for her to follow. Phyllis took her into the kitchen and grabbed a muffin. "Here."

"Thanks."

"Taste it, let me know if it's good or not. I ran low

on cane sugar, so I used what I had left of some light brown."

Samantha took a bite and moaned, "Oh, my God, it's so good. It's moist, fluffy, it's amazing. The kids are going to love them."

"I'm so happy, I was nervous it may not come out. You know, baking is an exact science; one deviation from a recipe can spell disaster. I thought I'd have plenty of sugar but ran low because I made the kids some hard candy on a stick," Phyllis said, pointing to a cardboard box that had dozens of candy-covered sticks poking out of it.

"That's so sweet," Samantha gushed.

"It is sweet," Phyllis joked.

"It sounds like I can bring you some sugar for payment," Samantha said.

"Nope, your payment was being my taste tester. It's a high-risk job and you survived."

"Absolutely not, I'm paying you; there's no ifs, ands or buts."

A loud banging on the door made them both jump.

"Huh, wonder who that may be," Phyllis said, rushing to the front door. She opened it and found Sanchez standing there, a look of urgency written on his face.

Samantha, seeing who it was, called out, "Everything all right?"

"No, ma'am, it's Luke. He got into a fight at school," Sanchez reported.

"Is he okay?" Samantha asked, pushing by Phyllis.

"No, ma'am, his arm was broken."

Samantha stepped out the door but hesitated when she remembered she was wearing the Uggs. She kicked them off and put her boots back on, grabbed her coat and ran out the door.

Cheyenne, Wyoming, United States

Conner wasn't surprised, but it still came as shocking to have it confirmed. He had always found Wilbur's strong opposition to most of his policies annoying, but he kept her around solely because she was smart, capable and he was open to hearing differing opinions. But knowing she was possibly working against him made him angry. He had more respect for his enemies. A traitor was the lowest form of existence and something he had zero tolerance for.

"You're sure she just didn't stop by for a drink?" Conner asked, wanting to hear something different than what he had been told.

Schmidt coughed and repeated what he told Conner moments before, elaborating on the information from one of his men who was in Pat's Coffee shop last night. "No, sir, she came in, went to the counter, asked for Pat, and then headed towards the back. She reappeared twenty minutes later, no drink in hand, no food, no bag, nothing, she just left."

"What time was this?" Conner asked, wanting to

make sure he had his facts straight.

"A bit past nineteen hundred," Schmidt confirmed.

Conner stood looking out the large window behind his desk. The cool fall air had turned the birch tree leaves a brilliant golden yellow. Like many people, fall was a favorite time of year for him and always brought back memories of him and Julia taking walks along the Potomac or going hiking in Northern Virginia. There was a simple joy he found in this time of year above the others. Summers were always too hot, and for someone who sweated easily like he did, the heat was an inconvenience more than anything, and winter too presented obstacles he'd sooner miss, like freezing rain and snow drifts.

"Let's bring her in, and let's try not to make a scene," Conner ordered.

"Sir, I have a different approach."

Conner didn't turn; he kept his eyes glued on the people and cars going by outside. "Go ahead."

"If we bring her in, people will notice her missing. She's too well known to have her just disappear. The minute her fellow traitors know, they'll scurry like rats. I say we keep tabs on her. I've been cataloging her movements and listing every person she comes into contact with. We know now she's feeding information to Pat, but who else might she be working with? I only just started tracking her. She has to be one of the leaders, so let's keep her active, thinking no one is watching. With your permission, I want to listen in on her calls."

"Fine, do it, do whatever you need to, but if you

come across a conspiracy to do our country harm and it's time critical, jump on it and bring them all in. Don't hesitate, act quickly," Conner ordered.

"Yes, sir."

Conner finally broke away from the window and faced Schmidt. "Christ, Major, you look like shit."

"I'm not feeling well today," Schmidt admitted.

"Now you say you're not feeling well. Either you have a high pain tolerance, or you're now willing to be honest."

"All things are in place for your speech later today. I can promise it will be exactly the thing that will give you the reason to come down hard on all these people."

Conner walked to his chair and sat down. "Nothing like a good false flag to get the people behind you to do whatever you want."

"It's not a bad thing, sir. We know these people wish to do us harm, so why not get them before they act. Even if it requires taking a few of ours out in the process, we're actually saving lives," Schmidt said, rationalizing their approach.

"What is it with people? They want us to keep them safe, but when we do the heavy lifting, they get all uncomfortable."

"It's easy for them, sir. They get the advantages of the safety but also the privilege of being righteous without the consequences of having to make a hard decision or do a damn thing. It's so typical. I would've thought the collapse would have changed some people, but it looks like that soft, warm and fuzzy perspective is still alive and well."

"I wonder if they comb the hair of their pet unicorn every night before going to bed," Conner joked, mocking his political enemies.

Schmidt chuckled.

"Major, I need you to go to that appointment. Everything will work itself out," Conner ordered. He was sticking to his demand that Schmidt conduct his follow-up appointments.

"Please, sir, my place is out there. I don't want to miss it."

"You shouldn't," Conner assured him.

Schmidt looked at his watch and saw the time slipping away. He had given his team the mission and it could be executed without him if need be. "I need to go now, then."

"Let me know how it goes," Conner said.

Schmidt got up and exited his office.

Conner immediately picked up the phone and called out. "Dr. Weston, please."

A moment passed.

"This is Dr. Weston."

"Doc, Conner here. Major Schmidt is heading your way. Don't forget what I told you yesterday."

"Yes, Mr. President."

Conner hung up the phone, looking at the clock. His speech was in five hours and his anxiety was rising. Just what types of fireworks did Schmidt have in store? He could hardly wait.

McCall, Idaho, Republic of Cascadia

"Why didn't you transfer him to the hospital?" Samantha barked.

Luke sat on the cot in the school nurse's office in visible pain. His right forearm had the telltale sign it had suffered a break. Halfway down the forearm it bent at a slight thirty-degree angle and the area around it was swollen and bruised.

"It's our policy not to administer aid nor forward a student to the hospital without a parent's consent," the principal said.

Frustrated, she looked at Luke and said, "C'mon, sweetheart, let's get that taken care of."

Luke stood up, his right arm cradling his left. His face contorted in pain as he took a step.

"I know it hurts, but soon we'll get someone who knows what they're doing to take care of you," Samantha said, her tone directed at the principal and nurse, who stood watching Luke walk out as if bystanders watching an accident. She cut her eyes at them just before leaving.

"It hurts real bad," Luke moaned.

"I know," Samantha said, patting his back.

"Ouch, don't touch me," Luke complained.

"Sorry."

They exited the front doors of the school and found Nelson rushing towards them. "I just heard. I came as soon as I found out." He stepped up to Luke and asked, "What happened?"

"A fight."

"How about we ask him all the twenty questions once we get him patched up."

"Let's take my truck," Nelson suggested.

They piled into Nelson's truck and headed to the hospital, which was a short drive away.

Sanchez followed in the Humvee.

Sporting a cast and feeling better from the painkillers, Luke was escorted by Samantha to the front waiting room, where Nelson sat patiently waiting.

Seeing Luke, Nelson jumped up. "Look at you, boss. You look like a badass with the cast."

"Ha," Luke said.

"Can I be the first to sign it?" Nelson asked.

"I think I should leave that privilege for Haley," Luke replied, his mind always considering Haley above all others.

Samantha rubbed his back, this time with no complaints from Luke, and said, "You're a good and thoughtful young man."

"That he is," Nelson said.

Seneca suddenly appeared through the hospital front doors. "I'm so glad I ran into you."

Samantha gave her old friend a hug and complimented her long hair. "I really love that you've grown your hair out."

"Oh, thanks," Seneca said, touching the dark brown strands that jetted from her tight-fitting beanie.

"This has to be the worst place to be discussing hair," Nelson joked.

"I like it," Luke said.

Seneca reached out and rubbed Luke's left shoulder. "You holding up?"

"Yeah, I'll be fine. Like Gordon says, what doesn't kill you will make you stronger."

"True words there," Nelson replied, his gaze fondly looking at Seneca.

Their relationship had now progressed to an intensely intimate one, and rumors that the two would get married were floating around, but to date nothing formal had been announced. But to see the two together, anyone could see their bond and attraction was obvious.

"How about I take you to pick up Haley?" Nelson asked.

"No, you guys go ahead. I'll see you tonight at the party?" Samantha asked.

"Of course, sure, but, um, can I ask what happened?" Nelson asked, his patience being taxed, wanting to know the cause of the fight.

Luke lowered his head and answered, "I don't want to talk about it."

Nelson tried to make eye contact, but Luke wouldn't look up. "You sure?"

"Maybe later," Luke said.

"Listen, tough guy, there's no reason to be embarrassed," Nelson said.

"I'm not embarrassed; I just don't want to talk about it," Luke said, his tone a bit snappy.

"No worries, but if you ever wish to, please just hit me up," Nelson said.

Samantha put her arm over Luke's shoulders and led him out. Once in the Humvee, Samantha asked the same question Nelson had, "What happened? I'd like to know."

"Like I told Nelson, I don't want to talk about it."

"I know you were hurt today, but I need to know, not because I'm being nosey, but if this has anything to do with Gordon or our position in this town, I need to know. If there are people that wish to hurt you because of who you are, they may want to hurt Haley too," Samantha said, calmly explaining why he should answer in simple terms.

Luke looked out the window, his breath fogging the glass.

Samantha waited a moment and asked again, "What happened?"

"Argh, you won't stop, will you?" Luke protested.

"Not until you tell me."

Luke resisted looking at her, but he finally confessed to what occurred, "Two boys were saying bad things about Gordon."

"Like what?"

"That he's a bad person, a murderer."

"You know that's not true, don't you?"

Luke looked at her and brushed his long bangs out of his face. "Of course I know that. I know he's killed people, but some people suck and deserve to die."

Hearing Luke speak like this was shocking. He had always been a more docile and sweet boy.

"They kept taunting me and I kept ignoring them until they mentioned Haley."

"What did they say about her?"

"They said she was a freak."

"A freak? Why would they say that?" Samantha asked, astonished to hear Haley described that way.

"Haley told someone in class that Uncle Sebastian visited her after he died."

"I see." Samantha sighed.

"They started yelling, 'Haley is a freak,'" Luke said.

"And?"

"I just exploded on them. I hit the first kid in the mouth, but the second kid tackled me. Next thing I know they're both on top of me and…" Luke said but hesitated.

Samantha could see he was emotional.

"Other kids came around, but no one helped me. They laughed as the two beat me up. Next thing I knew they jumped on my arm. I heard it snap," Luke said, his voice trembling.

"I admire you for standing up for your family," Samantha said, taking his hand.

He flinched and pulled his hand away. "Look what it got me."

"I'm proud of you and Gordon would be too," Samantha said, not one to chastise a child for defending the honor of a loved one. The world was different and fighting was a major part of it.

"If Sebastian were alive, he would teach me how to fight." Luke groaned.

"When Gordon returns, he will; I'll make sure of it."

"Stop bullshitting everyone, Samantha. I hear you lie to Haley all the time. You don't know if he's ever coming back."

Samantha recoiled from his statement and couldn't let it stand. "You listen here, I have to tell Haley that. She's a little girl. I can't fill her mind with thoughts that her father may not come back. She's not old enough to understand. I know she seems wiser than most six-year-old kids, but she's still young. Also, I know you've been telling her stuff, stop that. I don't want to hear you filling her mind with things. I know you got hurt today and I truly applaud you for standing up for your family, but don't think you can hurt me or Haley just because you got hurt."

Luke grumbled and turned away.

Sanchez pulled up at the school and cleared his throat. "We're here."

"Just sit here and think about what I said," Samantha sternly said as she got out.

When the door closed, Sanchez cocked his head and said, "Hey, kid."

"What?"

"I can't help but hear things, so I'll say it like this. Your mom is right."

"She's not my mom."

"Whatever, she's the next best thing to a mom a kid can have, and let me tell you, family is the most important thing in this world right now. I know she cares for you and you need to know things are bad out there."

"I know they are, I've been out there, okay," Luke snapped.

Sanchez spun around and looked at Luke. "Hey, kid."

"My name isn't kid." Luke glared.

"Luke."

"By the way, aren't you supposed to be nice to me?" Luke stated.

"Here's a four-one-one for ya, I'm not here to be nice, I'm here to keep your ass safe, nothing more, and your dad…Gordon would agree. Listen, I know you're pissed off because you got your ass beat today, but let me tell you something, use that ass beating as a positive—don't quit or ever give up. If you go back to school tomorrow and those kids come at you, fight back again even if they beat your ass again. Don't ever quit and don't ever show them they've beaten your spirit. Once they do, they own you."

"So that's your wisdom, go back and get my ass kicked every day? Whoa, you're like a philosopher."

"If you were my kid, I'd smack you in the mouth just for that comment. Fucking kids these days are only smartasses because they can get away with it. There isn't fear that your actions will result in negative consequences. Let me tell you, this world is not the old one. If you think you can open your mouth like that out there, expect that it might get closed forever."

"Can you please stop talking to me?" Luke complained.

Sanchez saw Samantha coming with Haley but wasn't

done talking. "Listen, if you want to learn how to fight, come see me tomorrow morning before school and right after school."

"Why?"

"Because tomorrow is your first day of combat training."

Mountain Home, Idaho, Republic of Cascadia

Gordon stood before his company commanders. All were experienced Marines with many years of service. Having a mission was something these men thrived on, and soon they'd have another.

Gordon had needed a night and the morning to make his decision, and he hoped it would work. The closer they got to Cheyenne, the greater the risk of aerial bombardment. So to minimize this threat, he had a plan of splitting his forces up into three smaller ones. This still might not stop Conner, but giving him three targets versus one just made sense.

After his briefing, Gordon opened the floor for questions.

"Sir, we have a month, maybe less, of food for my men. What's the timing for resupply?" a young captain asked from the back of the room.

"Yes, supplies, I should have mentioned that, so thank you for the question. Mountain Home has proven to be a gold mine. We will get your units resupplied tonight from the caches we've found. This includes water, fuel, parts and medical supplies on top of the food you'll need. If there is anything specific you need, let Corporal Jones know."

"I could use a beer," someone joked.

Laughter broke out.

"And a hot piece of ass to go with it," another Marine hollered.

More laughter.

Gordon didn't mind the joking and levity. These men deserved to let their hair down now and then.

Another officer raised his hand. "Sir, you said that the refugees are heading east with us."

"Correct," Gordon said.

The captain looked at his fellow officers and asked, "Aren't we using them like human shields?"

"Yes and no, I know it sounds horrible to say that some aspect of having them come along with us is for cover, but we're also providing them security. We can't take care of these people, and the best place for them to go is Cheyenne. We don't have the resources, but the United States does. Does that help answer your question?"

"Yes, sir."

A short and muscular major stood up and asked, "Sir, you didn't mention my company."

"Who are you with, Major?" Gordon asked.

"Charlie Company, One One."

"That's because I have something else for you. I'll detail that after the briefing."

"Sir, that's a bit unorthodox. It's best we all know our individual missions," the major suggested.

"I don't want anyone knowing just in case. What people don't know, they can't tell."

Some grumbling in the ranks distracted Gordon. Picking up that his decision to keep Charlie Company's special operation secret was not popular, he said, "It's not because I distrust you, it's because I genuinely believe that as we go further east, the chances of us being attacked will increase as well as the chances that some of us may get captured. I don't want anyone to spill the beans accidentally, and if they don't know what the beans are, none can get spilled."

An officer in the front row blurted out, "But that sounds like you don't trust us."

Gordon made sure to blunt that view. "Not true, not true. The war is more important than you, you, you, you and me. This is about winning our independence and nothing more, so don't let your egos get bruised so easily, okay?"

Several men nodded.

Gordon wanted what he said to sink in, so he repeated his question only louder, "Okay?"

"Yes, sir!" many of the men said in unison, most of them nodding their acknowledgement.

"Good, any more questions?"

A few more officers raised their hands and asked questions. Gordon promptly answered them until he had fielded every last question.

After he dismissed them, he called the commanding

officer of Charlie Company over. "Major Bergman, I know you have a ton of questions and I'm going to get right down to it. I've slated your infantry company for a special mission, one that is unconventional, but I know your men can tackle it."

Jones and John remained, but Gordon wanted time alone with the major. "Gentlemen, I wish to talk privately with Major Bergman."

They nodded.

John said, "Have a good night."

"You too," Gordon replied.

Both men exited.

"Where was I?" Gordon asked, fatigue showing on his face.

"You have a special mission for my company," Bergman replied.

"Yes. So do you think you're up for something a bit different?"

"Sure," Bergman said, curious as to what they were being tasked with.

"I feel one way to defeat Conner is to keep him bogged down with internal problems, you know, domestic issues, local attacks, bombings, day-to-day harassment."

Bergman nodded.

"I need your men to go into Cheyenne as refugees, it will be similar to how we penetrated the base here, but this will be on a much larger scale. You'll leave tomorrow with a group of legitimate refugees; I have a few five-ton trucks waiting to take all of you. They'll take you as far as

Rock Springs, Wyoming; after that you'll have to walk the rest of the way. We'll provide you with food and water, but you'll have to ditch some of your weapons before you enter the outskirts of Cheyenne. If you all bring in weapons, it will look suspicious. And you can't take comms in, nothing. Make sure you see Jones for some civilian clothes. You can't be wearing your uniforms."

"Roger that."

"How do you feel about this mission?"

"Whatever you need, but I never thought after fighting insurgents in Iraq and Afghanistan that I'd end up being one. And I hope you understand that a large chunk, around fifty-five percent of my men, aren't Marines but new recruits. I hope that you considered that when making your selection."

"Many in our army are new recruits, there's no escaping it, and I thought it best to implement them with the old Marine units. Having them in their separate or even segregated units might not have been as successful."

"I agree," Bergman noted.

"Get with Jones, he'll get you everything you need."

"Roger that."

"If you've got nothing more, may I be dismissed? I have a lot to do."

"Yeah, go back and inform your men, but please make it clear that this operation is secret. They can't whisper a word of this to anyone," Gordon said.

"Copy that," Bergman said.

"Good man."

Bergman stood up to leave but stopped short. "Sir,

why my company?"

"Your Charlie Company, you're the best, that's what I heard," Gordon replied.

Bergman's chest grew a couple inches hearing Gordon's answer. "This is kind of a suicide mission, isn't?"

"Doesn't have to be, just create as much mayhem, confusion and problems as possible. Be creative in your approach. You have experience with dealing with insurgents, take those lessons and apply them."

"Sounds good. I hope to see you back in McCall one day," Bergman said.

"Me too, I'll buy you a few drinks when I do."

Bergman exited the room.

Gordon stepped over to a chair and fell into it. His body ached and his feet were throbbing. Sometimes he felt like he was twice his age. He leaned back and began to process everything that had occurred and came to the conclusion that he did have big balls, as Jones said. He was putting everything on the line; he had made deals that threatened his leadership and was about to embark on a mission east without knowing if they'd even make it. Dividing his forces was risky, but keeping them together could be worse. The move east was more about finding locations to hunker down and play wait and see. Conner knew he was at Mountain Home and it was only a matter of when they'd get hit there. He needed to scatter his men and place them where Conner couldn't find them. If Bergman and his men were successful, he could then come out of hiding and attack the city. When that would be was unknown. He just hoped it worked because he also had to contend with Conner's Marine battalions in Olympia. To call what he was about to do a Hail Mary pass was an appropriate name for it. For Cascadia the war had only begun several months ago, but they were already in the fourth quarter and the clock was ticking.

Cheyenne, Wyoming, United States

Conner was shaking from the excitement. From a large window in the conference room, he watched the people of Cheyenne gather near the checkpoints of the green zone. He estimated there were thousands. If this went as planned, he'd soon have the moral authority to do anything he wanted regardless of the opposition.

Conner's assistant, Heather, stepped into the room and advised, "Twenty minutes, Mr. President." She left as quickly as she had arrived. He liked Heather; she was professional, prompt, courteous, and didn't ask any questions that didn't pertain to getting her job done; otherwise she kept her mouth shut. Plus she was easy on the eyes, something that was nice to have around.

"I guess I better get down there."

His assistant came back into the room and informed him, "Your doctor called."

"Okay."

"He said it's done."

"Good, let's get this party started."

Conner walked through the corridors of the main governmental building until he found the exit on the ground floor. Flanked by his security, he exited the building and into the cool late afternoon air. He paused and took a deep breath. "Ahh, fresh air."

The roar of people talking, laughing and some chanting echoed off the concrete and glass of the surrounding buildings. Apparently he wasn't the only one excited about his speech but obviously for different reasons.

Like a boxer who already knew he'd won his fight before the first punch was thrown, Conner strutted towards the raised podium. Flashbacks of the time months ago when he exited the tank ran through his mind. That was a powerful moment and he was confident this would be as powerful. He stopped just at the base of the stairs to the platform, took a deep breath and scaled the ten steps. Once on top he looked down on the masses gathered waiting to hear his pivotal speech. Some of them came thinking their resistance had won and he was there to capitulate, others came to see the man who had helmed the country since the attacks, and others just had nothing else better to do.

He raised his arms and a roar followed. Intermixed in the clapping and cheers were boos and hisses. He reached into his coat pocket and removed a folded stack of papers and placed them on the podium. Opening them, he chuckled that they were blank, not one word was written because he didn't need a real speech, all he needed to do was ad-lib until Schmidt's men acted.

In front of him were large sections of bulletproof Plexiglas. This was one mistake, as he wanted to give the image he wasn't afraid and hiding. He cursed under his breath, but let it go quickly, as soon it wouldn't matter.

With his index finger he tapped the microphone and could hear it echo.

He was ready, this was it. Leaning forward, he spoke, "Good afternoon, Cheyenne, good afternoon, America!"

The people roared, again a mix of cheers and boos.

"I want to thank you for coming. What I'm about to say will have a lasting impact on you."

Again the people sang out.

Raising his arms, he motioned for them to quiet down. "Now if everyone could lower their voices."

They heeded his call for silence save a few who continued their boos and jeers.

"I know not everyone loves me out there, but if you could respect the others who want to listen, I'd appreciate it and so would they."

"Dictator!" a man screamed.

Conner couldn't see the man, but when he searched, he could see the vast number of soldiers and security that encircled the massive crowd of thousands.

"Liar!" another person cried out.

"Now please, be respectful to those around you. If you intend on disrupting this speech, I will have you removed."

"Murderer!" screamed a woman from the far back.

Feigning irritation, Conner decided to use their outbursts to frame what was about to happen. "People, please. Show some respect. I know you dislike me and my policies and have even called for violence against the government, but I pray, I beg you not to resort to such tactics and to allow me to give my speech and allow those who came to listen without spewing your hate!"

A group of a half-dozen people raised a banner and began to chant, "Dictator, dictator, dictator!"

Those who had come to listen without interruption turned their own irritation towards the protestors. "Shut up, let the man speak!"

"Now is not a time to be disruptive, but a time to listen!" Conner called out, his voice booming over the large speakers.

"Dictator, dictator, dictator!" the group chanted, the cries being picked up by others through the crowd.

Conner could see the soldiers and security communicating and motioning towards the protestors. He tried to see if he could find Schmidt's men; he wondered if some of them were the protestors.

From his left a brick smacked the Plexiglas and bounced off. Conner recoiled and felt a sudden sense of excitement surge through his body. The brick was followed by a can of red paint and sticks.

He thought those must be Schmidt's men; this was perfect.

The crowd began to heave and push as the many innocents started to fear a riot was about to break out. The sound of the thousands crying, yelling and screaming began to drown out the chanting protestors.

The moment was coming, Conner knew it. Playing

into the scene, he said, "Please, everyone, calm down!"

The cries and screams intensified as people tried to leave, but the sheer number of people made it impossible as people pushed and shoved against each other.

The intensity of the scene below kept building like a crescendo until the sound came Conner had wanted to hear.

BOOM!

A massive explosion erupted off to his right about two hundred feet out. The concussion from the blast was so powerful he fell to the ground.

The cries and screams turned to wails and moans of terror as the crowd tried to run. People trampled over others in their rush to escape.

BOOM!

Another blast equal in force to the first erupted from Conner's left. He pivoted his head to see, but the red paint that had splattered the Plexiglas prevented him from seeing.

The volume of terrorized civilians was deafening.

Conner scurried to his feet to get a view of what was happening. He jumped behind the microphone, but before he could speak, his security grabbed him forcefully and pulled him away. They huddled over him and raced back towards the government office building. Conner craned his head around to get one last look and saw thick black smoke billowing. Shrieks and wails of horror echoed everywhere. Pandemonium and terror filled the streets. The plan had been executed beautifully; now he needed to close the deal.

McCall, Idaho, Republic of Cascadia

Samantha cradled Haley in her arms as she walked into the house.

Luke was close behind, his arm snug against his chest and his head hung low.

"Sweetheart, can you please turn down Haley's bed for me?" Samantha asked Luke.

"Can I turn on some lights first?" Luke grumbled. He still hadn't gotten out of his funk since the fight at school. He wandered to various tables and lit the kerosene lanterns that sat on top of them.

The lanterns bathed the mocha-colored walls of the great room and hallway in a warm orange glow.

Luke grabbed one and took it with him down the hall to Haley's bedroom.

Samantha grunted as she followed him. "Gosh, she's getting heavy."

Haley had fallen asleep on the drive back from the party, and once Haley passed out, she wasn't easy to wake up.

Luke did as requested and pulled the blanket and sheet down on Haley's bed.

Samantha plopped Haley into the bed and carefully removed her costume.

Not saying a word, Luke left the lantern and exited the room.

Finished with putting Haley to bed, Samantha went directly to Luke's bedroom. She found the door closed, so she knocked. Just above a whisper she asked, "Are you asleep?"

"No."

Samantha cracked the door and said, "Can I come in for a moment?"

"Sure."

She stepped in and walked to the side of the bed.

Luke was tucked in with his head propped up on two pillows.

"I wanted again to reiterate what I said earlier…"

"Are you going to chew my ass again?"

"Chew your ass? Why would you say that?"

"Well, you did."

"No, why would you say it like that?"

Luke looked away and replied, "No reason."

Samantha could see her goal of making things right was already going sideways, so she stopped her brief interrogation. "Um, I just wanted to say that I'm proud of you. You stuck up for our family and that is more important than ever. As you know, things are difficult with Gordon gone and the war. I know you'll hear lots of rumors and some might scare you, so I want to make you a deal. Come talk to me, ask me anything, and I'll be perfectly honest. I won't mince words, I'll tell you if they're true or not."

Liking what he was hearing, Luke turned and faced her. "Okay."

Samantha reached and touched his arm. "The thing is I need you to be strong. We both need to be strong for Haley and for each other. Family is all we have in this crazy world."

"I know."

"Please know that I love you and that I consider you a son. Your place is here with us."

Keeping with his minimal replies, he said, "Okay."

"Just so you know, Lance Corporal Sanchez spoke with me about the conversation he and you had earlier."

Luke's eyes lit up.

"He asked me if it would be okay if he taught you some tactical training."

Luke sat up; his head perked, anticipating the completion of her statement.

"And I said it was a great idea."

"YES!" Luke exclaimed.

"Here's what I expect out of you, though…"

"I know, make sure I do my homework first."

"No, this is just as important as homework. Heck, it's more important than learning algebra. I want you to take this seriously, train hard. I know your arm is broken, but I want you to dig deep, work around it. I want you to be the best because the Van Zandt family needs more warriors and little Haley needs a champion."

Thrilled, Luke lunged and gave Samantha a big hug. "Thank you."

She returned his embrace and kissed him on the head. "You're welcome."

"Ah, I hate to ask," Luke mumbled.

"What is it?"

"My birthday is in two weeks."

"Oh my God, your birthday. I'm such a klutz, with

all the craziness I never..."

"It's okay, I understand, but do you mind if I can have a cake?" Luke sheepishly asked.

"Of course, of course, I'll have Phyllis make one up."

"I was thinking you could do it. My mom used to make my cakes before and I'd help; it was something we'd do together."

She lowered her head to hide the tears that formed in her eyes. "I'll make the cake if you want, but I can't promise it will be good."

"Thank you."

"No, thank you," Samantha replied.

"For what?"

"For making me feel special," Samantha answered.

Cheyenne, Wyoming, United States

"What's the body count?" Conner asked, pacing the large conference room of the new fortified bunker located in the subterranean floors of the governmental office building.

"Last report was over thirteen hundred," Baxter replied.

The room was packed with Conner's inner circle and their subordinates. Immediately after the explosions, Conner's security detail brought him to the bunker, and shortly after his staff began to arrive. Conner didn't wait for advice but re-implemented martial law and put emergency procedures in place. He called out the local militia supervised by regular army soldiers. He wasn't wasting any time rounding up the opposition.

Looking around the table, two people were noticeably missing, Wilbur and Schmidt.

"Where's Secretary Wilbur?" Conner asked.

An aide to Wilbur answered, "We've been trying to reach her but no reply."

Conner looked at Baxter and cocked his head.

Baxter shrugged his shoulders.

"Is it possible she was a casualty?" an older air force officer suggested.

The door of the conference room opened. All eyes turned to see a weary Schmidt.

"Sorry I'm late, Mr. President. The doctor gave me something for the pain, and it put me to sleep."

"It's fine, Major, but you have some explaining to do," Conner said, feigning an irritated tone.

Schmidt hurried to a vacant seat and sat down.

"Let's bring Major Schmidt up to speed," Conner said.

Baxter looked at Schmidt and said, "Just shortly after the president took to the podium, insurgents began to protest by chanting then throwing objects in the direction of the president. Moments later two large bombs were detonated, resulting in mass casualties. The crowd panicked and fled, resulting in further fatalities."

"Do we know who's responsible?" Schmidt asked.

Conner barked, "Of course we know who's responsible. It's Pat's people and his little army of terrorists."

"What are we doing right now?" Schmidt asked, rubbing his face.

"I've declared martial law again and called up the militia to arrest all suspected terrorists and anyone associated with them," Conner said.

"Good, about time." Schmidt smiled.

The door opened briskly and a young enlisted soldier raced in and handed Baxter a piece of paper.

Baxter studied it. His eyes grew wide as he read further towards the bottom.

"What is it?" Conner asked.

"We've found evidence that Pat and Van Zandt's Cascadians might have worked together in this attack."

"Those bastards," Conner said.

Cross talk erupted in the room following Baxter's announcement.

"If we find that's the case, what do we do?" Schmidt asked.

Conner increased his pace and circled the large table twice before responding, "I want Pat and all of his followers arrested. I want them interrogated; get everything you can out of them. Squeeze them like a damn sponge for every drop of information."

"What about the Cascadians? If they're behind this, we must answer with something substantial," Schmidt mentioned.

Conner stopped, put his focus on Schmidt and replied, "We have to hammer them. We have to show the people of the United States and Cheyenne that we will respond harshly to any attacks against our civilian population."

"What does that mean?" Baxter asked.

The room drew quiet as all eyes were glued on Conner, waiting for his response.

"General Baxter, ready the bombers."

Sandy, Utah

The first time Annaliese asked if Hector could stay in the main house, Samuel was against it, but once again her persuasion had won out. For Samuel, he allowed Annaliese to get away with more than he used to because he felt guilty about Sebastian. He couldn't help but feel somewhat responsible. If he hadn't been so resistant to him but made him feel more at home, just maybe he would have stayed longer or never left at all. The thought of what happened to him and what could have happened to Annaliese made him feel horrible. He wasn't going to have a repeat of that, so he let her leverage him for much of what she wanted.

Hector now was considered a part of the family. He ate most meals with them at the main table and had his own room downstairs.

Like Annaliese, Samuel also enjoyed that Hector didn't talk much, but his reasons were different. The requirement for people to stay in their new community was directly linked to contribution and value. Hector didn't provide anything that Samuel saw, but Annaliese had taken to him, so he never questioned his being there. However, his interview process was hard and he had turned many people away. One of those interactions had occurred earlier that day.

"So I talked to a couple guys who came to the main gate. They wanted in, but something about them turned me off," Samuel said, taking a scoop of pasta from the casserole dish.

"Did they have that typical marauder look?" Annaliese joked.

"And what's that look?" Samuel asked.

"The *Mad Max* look with long dreadlocked hair, or bald, the bald thing Mad Maxey, with leather pants and a leather vest, lots of tattoos and body piercings everywhere," she joked.

Samuel raised a single eyebrow and asked, "What's *Mad Max*?"

"That movie, you know, with Mel Gibson."

"Nope, never saw it. I work for a living, remember."

"Uncle Samuel, that movie came out twenty plus years ago."

"I've always worked and had no time for silly movies like that," he insisted, taking a bit more pasta.

Hector sat watching the two chat. His eyes darted back and forth like a spectator watching a tennis match.

The LED lantern in the center of the table began to dim. Samuel reached out and tapped it. The lantern grew brighter.

"Time to pull another from the shed," Annaliese

said.

"No, this will do, just quirky," Samuel said. He missed having power and he missed his solar generators. After the lights went out, he got the ranch up and running off the generators. When the hospital came on line, he dedicated them to it.

Annaliese took a bite and asked, "So what was wrong with those guys?"

"I can tell you they weren't dressed like the people from the *Mad Max* movie. If only it was that easy to discern who is good or bad."

"Right, if people could wear badges saying good or bad, it would make it easier," she joked.

Samuel finally picked up that she was unusually happy. "So what's with you?"

"What? Nothing."

"You seem extra happy."

"Nothing new, really, except I did want to ask if you could ask one of the guys to build Hector parallel bars out back by the swings."

"Parallel bars, for what, is he becoming a gymnast?" Samuel cracked with his snarky form of humor.

"No, he's going to learn to walk."

"Good, then he can start helping around here a bit," Samuel said with a tinge of contempt in his tone.

"You've never commented on that before. I thought you could see he's a bit disabled," Annaliese said.

Hector watched the back and forth, growing annoyed.

"He was in the hospital earlier today helping out. It's

just taken him a while," Annaliese said.

Samuel looked at Hector and said, "Glad to hear it."

"Can you get one of the guys on it tomorrow?" Annaliese asked.

"Maybe, but we're constructing a new shed. How about next week?"

"Can't be earlier?"

"No, it can't. The shed is critical; the bars aren't."

Hector caught Samuel's gaze, blinked and nodded, signaling he was fine with the time frame.

"Anyway, I need you to start carrying around the place; you too, Hector. These two guys that showed up seemed shady and beyond that. They had some type of military uniform on, nothing like I'd ever seen before."

"Maybe they were wearing stuff they found at a surplus store," Annaliese suggested.

The mention of the uniform caught Hector's attention.

"I guess that's possible, but something about the uniforms seemed like they were legit, like they were in the army or something, but not our army."

Hector suspected who these men were but remained silent.

"What did they say?"

"That's just it, what struck me above all else was they didn't speak English well," Samuel said.

"They were foreigners?"

"Ah, yeah, they were," Samuel said and glanced over at Hector. "They sounded Mexican, you know, Hispanic. Their English was broken and they asked a lot of questions."

Hector looked down at his plate.

"What happened?" Annaliese asked.

"I told them to go away, and they did, but something told me these guys might be back, and they might bring some buddies with them."

OCTOBER 31, 2015

"Trick or treat."

Mountain Home, Idaho, Republic of Cascadia

Gordon shot up and looked around when the first blast rocked his quarters. He sprang from his bed, grabbed his trousers, and quickly put them on. He pivoted to grab his boots but jammed his toes against the chair. "Fuck, ouch!" he yelled. The room was pitch black and it was impossible to see. Having adapted to the new world, his instinct was to find his flashlight. His tactical vest was slung over the same chair; he ran his fingers over it and found his flashlight. He pulled it out and clicked it on.

Several more explosions shook the ground. Out the window, bright flashes lit the darkened sky.

Yelling came from the hallway and outside.

Seconds later someone began to bang on his door. "Van Zandt, we're under attack!"

Gordon shoved his feet into his boots and ran to the door; he flung it open and found Jones standing there. "Any idea where it's coming from?"

"It's aircraft."

Unable to combat jets, Gordon knew there wasn't much he or his forces could do but take cover.

"Have everyone find adequate cover to ride this out!" Gordon ordered.

A series of larger and louder blasts hit close by, shaking the officers' quarters.

"We have to get you below," Jones said.

"Where?"

"There's an underground parking lot," Jones said.

"I thought you said there was a bunker on site?" Gordon asked.

"Too far away, we need to get you and whoever's in here down in the garage now," Jones said, grabbing Gordon by the arm.

Gordon pulled back and said, "I'm coming. Let me grab some things."

"Come on, Van Zandt!"

"Fucking go. I'll meet you down there!" Gordon ordered.

Another series of explosions lit the sky; the concussion blew out the glass in the window of his room. Gordon fell to the ground, cursing and praying at the same time. He got to his feet and grabbed his vest, rifle and personal effects, including items from Haley and Samantha. Having those meant a lot to him, and those little trinkets had seen him through darker times, so he wasn't about to leave them behind.

With everything in hand, he raced for the door, but a direct hit on the quarters threw him to the floor.

Screams and yelling from inside the building told him the strike had been fatal for some.

Gordon got to his feet and ran towards the stairwell.

A myriad of flashlight beams darted off the walls of the hallway, as everyone on his floor was doing the same as him.

Thoughts of Samantha and Haley came to him as he prayed he'd make the stairs and get to safety.

A massive blast hit the far end of the hallway.

The sheer force of the blast tossed Gordon and the others like rag dolls. Flames jetted down the hall, barely missing him but catching others on fire.

Gordon looked up and saw the men frantically running around, their bodies engulfed in flames. A gaping hole replaced the far end as smoke and flames found an escape. Fear suddenly gripped Gordon when he realized the stairwell was where the hole now was. Needing a way out, he got back on his feet and headed towards his room. His only avenue of escape now was out the window and down the three stories to the ground.

The yells and screams were muted because his eardrums had been perforated from the intense concussion. Blood trickled out of his ears and down his cheeks.

Back in his room he hastily tied the sheets and blankets end to end and secured one end to the bed frame then tossed the other through the open window.

The ferocity of the aerial attack was now at its worst as the night sky was constantly lit by one explosion after another.

He donned all of his equipment, grabbed the makeshift rope, and stepped out of the window. He slowly lowered himself one floor, then another, and was only fifteen feet from the ground when a missile struck the top floor of the building. The subsequent explosion caused him to lose his grip and fall to the ground hard with the back of his head smacking the edge of a concrete sidewalk.

He opened his eyes to see debris raining down on him. He thought about moving, but a darkness he was familiar with was coming and there wasn't anything he could do. Relenting to his fate, he closed his eyes and blacked out.

McCall, Idaho, Republic of Cascadia

Sleeping in was something Samantha liked to do on the weekend, and knowing that her day would be long due to it being Halloween and they had a house party to attend, she wanted the extra sleep, but whoever was banging on the door wouldn't allow that to happen.

"I'm coming, I'm coming," she said, rubbing her eyes and catching a glimpse of the dimly lit morning.

Whoever was knocking began to bang louder.

"Hold on!" Samantha called out, wishing they would stop so as not to wake the kids. She unlocked the series of deadbolts and opened the door to find Charles, Michael Rutledge, Nelson and Seneca. Seeing all of them sent shivers down her spine and a cold chill across her body. "Oh no, what happened?"

"There's been an incident," Charles said then continued, "A horrible incident."

Samantha put her shaking hand over her mouth and

could feel her legs wobble.

Seneca pushed her way past Charles and embraced Samantha.

The worst imaginable images flashed before her eyes. "Is he dead?"

Charles didn't answer. He looked at the others then back to Samantha and asked, "Can we come in?"

"Answer me," Samantha declared.

"We don't know," Charles answered then stepped inside uninvited, followed by Nelson and Michael, who closed the door behind them.

Seneca walked Samantha to the couch and sat her down.

"What does that mean? What's happened?" Samantha asked.

"Early this morning Gordon's army came under attack, a fierce aerial and missile bombardment," Charles explained. "All we know right now is our forces have suffered greatly; to say they've been decimated would be the most accurate way of explaining it."

Samantha held her hand to her mouth and her stomach tightened. A strong sensation of nausea swept over her.

"The survivors are working to find other survivors and get an accurate accounting of all who have died," Michael added.

"It's a mess, a total disaster," Charles lamented.

Nelson sat next to Samantha and took her hand.

"How is it that you don't know if Gordon is alive or not?" Samantha asked.

Charles looked at Michael and Nelson before replying, "The building where he was last seen was destroyed. We don't know because we can't find him or a body."

"Oh my God, no, please, no," Samantha cried. Tears burst from her eyes and she began to breathe fast and heavy.

"What's going on?" Luke asked, stepping into the great room.

"It's nothing," Nelson said.

"No, I promised I'd tell him. Come here, Luke." Samantha beckoned, her shaking hand outstretched.

Luke approached and took it. He looked into her swollen red eyes and asked, "Is he dead?"

"They don't know, but the army he was leading has suffered greatly. It's not just us that might be suffering. We must think of everyone, all the others who also might have lost someone today."

Haley then appeared; she yawned and rubbed her eyes. "Mommy, you don't need to cry."

"Come here, baby," Samantha called.

Haley jogged over and jumped into her open arms. She wiped Samantha's tears away, leaned in and whispered, "Don't cry, Mommy."

"I can't help it, I'm just scared."

"Daddy will be fine."

"Oh, baby, I love your optimism," Samantha cried.

"I just know it, he's fine."

Samantha pulled Luke down to her and embraced him with her open arm. She then squeezed both kids tightly.

"We didn't mean to cause stress or alarm, but we thought it best to come over as soon as we heard of the attack," Michael said.

"It's fine, I want to know. What happens now?" Samantha asked.

Charles was still standing. He was too tense to even think about sitting much less relaxing. "We bring the survivors home and just pray that we can come back from this."

Cheyenne, Wyoming, United States

Conner had taken a break from the hectic war room to get a drink in his office. He asked Schmidt to join him because they had much to celebrate.

"Major, you are the best, and I don't throw that word around lightly. What you pulled off yesterday was perfection," Conner jubilantly said.

Schmidt coughed and replied, "Thank you, but that was all my guys. They deserve the praise not me. Hell, I wasn't even there, and for that I am deeply sorry."

Conner raced over to Schmidt's side and said, "Are you kidding me? I had the doctor give you that. I didn't want you there because I didn't want someone to implicate you. If you were passed out from medicine, then in no way could Wilbur say your men did anything. I just didn't know that traitorous bitch would skip out."

"Yeah, I checked with my team, and they haven't seen her since just before the attack."

"She must have gotten Pat out too," Conner theorized.

"She acted quickly following the explosions. She knew you'd come down hot and heavy. I just don't know how she got past my guys."

"Do you suppose she knew we were onto her?" Schmidt asked.

"I doubt it. She just figured we'd put the screws to Pat or some of her compatriots and they'd squeal."

"She'll get hers out there."

"What if she didn't leave, what if she and Pat are still here?" Conner suggested.

"They could be hiding somewhere, and if she is, we'll find her just like we found Saddam Hussein years ago, quivering in a hole."

"Triple your teams; no, put all of your assets to finding them."

"Yes, sir," Schmidt said and coughed loudly. He recoiled and hid his hand when he saw blood.

"I'm sorry."

"It's just a virus, that's what the doctor thinks."

"Major, don't lie to me. I've spoken with him. You can be honest with me, I'm the one friend you have here, and you're mine now," Conner said with a sentimental tone. He walked back and poured a fresh glass of scotch for him and one for Schmidt. He walked it over and said, "Take it."

"No, sir," Schmidt said, waving his hand.

"Take it, that's a damn order," Conner insisted.

Schmidt reached up with his weak and shaky hand and took the drink. "Thank you."

Conner tapped the glass and cheerfully said, "Cheers and congratulations on a perfectly executed operation."

Both men took a sip.

"What's the next play, sir?"

"Well, the reports from our surveillance drones say we've destroyed Van Zandt's army. I think we need to focus on finishing this. What would make me the happiest person on Earth right now is if we could bring him back here to stand trial. I'd say we send a few teams, but I don't want to risk losing them. Closely monitor the situation and find out if he's alive or not."

"No, sir, I say we go in and finish this up. Let's send some gunships followed by strike teams and kill them all, except, of course, for Van Zandt if we find him alive."

"You think we can do this and not lose too many?"

"Yes, sir."

"Then send some drones out first thing in the morning to get solid intel before sending your teams out."

"Yes, sir," Schmidt said, then took a sip of scotch.

Conner's phone rang.

"One sec," Conner said, picking up the phone. "Yes."

"Mr. President, General Baxter here. We found Wilbur."

Sandy, Utah

Annaliese bounded down the stairs into the living room of the house. She had just changed her clothes after having gotten dirty helping build the parallel bars for Hector. She'd bypassed Samuel by going to visit Marcus, a young man who now called the ranch home. He was in his mid-thirties and had been a general contractor before the lights went out. She discussed the project with him, and he informed her they'd take only a few hours to build once he did some quick measurements and gathered the materials. With Annaliese's help, the bars went up just as Marcus had said.

Hector did his best to contribute to building the bars and tried to focus on what work he could do, but his mind wandered to the conversation last night over dinner. Samuel was right; the two men who showed up weren't there to find a new home but to scout the property. He knew they'd be back, and he needed to prepare them without giving away how he knew this.

"What are you doing sitting here?" Annaliese asked Hector, finding him in the living room. He was facing the stairs as if waiting for her.

He held out a semiautomatic pistol.

"What's this?" she asked, looking at the firearm.

He nudged it towards her.

"I have one upstairs, I just forgot to put it on."

He again motioned with his arm by waving the pistol.

She stepped forward and took it.

"Is something wrong with it?"

"No," he answered, then pointed to her.

"I have one," she again reminded him.

He pushed it at her one more time but harder.

"Okay, I'll take it," she reluctantly said.

He then handed her a shoulder holster.

"Really?"

He nodded.

"Fine," she said, taking the holster.

He motioned for her to put it on.

She grunted but complied with his request.

"Where's yours?" she asked.

He leaned to one side, showing he had not one, but two pistols tucked in between his right leg and the wheelchair.

"Good, I wasn't about to take yours, but I see you're prepared. Did what Samuel said last night concern you?"

He nodded.

"We'll be fine; we've got a good number of people guarding the place."

He shook his head, protesting her last comment.

"Don't worry too much, we have a good system here, and we even have the bunker to fall back to."

He shook his head.

"Listen, I have to go help at the hospital. Are you coming over today?" Annaliese asked.

Hector nodded slightly.

"You want to come with me?"

"No."

"Okay, I'll see you over there," Annaliese said and walked off.

His eyes drooped. If these men did come back, the bunker would be worthless for two reasons: it couldn't hold everyone, and second, they'd come back with the means to breach it.

McCall, Idaho, Republic of Cascadia

When Samantha heard the knock, she prayed the news was good, but she braced for the worst. She hurried to the door, holding a lantern to light the way, and opened it to find only Nelson this time. The look on his face was somber and instantly told her no good news was to come.

"It's been all day and nothing new. What's going on?" she asked, grabbing and pulling him in.

He kicked his boots free of fresh powdery snow but stopped short of pulling his boots off.

She could see he looked defeated.

"Just tell me," she blurted out.

"Nothing new about Gordon, that's what has me upset. I wanted to come here and give you something, but I can't. It's a damn mess. Those who survived are working frantically to find others that might be trapped in the rubble of buildings. It's just a fucking disaster."

Seeing Nelson was suffering emotionally from the tragedy, she brought him over to the kitchen bar and sat him down on a stool.

"Let me get you something to drink," Samantha said.

"Wait, this is ass backwards. I should be taking care of you," Nelson protested.

"We're both suffering, and would you believe that giving love and caring to others is therapeutic?"

"I would believe that."

"I'm actually getting myself a drink, so I'll just pour an extra one," Samantha said, walking into the kitchen and pulling the cork on a bottle of homemade hard cider.

"You like Phyllis's special brew?" Samantha asked.

"It will do, thank you," Nelson replied, looking around the dimly lit space. "Where are the kids?"

"Luke is entertaining Haley by reading her some books, unless he's fallen asleep. He's really tired after some tactical training he received today from Lance Corporal Sanchez."

"Tactical training?"

"Long story, but it's keeping him busy and his mind focused."

"But his arm." Nelson groaned.

"He'll be fine; I'm more worried about his state of mind than his arm right now."

Nelson shrugged his shoulders, dismissing it all, and took a long drink of the cool cider. "Yum, it's nice and cold."

"That's the one blessing of it being cold outside; the cider is always the perfect temp."

"How are you holding up?" Nelson asked.

"Better since my meltdown this morning."

"It's okay to be upset."

"I can't afford to be upset all day. The last time I was, it affected Haley strongly, and until I know for sure what's happened to Gordon, I'll just be optimistic."

"You're a good woman, Sam, you really are."

"Speaking of good women, when are you going to make an honest one out of Seneca? What are you waiting for?" Samantha asked.

Nelson looked down at his drink, not wishing to discuss such topics. "I don't know."

Samantha brushed the long hair from his eyes and said, "Tell me what's wrong."

"After what she did last time to me, I just have a hard time…trusting her."

"That was another time, another world, another Seneca; things are so different now."

"I know, but I just can't seem to get that out of my mind." Nelson explained his thoughts on how Seneca had dumped him at the last minute, ending their engagement and disappearing from his life years ago.

"Just put that out of your mind, please. She hasn't said anything to me or anyone that I know of, but she's waiting. Ask her to marry you. She needs that commitment, I know she does. Get married, have babies."

Nelson looked up and said, "I love her, I do, I just wish that had never happened."

"It did, it happened, but that was years ago. Now put your big-boy pants on and nail that girl down."

"I'll think about it."

"Don't think. In fact, stop thinking, get out of your

head, and act using your heart. Nelson, I want you to hear me, are you listening?" Samantha said, grabbing his arm.

"I'm listening."

"The old world is gone. It died a while ago. This world holds no guarantees, nor does it ensure the grass is greener somewhere else. Look at what happened today. Enjoy your life. Live, love and procreate. Have a legacy."

"But what legacy do I give my future children? One that lives under tyranny and fear? I'm not sure if I want children; I would be terrified of what could happen to them every day."

"I know it's hard for someone who doesn't have a child, but believe me, once you hold that child, there are no regrets. A child is something so special. It's an expression of the love two people have for one another. Share that with Seneca; share that child with all of us. That child would be so loved and cared for, and I can think of no one better suited to have a little one than you and Seneca. My kids love you and look up to you, you're great with them, and when you have your own, you'll be even more intense in your love for them."

"You think so?"

"I know so. After you have your first child, you'll come to me and say, 'Wow, you were right.' Having a baby is the most life-changing event a person can have. Even if I find out that Gordon is dead, he still lives on in Haley; I can look at her and see him. Half of him is her, so he lives on past death."

"Wow, so powerful."

"I don't mean to be pushy; I just know when I see

someone who's getting in their own way. Go home tonight and tell Seneca how much you love her, then get on your knee and beg her to marry you!"

A broad smile stretched across Nelson's face as he thought about everything that Samantha had said. Deep down he saw the wisdom and accuracy in her declaration. He was in his head. He knew how violent and unpredictable the world was and that Seneca could be taken from him tomorrow. "Okay, I'll do it."

"Bravo," Samantha said, holding up her half-full glass.

Nelson raised his and said, "To getting married."

"To babies."

NOVEMBER 1, 2015

"Come what may, all bad fortune is to be conquered by endurance." – Virgil

Mountain Home, Idaho, United States

Gordon opened his eyes but saw nothing but black. He looked up, down, left and right, but he was surrounded in darkness. He lifted his head and instantly was met with a sharp pain. He waved his right hand out in front of him but discovered a coarse and jagged slab of concrete just a foot from his face. Using his hands, he surveyed the rest of the darkness to discover he was encased in debris, mostly concrete but tiles and other miscellaneous things. Panicked, Gordon began to push the debris above him, but it didn't move. He turned his attention to his right and began to make progress with his pushing and pulling until large pieces fell away, exposing the outside. Fresh air rushed in, and he stuck his head up and breathed the cool, crisp air.

Having reached the surface, he became calm. He could see that it was even dark outside. Assuming it was still the same day, merely hours later, he pried himself free and rolled out of the concrete tomb. The night made it impossible to see much, but what fires remained from the attack still burned brightly. His body ached and his head wasn't much better; a dull throbbing pain emanated from the back of his skull. He pulled the flashlight from its pouch and turned it on. From his vantage point he could see the building where he had been staying was nothing but rubble now. All around him he found the same thing.

Each labored breath he took, he could hear it in his head. Blowing out his eardrums not only made it difficult to hear, but Gordon found it quite annoying.

"Hey, anyone here, hey!" he called out.

Moaning, cries and screams filled the air.

Shadows darted around as people raced to help the wounded and trapped.

Gordon stood and began to walk around, shining the bright beam of his light in every direction. Everywhere the light touched, he found destruction and bodies.

"Jones?" he hollered, but no reply came back. "John Steele!" he yelled, but they didn't reply. The only sounds that came were of the poor wounded souls and those few survivors who were doing their best to help.

The pain in his head grew worse as he meandered through the endless remains of what had been Mountain Home.

As he came upon more and more bodies of his fellow Cascadians, he suddenly realized that this could be it, this could be the official end of his army and with it the dream and vision that would be a free and independent republic. More importantly for him, it also meant that his family would be in jeopardy. Had he made a mistake? Had he miscalculated? Should he have taken Mountain Home? Was McCall next? Were they attacking it now?

Endless questions plagued his mind, but the number one thing that kept popping up was if this entire expedition was a mistake, but was it only a mistake because he lost? Nothing is considered a mistake until you lose, right? Making bold and risky moves are great if they're successful. You get called a genius for doing such things but a fool if you fail. Was he a fool? Had his hubris caused this, or was this just war? War is always sloppy, bloody and unpredictable. The badgering thoughts made his head hurt worse.

His deafened ears kept picking up the moaning and weeping of his now defeated army. A withering fatigue struck him, so he stopped to rest along a concrete wall. Letting gravity work for him, he slid down until he rested on the ground. His body had been maxed. It was tired, dehydrated and hungry, but also emotionally depressed. Unable to remain conscious, he rolled onto his side and passed out again.

Sandy, Utah

Hector didn't wait for the sun to fully rise before going out to the parallel bars. Annaliese had asked him to wait for her, but he couldn't. He cursed the wasted time lost in his depressive state. For months he didn't have the energy or desire to do anything but sit in his chair. His condition, specifically his physical appearance, had taken him to a dark place emotionally, even considering suicide. The only thing that stopped him from taking such a dire step was his deep Catholic roots.

Things were different now. Like a light bulb being turned on, he suddenly wanted to walk. Actually that wasn't entirely accurate, he needed to walk. Soon something bad could come, and he needed to have the confidence and strength to help Annaliese and the community.

"Argh!" Hector cried out as he fell to the hard ground.

Determined, he lifted himself to his knees, gripped the bars and pulled up. Steadying himself, he shuffled his left leg forward then his right. He had strength in his legs, but with the legs not being set correctly, it created a tremendous amount of pain. Biting down, he took a few more slow steps until he reached the end. He paused, turned around and headed back. He did this a dozen times. Stopping at the end, he looked past the bars, across the yard to the hospital. The walk had to be a hundred yards. He dared himself to take the challenge, but something warned him the pain would be too great. Afraid, he turned around and went back and forth on the bars. He stopped again at the end and looked at the hospital. The sun was just rising now past it. It was a new day, and he now felt he needed to go for it.

His legs were trembling from the pain, and a steady sweat streamed down his face and soaked his clothes.

People began to emerge to start their day. No one took notice of him as he stood at the end of the bars. He watched them stroll from the barn to the shed and other outbuildings. He was jealous of their ease of movement. Memories of his life before came rushing back. He had been a handsome and charismatic man, athletic and agile. That was all gone now, taken away in an instant and replaced with a crippled and disfigured man, or freak, as he'd call himself in his head. All he had left was…he couldn't give an answer.

"Look at you!" Annaliese hollered as she came out of the house.

He nervously looked at her and almost lost his grip on the bars, which would have sent him tumbling to the ground.

She rushed down the stairs and over to him. "How long have you been out here?"

He shrugged and then decided to speak the best he could. "Hour."

"Look at you, big man, another word," she joked.

Speaking brought pain as well, his vocal cords had been severely damaged from the intensely heated fumes he'd inhaled.

He pointed his head forward and said, "Thrrr."

"Another word, this is a big day for you," Annaliese said but didn't quite understand what he had said.

"Thrrr," he said again and pointed his head towards the hospital.

"You want to go over there with me? Let me get your wheelchair," she said, walking to get it.

"No."

"So you don't want to go over there?"

He slapped his hands on the bars, gulped hard to

lubricate his throat, and said, "Walk."

"No, that's too far. You only just started this morning; that's too aggressive."

"Walk," he said. He took in several deep breaths and closed his eyes. In his mind's eye he watched like a spectator as he made the distance with no problems, ending the journey by going inside and sitting next to the woman who was dying.

"Hector, I don't…"

He took one last breath, opened his eyes and pushed off. The first five steps went fine. When he placed his right foot down on the sixth step, an electrifying pain shot up his thigh and into his hip, causing him to pause. He steadied his footing and continued. His eyes were fixed on the door as he took more steps.

Annaliese came up behind him but made sure not to distract him.

Others began to notice his journey and stopped to witness it.

The red door grew closer and closer.

Annaliese bit her lip, nervous that each next step would be his last.

As the large red door grew closer, his confidence rose and the pain subsided.

He could hear people talking, but he pushed their voices out of his mind and concentrated.

Ten more steps.

Annaliese was beyond frightened for him, but now hope began to replace that fear as he was closing in on his goal.

Thirteen more steps, he was two-thirds of the way there.

He paused when the pain returned with a vengeance, stopping a mere ten steps away. The pain had now spread to his lower back and up his spine. Sweat poured off his face and dripped to the dusty ground.

The onlookers began to cheer, "Hector, Hector, Hector!"

Their voices weren't a distraction now. He used them to gather the strength to continue. Nine steps away, eight, seven, six, five.

Annaliese came up right behind him now and readied to embrace him.

Four, three, two and he stopped. The door was four feet away; he had made it. He turned his head around and looked back past Annaliese to the bars and the wheelchair. Full of pride, he faced the door and took his final step.

Cheers erupted around him as his fellow neighbors came rushing towards him. They knew how important of an accomplishment this was and were all so proud of him.

Tears broke from his eyes as he too knew how great it was. It had been hard, but it proved to himself that he could recover a piece of him that he thought had been taken away.

Warren Air Force Base, Wyoming, United States

Conner stood above Wilbur's corpse and thought how someone like her could turn against their country. She had been raised in a military family. Had joined the Air Force, risen to the respectable rank of major, gone on to work within the government to eventually become the secretary of state, but suddenly one day thought it was best to throw that all away. For what? he thought. Did she think she was smarter than him? Did she think she had an opportunity? Was that it? Like they always say, in chaos there's opportunity. Was she driven by hubris, pride or ambition? He'd never know now because there she was lying on a cold stainless steel bench, dead. A single bullet to the brain did the trick. One single piece of lead ended her life. But why? he kept asking himself. Why did people keep betraying him, why did they keep betraying their country?

"Where did you find her?" Conner asked Baxter.

"We found her in an alley. Her pockets were empty. She had nothing on her," Baxter replied.

"But who killed her, any suspects?"

"We think it was either a random crime or she was targeted."

"Forget the random crime. One of her compatriots killed her so she wouldn't speak. She was a traitor and they took her out. What's the old saying? Dead men tell no tales."

"If we find Pat, maybe we'll get an answer," Baxter

said.

"Keep patrolling, I don't think he's left the city. I think that slimy bastard is still around."

"We'll find him, sir."

Conner pulled the sheet over Wilbur's pale face and said, "Dispose of the body immediately."

"Yes, sir."

"And that means just dump it, preferably naked on the prairie so the coyotes and other vermin can eat her. She doesn't deserve a respectable burial."

Baxter turned stoic hearing Conner speak that way about her.

Not hearing a response from him, Conner asked, "Did you hear that? Just dump the body, nothing more. I don't want to waste the manpower or time."

"Yes, sir," he replied, biting his tongue.

"Now walk with me," Conner said, stepping away from the body and heading towards the exit of the base morgue.

Baxter took one last look at Wilbur's draped corpse before following Conner. He caught up and began to walk next to him.

Conner looked up at Baxter, who was a tall and imposing figure. "You know I take counsel from Major Schmidt, but I respect your guidance too. You've been a team player and strong advocate for my policies. What do you think our next step should be?"

The only thought that ran through Baxter's mind just then was reaching down and placing his large hands around Conner's throat and strangling him. He had not only respected Wilbur but had grown to care for her even though she didn't reciprocate those feelings, and now she was dead. He blamed Conner even though he knew Conner wasn't directly to blame, but if this man wasn't in charge, things could have been different.

"General Baxter, did you hear me?" Conner asked.

"Ah, yeah, um, no, sorry, I was thinking about things. I was thinking of who might have murdered her," Baxter answered, clearly flustered.

"What do you think our next step should be? We're close to finishing off all the secessionists and putting this chapter in our history behind us."

"It does seem like we're turning a corner," Baxter said.

"Yes, things are getting better."

"But not internally, these terrorist attacks are disturbing. How did Schmidt not catch this?" Baxter asked. Major Schmidt was responsible for all security and defenses of the city and government agencies.

"We'll dive into that, but now is not the time to point fingers and cast blame but find solutions. Obviously we can't implement Project Congress or even think about lifting martial law and the anti-protest laws."

"Why not? Why should we allow a few to dictate to the many? Why can't we move forward with those things while simultaneously increasing our antiterrorist policies?"

Conner stopped and said, "You sound like Wilbur."

Baxter stopped too and turned to face Conner in the narrow hallway. "I'm not sounding like anyone. I'm my own man and I think we can do both. We have to be principled and not drift too far away from what our founders intended."

Conner's eyes pierced Baxter as he found what he was saying counter to what he wanted. However, the points he made weren't far from what he used to say before. When he was in Congress, he'd uttered similar things, and it was right then he realized how much he'd changed. He believed in the dream and vision of the Founding Fathers, but how could he maintain that vision or keep those principles when fighting against an enemy that required him to abandon such things. Even Abraham Lincoln had to discard the Constitution so he could save it. No, Conner couldn't give up now. He was close to having total victory, and the last thing he needed was a pesky Congress constantly challenging his authority. He needed to get the job done first, and once there was peace, he could then look towards reestablishing the republic.

"I hear what you're saying, General, and I agree, but let's finish the job then turn all of our energy to restoring the old system."

"As you wish, sir," Baxter replied, not wishing to debate the issue.

Mountain Home, Idaho, United States

Gunfire woke Gordon. Confused and disoriented, he sat up and found the dawn had come and with it a large US strike force of what must have been two dozen helicopters with a hundred heavily armed soldiers.

The whirl and whoosh of helicopters flying over turned his attention skywards. There he witnessed Apache gunships opening fire on his men with their M230 chain guns. The 30mm rounds rained down and shredded his people.

Automatic small-arms gunfire to his left brought his attention there only to see a team of American soldiers shooting some of his men that were attempting to surrender.

This was a clean-up mission. There was no negotiating or appealing to a greater good. This was war in its most brutal form.

The thought of trying to rally a defense popped in his head, but as he surveyed the scenes all around him, he saw it was fruitless. His army was in disarray and there was no forming a meaningful defense, they were all on their own. If Gordon was going to survive the onslaught, he needed to get out of there fast.

A rush of adrenaline shot through his body as he got up and ran for cover.

In between the gunfire and helicopter noise, the cries and screams of his people rang out.

Ignoring the pain that riddled his entire body, he sprinted west towards the refugee camp.

People were running in every direction, trying to avoid the assault, but with each turn they'd encounter American forces that showed them no mercy.

Having planned his own assault on the base, Gordon

was familiar with the layout and knew that if he could make it to the far western edge, he'd be able to take cover along the Snake River.

His heart pumped heavily as he sprinted and leapt over bodies and debris. The camp, a glorified tent city, extended for half a mile. Row after row of green or white general-purpose tents had been the home of thousands of homeless Americans. Now it was a graveyard as Conner's first aerial bombardment didn't spare them either. Hundreds of tents lay destroyed and burned while their occupants lay on the ground dead. It became apparent that Conner didn't intend on fighting with any honorable or moral code. While Gordon didn't hesitate to kill a military officer, there wasn't anyone who Conner wouldn't kill as long as it fulfilled his goals of defeating Gordon and his fledgling army. How could he win against someone who was willing to fight like that? Could he? Did he have to fight the same way? That was something he just couldn't do.

Gordon made a hard left for a hundred feet to dodge an encounter with some American troops, but when he turned back to the right around a tent, he ran into two of them, literally. Thinking quickly, Gordon kicked the first one in the stomach with a front kick. The soldier flew backwards. Gordon pulled his pistol and shot the man without aiming or extending the pistol. That man dropped to the ground but wasn't dead. Gordon stepped forward and pulled the trigger two more times, hitting the other man in the head; he then pivoted and shot the soldier on the ground. With the threat gone, Gordon continued to race towards the far western edge.

The cold air burned in his lungs as he ran as hard as his legs would take him. With a linear focus, he headed towards a fifteen-foot chain-link fence two hundred yards ahead of him; the screams and cries for mercy pushed him harder. There was no surrender or mercy to be found, only death, and dying today was not on his agenda.

He reached the fence and paused for a microsecond. Should he climb or cut through? Scaling the fence would skyline him. He reached back and pulled out his trusty Leatherman tool, flipped it open and clipped the links that connected a side of the fence to a pole. He pushed his back through first then squeezed his body past. After clearing the fence, he took one last look at the continuing chaos on the base. The only word that came to mind as he saw the circling helicopters and heard the roar of gunfire was massacre. He took one more look then sprinted west towards the Snake River that lay a quarter mile away.

McCall, Idaho, Republic of Cascadia

For the third time in twenty-four hours, loud banging at her front door made Samantha's heart jump. She raced through the house, putting on her robe as she went.

"Samantha, hurry up, open up, please!" Nelson yelled.

"Hold on, wait!" she said, unlocking the deadbolts.

She threw the door open and found Nelson with a panicked look on his face. "You have news, obviously?"

Nelson pushed past her and entered the house.

Samantha looked out to the driveway and saw two vehicles. One was Nelson's old pickup and the second was the Humvee she used. It was running with Sanchez behind the wheel.

"Sam, we have to evacuate you immediately, all of you, now!" Nelson barked, running down the hall. "Haley, Luke, get up. We have to go!"

"Nelson, what's going on? Are we under attack?" Samantha asked, following him.

Nelson was in Haley's room. "Sweetie, get up, get your things. We have to leave."

Samantha came into the bedroom and stopped Nelson as he was walking out to go get Luke. "Stop! What's going on? Tell me!"

"The army in Mountain Home has been taken out, completely," he said, pushing past her again en route to Luke's bedroom.

She grabbed his arm and held him. "I know that already. What's different?"

"An hour ago they were attacked again, but this time Conner sent in ground troops. They systematically wiped everyone out."

"What about Gordon?"

Lowering his voice and tone, he replied, "Still nothing, we don't know."

"How can that be?"

"Sam, it's been confusing there. It's a train wreck of

biblical proportions, and now they've gone in and slaughtered everyone else. They didn't show mercy, they just gunned everyone down."

"Are they heading here?" Samantha asked, fear gripping her.

"We don't know, but we're not taking chances. We're getting everyone that is nonessential out of town and to the safe houses west of Lake Cascade."

"We have safe houses?" Samantha asked, surprised but happy to know these things were thought of.

"Yes, now enough questions. Put together your stuff."

"I already have bags packed; they're in the garage. Gordon had us put them together months ago."

"Where are they? I'll have Sanchez load them up. Get the kids and meet me outside in five minutes," Nelson said and pulled away.

She grabbed him again and asked, "Do you think they're coming here?"

"I don't know, but why wouldn't they? Needless to say, we can't take any chances," Nelson replied and marched off.

Samantha turned her attention to Haley, who shocked her by being ready with another small bag and a stuffed animal under her arm. She turned to call Luke but found him also ready. "Well, you two are fast. Let me throw some clothes on. I'll be right back."

Luke watched Samantha run into her bedroom. He looked at Haley and said, "Don't be scared."

"I'm not."

Raising his eyebrows, stunned to see her so calm, he asked, "Do you somehow know we'll be okay?"

"I don't know what's going to happen. I'm just not scared."

"Well, I'm a bit nervous. Come on, let's get in the truck," Luke said, putting his right arm over her shoulders, and walked her out.

Lake Cascade, Idaho, Republic of Cascadia

The Humvee that brought Samantha and the kids was one of a convoy of vehicles. After receiving a call from John Steele concerning the massacre at Mountain Home, Charles passed a directive to evacuate McCall of all nonessential personnel.

Samantha wasn't as harsh on Charles as Gordon was, but she still lacked complete confidence in his abilities as a leader. He seemed smart and his attention to detail as it pertained to governmental policy-making was top notch, but where he failed was his ability to communicate. To Samantha, this also seemed to be an area of weakness for Gordon too, especially if he was acting hotheaded. However, where Gordon prevailed was people naturally trusted him; he gave off an air of confidence that Charles fought hard for. Deep down Charles knew this, so he would replace confidence with arrogance and cockiness, not an attractive trait for a leader. Samantha could see through him and knew he felt insecure about being in charge.

The decision to evacuate many from McCall was sound, Samantha thought, and Gordon would have approved too. What Charles's next step would be was what made Samantha nervous. With Gordon missing and his army gone, there was a power vacuum that no doubt Charles would exploit. She just hoped his vanity didn't trump his practicality.

The long convoy of vehicles pulled up to the lodge at Tamarack Resort. It was a five-story mid-rise building that had served as the resort's main hotel and condo lodging when it was operational. The resort was billed as a four season destination resort with everything from skiing in the winter to golf in the summer. Samantha and Gordon had gone there numerous times before the lights went out and found it to be a wonderful place. Now the resort sat empty, and many of the second or vacation homes on the property were vacant. A few wandering groups had found shelter and squatted there, but soon after declaring its independence in July, Gordon, Charles and Michael Rutledge made a decision to secretly occupy the property for use as a refuge if McCall was ever threatened. Its location and access made it ideal. With limited access, it made it very defensible, and with the back side of the property backing up to tens of thousands of acres of open space, those hiding there could disappear into the wilderness if its boundaries were ever penetrated. Flanked by West Mountain to the west and Lake Cascade to the east, the resort was situated perfectly and provided the perfect location to hide out.

The lodge would be used to locate those in government and their families while others were given access to the hundreds of single-family structures that dotted the landscape across the four-thousand-acre resort. Another reason the property was ideal was it had infrastructure like roads, wells with massive holding tanks, and an abundance of natural resources and wildlife.

Samantha stepped out of the Humvee and looked up at the Tudor-style lodge with its white plaster and dark stained wood trim.

Haley jumped out behind her and took her hand. "Will we be safe here, Mommy?"

"Yes, we will," Samantha replied.

Luke was getting out, but Sanchez stopped him. "Just because you moved doesn't mean your training has ended. Be ready to go at seventeen hundred."

Luke hadn't memorized military time, so he paused to subtract the difference from twelve and seventeen. "Got it, five o'clock."

"Meet me in the parking garage below the lodge," Sanchez said.

Wanting to sound like a military man, Luke replied, "Roger that." He got out of the Humvee and looked up at the towering lodge. "Cool."

Charles exited the lodge and briskly walked to the group that had gathered out front under the large porte cochere. "Welcome all, I know our hasty evacuation has some of you scared, and I would be lying if I said I wasn't nervous myself, but please know that your government is looking out for you. Some of you may know, but many of you don't. Our army to the east is gone; it has been destroyed by President Conner's forces. The defeat was total. We have lost most of our fighting men and women, and sadly one of those missing is our supreme military leader, Gordon Van Zandt. The last report we received was from his second in command, John Steele, and he reports that only a couple dozen were able to flee the secondary attack."

A woman raised her hand. "Secondary attack?"

"Yes, at dawn a large ground force landed and engaged what remained of our army there. The attack came as a surprise and caught our forces unprepared. The attack was a rout."

Gasps and unintelligible cross talk began.

"So we could assure your safety, we decided to bring all nonessential personnel here. We don't know if McCall will be attacked next, so we didn't want to take a chance."

A man called out, "Where is the other army, I thought we had two?"

"We do. Master Sergeant Simpson has those forces just a few days west of here. They are rushing back to provide security for the city."

"How long will we be here?" a person yelled out.

"We don't know. We will monitor the situation daily and make our determinations based upon what we can find out. So without a date set, I'd suggest you just prepare yourself to stay here for a bit."

"How long?" the man asked again.

"I don't know, but just frame your mind that it could be for a while," Charles answered as best he could.

The cross talk and chatter grew in volume.

"We will operate the lodge here like a commune. We will have food prepared for you two times per day. It will be served in the restaurant located on the lobby level. We ask that you ration your water and adhere to the nighttime lighting policy."

"What's that?" a woman called out.

"No lights after dark except for candles at night, and then the drapes and curtains must be drawn."

Several people grumbled.

"I know, I know, but if you look directly across the lake, there you'll see Highway 55. We don't know who may be coming, and we don't want to draw attention to ourselves here. This place is our secret, and we intend on keeping it that way."

Many people nodded after he explained the security reason for the lighting policy.

"Any questions?" Charles asked.

"What time will the two meals be served?" an elderly man asked.

"Mornings at seven and afternoons at five."

"Do the bathrooms work?"

"Great question. Don't use the bathroom unless you want the sewer to back up in your room. We have made the two bathrooms in the locker rooms on the lobby level operational. There's toilets and showers there. Please use those only."

Charles looked around for other hands, but everyone seemed content. "Since there's no further questions, please head on in. See Teagan for your room assignments."

Everyone slowly herded into the lodge, including Samantha and the kids.

"Samantha, can I speak with you before you go in?" Charles asked, stopping her.

"Sure."

Seeing Luke and Haley, he said coldly, "Without the kids."

"Ah, yeah," she answered. "Luke, go ahead and find out our room. Wait for me in the lobby."

Luke nodded and took Haley inside.

"What can I do for you?" Samantha asked.

"First let me express my deepest—"

Samantha raised her hand and said, "No, no, no, don't say condolences. We're not sure he's dead."

"You're right. I'm sorry, that was a bit insensitive," Charles said.

Samantha was suspicious if it was just insensitive or he was trying to mess with her emotions.

"Gordon played an important part in our government. He had a following of people that knew him and trusted him."

"You keep referring to him in the past tense; I for one don't believe he's dead."

"I apologize, it's not intentional. So can we count on you if or when we need you?"

"What can I do for you?"

"I wanted you to know that we'll take care of you and the family until his return."

"Why, thank you, but I've got a good support group

now. I know you must be busy with the business of governing."

"That's for sure, we're quite busy."

"Is that all?"

"Actually, it's not. My girlfriend, she's kind of an acquaintance of yours."

"Yes, Joyce," Samantha said, referring to the one woman in town she disliked more than President Conner, she would joke. They'd had a run-in months ago and never reconciled.

Charles had met Joyce when he first came to McCall, and the two hit it off.

Joyce's husband, David, had abandoned them right after the lights went out, leaving her with their two boys, three and five years old. Joyce was prone to drinking heavily and was not shy about giving her affections to as many men as would receive it.

"I'm back in town and I'm incredibly busy, so I can't spend time with her. She feels bad about the last time you two were together and would like to come see you to apologize, but she's afraid you'll refuse."

All Samantha could think was he was right, she would refuse her but add a bit more by telling her to go fuck off, and that was a strong word for Samantha.

"She never really had a chance to meet people when she was in Olympia, and now that she's back, she's a bit depressed."

Samantha knew where that depression came from but bit her tongue.

"Could you do me a huge favor and invite her over

for a drink, or maybe have her and the kids over for lunch sometime, like tomorrow or something?"

Feeling it was important to be candid, Samantha confessed, "Charles, you do know what happened the last time I saw Joyce, don't you?"

"Yes, and she feels really bad about it. I can attest that she's a changed woman."

"The last time I saw her she called me a snobby bitch for…I don't know what, she just wasn't a nice person and said some horrible things. And might I add she doesn't treat her two boys very well. She rides the razor's edge between neglect and criminal neglect."

"Now you're being too harsh. Please, she doesn't have any friends, and I thought that since you're kind of in the upper echelon of wives here, you could maybe bring her under your wing."

"I just don't think that would be appropriate."

Charles looked at the ground and kicked a small stone away as he thought about what to say. "You know, Joyce said you'd react this way."

"What way is that? I'm just telling you what happened and what I've witnessed. I'm not alone, ask anyone from the auxiliary about Joyce's behavior."

"I thought you were a bigger person and could forgive. She's a different woman now, she's been changed by everything. Going to Olympia and seeing what we're doing shifted her thinking."

Samantha hated being branded as the bad person, but she just didn't care for the woman and swore she'd never associate with her again.

"You know, forget it, I'll tell Joyce that it just won't work out. You have yourself a good day, Samantha," Charles said and briskly walked away. "I'll let you know when I hear anything about Gordon."

Frustrated by being put on the spot, Samantha called out, "I'll have her over for lunch tomorrow, but tell her she needs to be on her best behavior and her boys need to as well."

Charles turned around and said, "Thank you. I'll let her know and, by the way, she's in room 506."

Not happy about the situation, Samantha headed towards the lodge.

Inside, she found Luke and Haley waiting alongside Nelson, who had come out as well to help with the transition. A strong mold smell hit Samantha first; this caused her to pause and look around. Only a few lanterns were lit, and with the lobby's ceiling being low, it made the space very dark.

"What did Charles want?" Nelson asked, jumping up. He had been watching them through the front doors and was curious to the point of being nosey.

"He wants me to entertain Joyce."

"Joyce, the lush Joyce?" Nelson asked.

"Yes, that woman is a train wreck," Samantha complained. "Did you hear what happened last time?"

"Yeah, Gordon told me. She got all drunk and started screaming and calling people names. And oh, didn't she toss stuff around, like turning tables up and stuff?"

"That's the time. She's just crazy. She doesn't pay

any attention to her kids; they run around like animals, cause trouble, and they whine like little babies. I wanted to like her, but after all the nasty things she's done and said about me and my friends, I just don't want to be close to her. She's negative and that's the last thing I need right now."

Nelson chuckled.

"What's so funny?" she asked.

"Oh, nothing."

"No, what's so funny?"

"The world ends and women still find a way to be catty, just funny that's all."

"At first I felt sorry for Joyce, but I can see why David left. She's not a nice person. She pretends to be, but she has some real issues."

"We're in the penthouse!" Haley squealed with excitement. She had been trying to be patient but couldn't any longer.

"Ooh-la-la." Samantha laughed. She caressed Haley's plump cheek and decided she didn't want to discuss Joyce any longer. She needed to put her attention on her kids right now.

Luke snatched the key from Haley's hand and said, "I've never seen a penthouse. Let's head up."

"Don't be so excited, it's a four-story climb up the stairs," Nelson informed them.

"Last one up is a rotten egg," Luke yelled and sprinted towards the stairwell.

Haley chased after him.

"So are you going to do it?" Nelson asked, wanting

to know the outcome of Charles's request.

Samantha shot him an irritated look and said, "I had no choice, he put a guilt trip on me. So I'm having her and the boys over for lunch tomorrow."

"If it helps, I'll have Seneca stop by. She's arriving here tonight, and we have a room just below you on the fourth floor."

"Say, what room are we in?" Samantha asked.

"505," Nelson answered.

"Shit!" Samantha groaned.

"What?"

"We're across the hall from Joyce."

Grandview, Idaho, United States

Gordon reached the Snake River and with it a covered natural avenue for him to flee west. Disregarding his physical condition, he pushed west, stopping along the way to adjust his gear and take short breaks. Accustomed to the luxury of having a phone, he was distraught when he found his phone was broken, more than likely from the fall. Unable to communicate, tired, aching and hungry, he kept moving.

With his hunger plaguing him, he stopped on the outskirts of the tiny town of Grandview. Being careful as usual, he surveyed the town and couldn't see any movement. In fact, the little town looked abandoned. It was not unusual, considering the staggering death toll that had befallen the country since the lights went out back in early December last year. The estimates done before said ninety percent of the United States population would die, and from his experiences on the road, he could believe it. Each time recon teams would return to McCall, they would report finding fewer and fewer people, so finding a small town like this empty was not a surprise, but he didn't just stroll into towns without at least surveying the area.

Feeling confident the town looked clear, he headed in.

To call the town small was an overstatement, Grandview was the proverbial 'don't blink or you'll miss it' kinda place. With his rifle at the ready, he left the cover of the riverbank and headed into town.

He thought of finding a market or store, but that was a foolish idea. The supplies there would have been exhausted within days of the attack. Instead he chose the first house he came upon.

He scaled the wood steps of the back deck and walked to the door. He peered through the grimy glass and saw no one. He stepped back, ready to kick the door in, when the simple idea of checking the doorknob popped in his head. Grabbing the cold bronze handle, he turned it and, *click*, found it unlocked. "What do you know?" He laughed. With a turn and a shove, he pushed the door open and was greeted with an intense pungent smell. After months of living in the new world, he recognized the smell as rotting flesh, not fresh but someone who had died a while ago. He recoiled and stepped back outside. The positive was the room he had stepped into was the kitchen, and it looked like it had never been ransacked; the negative was he'd have to deal with that smell. He tore off his pack, found a bandana and tied it around his face. Smelling his stale sweat was preferable to the grotesque aroma of human flesh past its expiration date.

The kitchen was a gold mine. The cabinets and pantry were stuffed with canned foods, and on the floor of the pantry was a case of bottled water. With a vast selection of food, he found himself being a bit picky. His eyes lit up like a child when he found the Chef Boyardee spaghetti with meatballs. "Jackpot!" He opened his pack and began to stuff in those and other cans that looked appealing.

Not one to just walk away from finding an untainted house, he decided to go look for other items of value, specifically more weapons, ammunition, batteries and medicine. He also needed a coat, the cold fall weather was getting to him.

The living room was vacant. The thick layer of dust on the wood coffee table told him this place hadn't been occupied for a long time. Off the living room, a hallway led down to four doors. Obviously these were bedrooms, and behind one or more he would find the source of the smell.

Coming to the first, he tried the door. It was unlocked. He opened it and looked inside to find a child's bedroom with Transformers posters, toys and model airplanes hanging from the ceiling. He noticed the bed was made; how odd, he thought. Knowing that room would hold no value, he moved on. The next door opened up to a bathroom. There he went looking for medicine and found Tylenol, Advil and cough medicine. He also took the toothpaste and unused toothbrushes. Maintaining proper dental hygiene was critical, as dentists weren't available at every strip mall or medical office anymore. He stuffed all of it into his pack and moved on. The third door was another child's bedroom, this one a girl's and, by the type of toys and decorations, a girl around Haley's age. Again the bed was made and the room tidy. The overall tidiness reminded him of Samantha; she would be that person who would make sure the rooms all looked good even if she was about to die. He summed it up to a compulsive disorder, but for them at home, her disorder kept the order around the house, and he wouldn't have it any other way. The last door had to be the master bedroom and the location of the bodies. He tried the handle, but this time it was locked. He went to kick it but stopped short of doing so. What would he really find there of value? Did he really need to see what he already imagined he'd find, a small family huddled together on the bed, all victims of a murder-suicide? What possibly could he really need in there? Not needing to satisfy his curiosity and having seen enough death, he stepped away and exited the hallway into the living room. There he saw a small closet next to the front door; again he hit pay dirt. A men's extra-large Gore-Tex coat hung there as if it had his name on it. Besides the negative of being on the run, his escape had worked out, as had his finding everything he would need for the long hike back home.

After stuffing the coat in his pack, he looked up and saw several remote controls sitting on a side table. He pulled the back off the first, but the batteries had gone bad and leaked. He tossed the remote and pulled the back off the second to find four AAA batteries that looked good. He dumped them into his pack, and then did the same to the two other remotes. Batteries had become a currency in the new world, and leaving any behind would be like stepping over cash on the floor before the lights went out.

Back in the kitchen, he went looking through the junk drawers for more batteries, flashlights and other smaller items of value. He came upon a roll of string, matches, a lighter, small sewing kit and toothpicks. Nothing was worse than having food stuck between your teeth. This thought made him think about brushing, something he hadn't done in over a day.

He had stuffed his pack with as much food and water as he could as well as stuffing his belly. He took some Advil, brushed his teeth and was about to head out when he spotted some writing on the back of the white pantry door. He looked closely and saw it was hash marks, names and dates. He knew what they were, and seeing it made him sad and homesick. It also reminded him that so many people had a lot more in common than not. This young family appeared to be loving and well taken care of, but for some reason the fear and uncertainty of the new world was too much. The father must have imagined his children and wife wouldn't survive or could die a horrible death at the hands of a marauder or bandit, so instead he thought it best to kill them. Of course, this was all a guess, as he hadn't seen what lay behind the door, but it made sense. He wondered how often this had played out across the country as some people gave up hope and took their own lives. This was something that never crossed his mind. His will to live and mind-set prevented that from ever happening, and surviving was all about mind-set above all else. Of course skills and resources were critical, but these people had resources and possibly could have had some skills, but it was the mind-set that said life wasn't worth living without the luxuries and conveniences of modern society that led the father to take the lives of his innocent family.

He reached out and touched the names. He could tell by the spelling that the children had written their own names. He imagined the little girl being Haley writing her name on the door, excited to have finally grown three feet.

Yes, many people were similar, but there wasn't enough similarity to keep the world from falling into chaos. If society could have come together, there wouldn't have been a collapse. Of course, life would have changed drastically, but if people would have worked together, the apocalypse would never have happened. It wasn't the EMP that wiped out society, society wiped itself out with the moral decay of society coupled with a lack of skills. Preparedness sprinkled with an appreciation for one's neighbors would have prevented much of the death. When society became morally bankrupt with a focus towards one's own well-being above the greater good and a desire for the hedonistic pleasures, how could it come together? We were doomed. It really didn't matter if it was an EMP, financial collapse, nuclear war or pandemic, those were but the fuse.

His homesick feelings turned to disgust as he processed all of it. Needing to get past this feeling, he slammed the pantry door, slung his pack and left the house to find a place to lay his head and get some real rest.

Cheyenne, Wyoming, United States

If there was one thing Conner enjoyed when he could, it was his nightly routine. When his schedule permitted, he'd fix a cup of red rooibus tea with fresh milk and settle in to read a book. Shortly after arriving in Cheyenne, Pat introduced him to the tea, and before long he was making a cup each night. The rich, subtly sweet and smooth tea was one of the best things he'd ever had, and when you added creamy milk, it was purely divine, or that's how Pat would describe it.

With his tea and book, he walked to his den and relaxed into the thick cushioned leather chair.

Having to spend most of his time reading documents, memos, and reports, finding the time to escape in a book made for the best entertainment. Tonight's read was a Louis L'Amour classic Western. He had only recently discovered L'Amour and found his books not overly complicated and verbose, just fun, exciting reads with plenty of action and set in an age when men were men.

Sitting comfortably, he opened the worn paperback and flipped to chapter one.

The phone next to him rang.

He cut his eyes at the phone and questioned if he should answer it.

The phone rang again.

Having only read two sentences, he grunted and placed the book down. "This better be an emergency." He grabbed the receiver and answered, "President Conner."

"Brad, it's Andrew."

"Hey, is everything okay?" Conner asked his old friend and vice president.

"Did I catch you at a good time?"

"Just settling in for the night with what I hope will be a good book," Conner replied. He was happy to hear his old friend's voice. Their friendship spanned decades, from college to politics they remained tight and steadfast. From being in each other's weddings to even having the honor of being godparents. Theirs was a rock-solid friendship.

"I need to talk," Cruz confessed.

Conner sat up and said, "Sure, what is it? You sound upset. Is the family good?"

"Yeah, the family is great. They're a bit tired of living underground, or at least the wife is, but the kids are enjoying it."

"Good, good."

"Brad, it's about the tactics being using against the secessionists."

"Oh no, not you too." Conner sighed.

"It's a public relations disaster, and to be quite honest, your legacy in history might be tainted," Cruz opined.

"My legacy? I'm not even thinking about that just yet. One thing I don't want on my legacy is I was the president who presided over the total collapse and breakup of the nation. I don't want to be the last president of the United States."

"I know what you're doing is in the best interests and I know you, but it's troubling to some degree. Listen, Brad, these aren't some rag head terrorists in Iraq, these are Americans, and they're feeling disenchanted with our response. Now it's not our fault entirely; they have a right to be angry."

"Andrew, I don't treat them like Americans sometimes because they don't consider themselves Americans. I have to do some heavy lifting here to make sure this thing doesn't go under. We're like sailors on a leaky ship; we're constantly having to bail water out. These people don't want to talk; they just want to make demands."

"Brad, I know it's tough, but some of the things we're doing might be making things worse. I know I haven't been privy to many of the discussions and policy planning in regards to the conflicts, but I'd like to be. With Secretary Wilbur dead and Major Schmidt ill, I think it's best I play a greater role."

Conner smirked and replied sternly, "We're doing our best with what we have, and to date we've been successful. I think we need to look at the results before we criticize the actions."

"You know as well as I do how fluid these things can be, and when you take out one leader, another takes their place."

"Andrew, I appreciate the concern, but we have this handled. You're doing a wonderful job managing the reconstruction. I need you focused on getting the grid back up. That is critical and I can't have you dealing with this stuff."

"I spoke with the Australian Prime Minister today and even he mentioned how we're conducting these operations. It's becoming a bit controversial."

"We're fighting little wars everywhere, Andrew. These aren't protests, these are shooting wars. These people mean business and are willing to fight to separate. We can't treat them like they're common criminals, these are enemy combatants. Plus, you should know I'm doing my best to avoid civilian casualties. I know we've made some mistakes, but I'm fighting with one arm behind my back sometimes. After what Schmidt did in Idaho, I've heard nothing but heartburn from foreign leaders and from people in my cabinet. That was a mistake, we learned our lesson, but we can't stop, we can't let these people carve up what's left of the country."

"I'm not saying we give up, I just think we need a more comprehensive approach. We need to find those leaders who are more moderate. Those who don't wish to separate but have their needs met. A lot of this started because we didn't respond fast enough. The

people were left to fend for themselves. It's natural for people to want independence or to separate when they've been taking care of themselves. Brad, I was there, sitting in this damn bunker months ago when we discussed these issues. We made the tough decision then to stop resupply. When the other bunkers were destroyed, we stopped sending out aid, we caused this. We all did. This is the chickens coming home to roost."

Conner held his comment and thought about that time when they decided to withhold aid to the states. At the time resources were limited and the priority was continuity of government. That policy proved effective, but it did leave millions of Americans in FEMA camps without support for months. They did abandon them for a period of time.

"Brad, you there?" Cruz asked after waiting for a moment but getting no response.

"I'm here, you just have me thinking is all."

"Good, I want you to think."

"I think all the time, Andrew, that's not a fair thing to say. I think every single day about how I can get this country back on its feet. I think of the two hundred and fifty million dead. It plagues me to a point because I can't stay there; I can't remain in that place that obsesses over those dead. I need to think of the future, and if we don't stamp out these rebels, there will be no future. I know some of the tactics we've deployed have been rough, but I can't tiptoe around sometimes. We don't have the manpower or equipment we used to have; I have to use it wisely. I'm sorry if you don't approve of how I'm running the wars, and I don't give a fuck what the Prime Minister of Australia thinks. He has had the luck of not having to live in this environment. It's so easy for him to sit in Canberra and toss around lofty principles when he doesn't live under the threat of his country being broken up and destroyed; I do. And when it comes to my legacy, I don't care if people say I was hard on some rebels here or there, I'll ultimately be judged on if I kept us together as a nation, period."

Cruz sighed loudly. *"Like I always say, I have your back, and everything you just said rings true for me, but I can't help but think we've got to tone it down just a bit. Maybe arrest these rebel leaders, take them to trial. Instead of rushing in with tanks or troops, we rush in with supplies, food, and medicine. In the end the people of those states or cities will determine their own destinies. If we can show we're the best show in town, they won't leave us, they'll throw out those leaders and stay with us. We just have to show that we're worthy to stay with by proving we're that same generous and lawful nation we once were."*

"Were? Oh, c'mon, Andrew, you sound like a damn progressive. We are still generous, we are still lawful, it's just that an omelet doesn't get made unless you break some eggs."

"Hold on, I didn't mean to say we were unlawful and not generous. Of course we still are, but we can be better. We have to show the people of these states that we can take care of them. Think of it this way, ninety-eight percent of those people only care about taking care of their families. They don't care where the food comes from; they just want to feel safe and be able to provide. If we can do a better job than those who are calling for separation, we will win. Running in there and slaughtering people doesn't win over their

hearts and minds."

"They're traitors, and traitors have to be dealt with severely."

"Of course they do, but let's work with the locals to help get rid of them after we show we can provide the basic things they need. Going in there guns blazing and leaving a trail of death doesn't feed the children, it doesn't get the grid back up..." Cruz said then paused. *"Does any of this make sense?"*

Conner didn't answer right away. He was feeling judged by his one true friend. His white-knuckled grip on the phone began to make his hand ache.

"I didn't call you to bitch and complain. I want our great nation to prosper and remain intact, I just think there's a more subtle way to go about doing it."

"Okay."

"Not every solution is a military one. These are Americans we're talking about, not a group of Muslims. We share a culture with these people; we share a common bond and history. Our efforts years ago in the Middle East weren't as successful as we hoped because those people don't think like we do. That's not the case here. Those people in Washington, Oregon, Idaho, Arizona, Georgia, all of them are Americans. We can keep them with us by showering them with resources not bombs."

Conner's gut twisted the more Cruz spoke. He couldn't help but feel his best friend was harshly judging his efforts. This hurt him to feel this way.

"Are you hearing anything I'm saying?"

"Yes, loud and clear."

"I know it's getting late, so I'll finish by saying let's reexamine our approach, okay? And I want to be a part of future planning. I

have the ear of those nations who are supporting us, and I believe I can get them to double or triple their supply shipments. If I can do that, we don't have to conquer these people with tanks but with crates of MREs."

"Okay," Conner repeated. It was the only thing he could mutter without losing his temper.

"Okay, meaning I can help and be a part of future planning and policy?"

"Sure. Hey, I'm really tired, can we pick up the conversation again tomorrow?"

"I said what I wanted, but we should talk again tomorrow," Cruz answered.

"Good, thank you for the call," Conner said, faking a happy tone.

"Good night, Brad," Cruz said and disconnected the phone.

Conner placed the receiver down and relaxed as best he could into the chair. He thought for a few seconds about the call and was left feeling angry, disappointed and deeply hurt. All he wanted was to see the country flourish, but every time he made a bold move to secure that, people complained. It was so easy for them; they ultimately didn't hold the responsibility, he did. If it failed, Cruz wouldn't stand up and take the bullet, so to speak. As Harry Truman said, 'The buck stops here.' That was truer now than ever before. His policy was working; the secessionists were being defeated, allowing him to focus the country's energy and resources towards reconstruction. However, what vexed him was how everyone except for Schmidt didn't see the big picture.

They were more concerned with how things looked than what could be if he lost control and allowed these states to secede.

He heard every word Cruz said and he would allow him to participate in the debate, but he would keep pressing forward with his plan until every rebel secessionist was gone.

He took a deep breath and exhaled heavily. Needing a break from it all, he picked up his tea, took a large sip and thumbed the book to chapter one again. Tonight he'd let Cruz's words marinate. He had been friends with this man a long time. He felt in his heart that he was right, but for this one time and because of its source, he'd sleep on it before making a decision that would change everything he'd put into place.

NOVEMBER 2, 2015

"Everyone is handed adversity in life. No one's journey is easy. It's how they handle it that makes people unique." – Kevin Conroy

Grandview, Idaho, United States

Something wet and warm kept touching Gordon's face. At first he thought it was a dream until he opened his eyes to discover a dog hovering over him. He pushed the dog away and sat up, but the enthusiastic hound came back for more licks.

Gordon put up his hands and said, "Easy, boy, easy."

The dog, a large pit bull terrier, kept licking. The more Gordon resisted, the more the dog tried.

Giving in to the animal's love and affection, Gordon smiled and said in a soft tone, "Hey, boy, nice to see you too."

The dog began shaking its rear end and wagging its tail in excitement.

"Urgh, your breath stinks, but some doggie loving is not a bad way to wake up," Gordon said, scratching the dog on the head.

The sun was up, and by its position, Gordon guessed it was early morning. He looked around the bedroom of the house he'd broken into and couldn't figure out how the dog got in. He could have sworn he'd locked the bedroom door, and he definitely remembered securing all the doors of the house. But lo and behold, the bedroom door was cracked open. A tinge of fear hit him; he stood up and grabbed his pistol.

When he reached the bedroom door, the aroma of food cooking hit his nostrils.

Disturbed and somewhat freaked out, he went back to get his pack and rifle.

The dog wouldn't stop poking his leg with his muzzle.

"Get away," Gordon said, brushing the dog away.

Still the dog wouldn't listen and kept right on trying to get attention.

He grabbed his pack, slung his rifle and went to the single window that overlooked the backyard. He glanced outside but didn't see anyone. With a flip of the latch, he unlocked it and opened it. A screen was the next obstacle; instead of trying to remove it, he just cut it out. With the screen gone, he tossed his pack out and ducked to climb through.

Watching him, the dog got excited and barked several times.

"Sssh!" Gordon snapped.

The dog barked a few more times.

The window wasn't large, and for him, a man whose muscular frame towered over six feet, it made the effort more difficult. His head, right leg and right shoulder were through, but as he went to touch the ground, the muzzle of his rifle got hung up.

The dog was now excited and wouldn't stop barking.

"Goddamn it, shut up," Gordon grumbled, trying to free the muzzle from the edge of the screen.

"Why are you running off?" a raspy male voice asked from the doorway.

The voice scared Gordon, who was in a compromised position. He turned to see who it was but lost his balance and fell out of the window. The rifle became unstuck as he went, allowing him to fall to the ground with all of his weight on his right side. He scrambled to get his pistol after hitting the hard ground.

"Gordon, stop freaking out," the voice now said from the window.

Hearing his name, Gordon looked up to see John Steele.

"Your voice, I didn't recognize it," Gordon said, astonished to see his friend.

John touched his throat and said, "I think I have laryngitis or something, been like this since yesterday. Maybe it was all the screaming I was doing."

"You fucking scared the shit out of me." Gordon groaned, exhaling heavily. He sprawled out flat on the ground with his pistol still gripped in his hand.

"I tried to wake you, but you wouldn't get up, so I just let you sleep," John said.

The dog jumped up and looked out the window, its tongue hanging out.

Gordon lifted his head and asked, "What's up with the hound?"

"She started following me yesterday afternoon," John said, patting the dog on the head. "You hungry?"

"Yeah," Gordon said, getting up.

Inside, Gordon sat at the dinette table in the kitchen. His heart had returned to its normal rhythm following his little scare. "How they hell did you find me?"

"Just chance," John said, putting a plate of corned beef hash in front of Gordon. "I managed to escape the attack and headed west; I remembered the river. I thought it best to follow it."

"That was my thought too," Gordon said, shoveling a large forkful of hash into his mouth.

John put his index finger to his head and said, "Great minds think alike."

"I'm so happy to see you," Gordon said, stopping his eating to appreciate his friend.

"I was shocked when I broke into the house this morning and, voila, there you were sleeping in the fucking closet. I'll tell you, man, you can't sleep so deep, if I wasn't your friend, you'd be dead."

"My luck, I guess, it was you, but my body must have needed it," Gordon said. The look on his face grew tenser and he continued, "I can't believe the army is gone. It's a real shocker."

"A few of us got out. I was able to call back to McCall and let them know," John said, sitting down across from Gordon with a full plate of hash.

"You have a phone? Great, let me see it," Gordon said, excited about the prospect of calling home. He wiped his mouth and held out his hand.

"Phone's dead."

"Fuck."

"Yeah, sorry."

"How many got out, that you saw?" Gordon asked.

"A couple dozen, I'm sure there were more. By the way, when I talked to Charles, he was in McCall with the committee. He told me they were going to evacuate all nonessentials."

Hearing this made Gordon happy, as he didn't know if Conner would bomb McCall. "Great, he finally did something worthy of applause."

John laughed and said, "You really don't like him, do you?"

"I like him, when he's not around, unavailable, not in charge and just completely off my mind," Gordon quipped.

"Ha, that's funny. But he really pissed you off."

"I'm just not a fan of people who deliberately undermine me and spread lies for their own benefit."

"Who is?"

"Anyway, we need to get home."

"Agreed."

"So our next step is to find a car and get the hell out of here."

Lake Cascade, Idaho, Republic of Cascadia

"Since I'm up, can I get you anything, a drink?" Samantha asked Joyce.

Joyce held her glass in the air and said, "I'll never

turn a drink down."

Turning around, Samantha rolled her eyes and thought to herself that Charles flat out lied. She was still drinking, for one, and her kids still looked neglected. From the instant she showed up at her door minutes ago, she could tell Joyce had already been tipping the bottle back.

A tap on the door gave Samantha a reason to smile.

"Oh, someone else is coming over?" Joyce said, already slurring her speech.

Samantha ignored Joyce and opened the door to find Seneca there. "Hey, welcome."

Seneca stepped in, gave Samantha a hug and looked around. "Wow, this place is great." She scanned the large suite and was impressed by the twenty-foot ceilings and the far wall with its large windows that went from the floor to the eaves. She headed directly towards them, passing by Joyce. "You've got a great view."

"It's not bad for an evacuee shelter," Samantha said.

"I thought my room was nice. I'm on the fourth floor."

"Is it like this?" Samantha asked.

"God no, it's like a large hotel room, not fancy like this."

"Well, I'd trade it all in just to know if Gordon was safe, much less alive," Samantha lamented as she walked into the living room.

Seneca raced to Samantha, took her hands in hers and said, "I'm so sorry, I'm such a fool, coming in here talking about rooms and views. I'm an idiot."

"Yep, kinda," Joyce blurted out.

Seneca shot Joyce a look and said, "Hi, Joyce, what a surprise to see you back in the area."

Joyce didn't reply; she raised her empty glass and pretended to cheer.

"No word?" Seneca asked.

"Nothing."

"I've known Gordon for a while, I'm sure he's fine. I bet he's heading back here pronto."

Not wanting to really discuss it beyond a mention, Samantha changed the subject. "I was just getting Joyce a drink, can I get you one as well?"

"Sure," Seneca said.

Samantha went to the kitchen and brought back a bottle of hard cider and two glasses. She filled Joyce's then topped off the other two.

Joyce took a sip quickly then offered, "Should we toast something?"

Looking uncomfortable, Samantha replied, "Nah, let's just drink."

"I'm fine with that," Joyce said, taking a large swallow.

The afternoon was spent finishing off two bottles of cider, chatting and even gossiping.

Samantha found Joyce to be a bit more relaxed than before and actually funny. However, she still lacked any tact, and the more she drank, the more she talked, and everything she said wasn't nice or appropriate.

"Sam, you have to see Olympia, it's so nice. I mean, it's not like a real city, but it beats this little shithole," Joyce mumbled.

"I've never been, I suppose I'll visit sometime in the future," Samantha said.

"Me too, I guess I'll have Nelson take me there sometime once this has all blown over," Seneca said.

After her comment, Seneca realized it was not necessarily appropriate. "There I go again, saying something stupid."

"Oh, don't worry about it," Samantha said.

Joyce picked up the second bottle and turned it upside down, filling her glass to the top and empting the bottle. "You know, Seneca, I'm tired of self-censoring. If I have something to say, I say it. Fuck that PC bullshit," Joyce said.

Haley came into the room and went directly to Samantha. She leaned in and whispered, "Mommy, one of the boys pooped his pants."

Samantha leaned back and looked at Haley. "Who?"

Haley was acting embarrassed and didn't want to say it loud, so she again leaned in and whispered, "The little one."

"Are you sure?" Samantha asked, stunned to hear the complaint.

"Yes."

"Are you sure he just didn't, you know, pass gas?" Samantha asked.

Luke stormed into the room and blared, "Um, Joyce, your youngest took a crap in his pants then took them off and tossed it at me."

Samantha shot to her feet and said, "He did what?"

Luke shivered, clearly grossed out. "Yeah, he crapped his pants then threw it at me. The boy is a little brat."

"My boys are not brats!" Joyce declared. She stood up but needed to brace against the couch for fear of falling over.

"Excuse me, I'll be right back," Samantha said and headed towards Luke's bedroom. When she was a few feet away from the open door, she could smell fecal matter. Laughter and chattering was coming from the room. Samantha looked in and saw exactly what Luke described, Joyce's youngest had his pants off and a dark stain was present on the far wall. "Hey, Joyce, Luke wasn't lying."

Joyce pushed Samantha aside to enter the room. "I can't believe you two, that's disgusting."

"I'll get something to clean this up," Samantha said and walked away.

"You come with me, and you, how could you let your little brother do that?" Joyce yelled, smacking her oldest in the face.

"I'm sorry, Momma," the oldest boy said.

Samantha rushed back in with several rags and all-purpose cleaner.

"I think its best I take these fucking animals home," Joyce said, grabbing both of her children by their necks and pushing them out the door. The youngest boy whimpered as Joyce squeezed his neck hard. "You two fuck everything up all the time. I was just trying to relax, but no, you have to act out."

Samantha watched in disgust as Joyce shoved and tormented the boys until she closed the door of her room behind her.

"Mommy, that was gross," Haley said.

"You bet it was," Seneca agreed.

Samantha slammed the door, turned and said, "That woman is never allowed over here again, ever."

Cheyenne, Wyoming, United States

Conner had woken that morning feeling refreshed and his mind was clear. He attributed his clarity of purpose to Cruz's late night phone call. He knew what he needed to do, and he was going to make sure it happened right away.

With confidence in his step he headed into the hallway from the elevator. He was quickly met by his executive assistant. "Mr. President, everyone is gathered in the conference room."

"Excellent. Oh, go find me an egg sandwich," Conner said cheerfully. He strutted into the conference room and closed the door.

Encircling the large table was his entire team of cabinet members and their aides. General Baxter sat at the far head of the table, with Schmidt sitting in the middle; his condition had definitely not improved.

Sitting in for Wilbur was Edward Williams, her undersecretary. He was an older man, in his late sixties, and had spent many years in public service.

Conner came in and took his seat at the other end of the table. He looked at each person, smiled and said, "Good morning, everyone."

Everyone gave their greeting.

"Mr. Vice President, you on the line?" Conner asked.

Cruz was on speaker and replied, "I'm here."

"Good. Everyone, I want to tell you that the vice president and I had a great conversation last night. He wants to play a greater role in counter-secessionist policy-making, and how could I say no? The more good minds we have working on this, the better. Now, let's just jump right into this. We have several topics to discuss this morning. General Baxter, update us on Cascadia."

Baxter cleared his throat and read from a folder in front of him, "Van Zandt's Cascadian army has been destroyed. The bombing operation followed by the ground-aerial assault made the force ineffective. We believe some got away, but they're not enough to make a difference. Unfortunately, the bombing and raid also killed all of the refugees that were housed there."

"How were they killed?" Cruz asked.

"Sir, when we targeted the base, we hit everything."

"Why?" Cruz asked.

"Sir, because we believed Van Zandt's forces had intermingled with the civilian refugees," Schmidt answered.

"Brad, how could you target civilians deliberately?"

Cruz asked, unaware and shocked by the news.

"It was a tough decision, one we didn't take lightly, but if we were going to destroy Van Zandt and stop his advance, we needed to make sure we got as many as possible, plus we had some reports of the NARS virus there just days before. The place was probably contaminated anyway," Conner explained with confidence.

"If this gets out that we targeted civilians on purpose, it will cause an uproar in the international community," Cruz barked.

"It had to be done. Van Zandt's army is gone; the threat has been neutralized," Schmidt said.

Baxter glared at Schmidt.

"Andrew, don't get worked up, we've all but won the war against Cascadia. All we need to do now is find their leadership and…"

"Arrest them," Cruz offered.

"We can arrest them, but we'll also kill them if they don't come nicely," Conner said, adding to Cruz's comment.

"In light of what happened at Mountain Home, have you drawn up a plan yet to deal with what's left of Cascadia?" Cruz asked.

"Yes, sir, the president asked me to and I have it right here," Schmidt said.

Conner nodded to Schmidt as a signal for him to give his plan.

Schmidt coughed then began, "We currently need to locate where they might be. The leadership, however, we think they may have fled to McCall. Once we locate them, we will send a strike team to neutralize them."

"Have we reached out to them to see if we can talk them down now that they've lost Olympia and one of their armies?" Cruz said, offering a solution that didn't require military action.

"No," Schmidt replied.

"Have we thought about that? Maybe they want to talk," Cruz said.

Schmidt looked at Conner, who only smiled and nodded.

"No, sir," Schmidt replied.

"May I offer that as a solution? Maybe, just maybe these people don't want to die? We can offer them something. Brad, you're a student of history, even Lincoln forgave those Confederates who surrendered. He didn't kill everyone."

"That is true," Conner said.

"Andrew, I think Major Schmidt will take that into consideration," Conner offered, the smile on his face broader than ever. He was glowing, almost jovial, like a kid ready to explode with excitement.

Schmidt and Baxter both took notice but didn't know what was going on with him.

Several of the other cabinet members chimed in and offered ideas and possible solutions since Cruz gave his opinion.

Conner sat and enjoyed his egg sandwich as he watched the back and forth and open discussion. He looked at the clock and saw that fifteen minutes had gone by and nothing new was being proposed. "Might I say we've come up with some interesting proposals on the subject of what to do next with the Cascadians. Let's move forward with how things are progressing with our investigation of the speech bombings."

Like Conner, Baxter had been sitting on the sidelines too for most of the meeting, watching the open discussion. "We are no closer to knowing who did it exactly, but we still suspect the Cascadians and Pat's resistance group worked together. As of this morning we have arrested two hundred and nineteen people and another six hundred are under suspicion, but we aren't moving on them."

"Under suspicion means you take them in. Get on it ASAP," Conner ordered.

"Yes, sir," Baxter said, then went into more detail about what information they had garnered. Everyone remained quiet and no one asked any questions. "And to finish, we still don't know the whereabouts of Pat. His coffee shop is closed, obviously, and we've taken the place apart. We have found some interesting evidence that will help us make a case of treason against him, but nothing yet that gives us any clues to where he might be."

Hearing that, Conner relaxed back in his chair and tried to recall if out of the many conversations he and Pat had, he'd mentioned any specific place; then he remembered that Pat had been in the air force, more specifically he'd been part of the security forces guarding nuclear bunkers northwest of Warren Air Force Base. "You know something, Pat told me he had been an enlisted man guarding the nukes years ago. I wonder if he's out there. Do you suppose he has a hideout somewhere out there in the silos?" Conner asked.

Schmidt nodded his head, liking what he heard. "I'll get some teams out there immediately."

"Wouldn't we have seen him?" Baxter asked.

"Not necessarily, after the blasts there was a lot of confusion. He could have slipped right out."

"But we think he murdered Wilbur. The timing of her death indicates that would have been hours after," Baxter said.

"That's true, but it doesn't mean he still didn't manage to escape or find a way out," Conner said and looked at Schmidt. "Send your teams right away. I want them to go over every inch out there."

"Yes, sir."

"Any other topics we need to discuss?" Conner asked. No one suggested anything new, so Conner continued. He stood up, adjusted his pants and tucked in his button-down shirt.

"How much longer are we going to be? I have a call with the New Zealand Minister of State," Cruz asked.

"Don't go, Andrew, I need you to hear this; in fact, it's critical you hear this," Conner said.

"Very well," Cruz replied.

Like he did every time he had something important to express or was feeling a lot of emotion, Conner paced the room. He found that his mind was sharper and more articulate if he moved around while talking.

Baxter and Schmidt could see his excitement; it was

like he was electric.

"My journey to president of the United States was unique; few men have taken the job by succession. I'm definitely the only Speaker who has had the privilege, and a privilege it is. I was thrust into this position within hours of the attacks on December 5. To say I wasn't scared would be a bold-faced lie; in fact, I was terrified. I can still remember looking at my reflection in the bathroom mirror at Tinker Air Force Base. I had just been briefed on what had happened and how dire it was. I had been told I was the next in line because the president and vice president were dead. It was something I never could have imagined, but I stepped up regardless of my fear and took the oath. I knew I needed to work fast and get a vice president just in case something happened to me, and I didn't know of any other man than Vice President Cruz to be that man. He represents what is so great about our country. He is a great man, an honest man with a high level of integrity, much higher than mine; in fact, Vice President Cruz is a better man than I am." Conner paused and thought.

Eyebrows were raised and some were giving each other odd looks. The speech he was making seemed out of place.

"I have done my best to keep this country together and to get it back on its feet. I'm not saying every decision I've made was great or worked, but damn it, I made a decision and own those. No one can quite understand the awesome responsibility of this office except a person who has taken the solemn vow. To date,

I have stopped those hell-bent on ripping this country apart, I have established trade lines with those nations not affected, and so far we've been able to get much-needed supplies to those governors so they could get it directly to the American people. I have, along with Vice President Cruz, worked diligently to get the grid back up, and I can report that things are progressing nicely. I understand that some of my decisions have caused political problems for our government and might even have been the cause for some of the discontent that has turned into violence on our very streets out there. For that, I'm sorry, had I known my decision would have resulted in injury to my country, I wouldn't have done it. Now I hear and even see that it's not even about my decisions; there are many people who dislike me and will never in their lifetimes believe I can do anything right. They call me dictator, tyrant, murderer, you know the names, you've heard them. For them, it's about me, not my policies. This is why after a great conversation with one of my oldest and dearest friends last night I have made what will be my last executive decision. So that my country can move forward and have a clean slate, I am submitting my resignation as president of the United States effective immediately."

Gasps and cross talk erupted.

Conner raised his hands. "Please, let me finish. Vice President Cruz will assume the position, one he so honorably and professionally held while I was captive months ago. He proved then to be the man I've always known him as. With him, he can take the flame of liberty and extend it much further than I. His ideas and proposals will be the best to keep this country together. Without me in the way, he will be able to finish the work that I started last December."

"Brad, um, Mr. President, I don't…this comes as a shock. You don't have to do this," Cruz said, stuttering and stumbling over his words.

"I do, my country is more than me, and you brought up some great points last night. I have given my country all I can right now. If we are to go forward, the country needs a leader that inspires and has credibility in the eyes of all Americans, especially those in the resistance and secessionist movements."

Schmidt's face turned ashen, his jaw hanging open.

Baxter couldn't hide his excitement and was grinning from ear to ear.

"Brad, now is not the time to quit, you even said so yourself," Cruz begged.

"No, I thought about this. I'm an impediment. The country needs you now."

Cruz was silent as he pondered the immensity and significance of what was happening for him.

Two people raised their hands to speak like school children.

"No questions, this is a statement I'm making, and it's pretty cut and dry. I've had my letter of resignation already drafted. All I need to do is go sign it and turn over the keys, so to speak," Conner said.

"I think we need to talk in private, Brad," Cruz mumbled.

"No, no talking, I've made up my mind," Conner

stated.

"When do you need me up there?" Cruz asked.

"How about we do this in the morning? Be here by nine," Conner said.

"Very well," Cruz replied.

"Good, I look forward to seeing you tomorrow morning, then. And the rest of you, go do your jobs and serve our great republic with honesty and fidelity. It has been an honor to work alongside you. You all have distinguished yourselves, thank you," Conner said as he took his spot in front of his chair.

Baxter stood and began to clap.

One by one the others did the same until everyone was standing and giving Conner a rousing applause.

Grandview, Idaho, United States

"Who would have thought this little town would have been so plentiful with food, water, supplies and now a car," John said, sitting behind the wheel of a partially restored Jeep CJ-3.

Gordon just stood silently and watched John replace the battery with one from a new model car.

Bent over the engine, John worked diligently in hopes the old Jeep would fire up once the battery was installed. "God, I hope this thing runs."

Still silent, Gordon stared off, his mind consumed with the loss of his army and the safety of his family. He was happy to know they had been tucked away, but with only a smaller force left, how could they defend the city if Conner insisted on bombing it. Of course, this scenario was always a possibility, but like so many things in life, you consider them, but when they actually happen, it's surreal and shocking.

John snapped his fingers. "Earth to Gordon."

Gordon shook his head and blinked rapidly. "I have a lot on my mind."

"So do I, but I could use some help here," John insisted.

"What can I do?" Gordon asked, setting his rifle down against the side of the Jeep.

"I saw a hand pump over there next to the bikes. We need to get these tires inflated."

"A hand pump, Christ, that will take forever," Gordon complained.

"Unless you see a compressor around here, I don't know how else we'll get these tires pumped up," John complained.

"You're right," Gordon said and went to get the pump.

"What's up with you? I know we're dealing with a lot of shit, but you seem shaken. I've never seen you like this," John said, his head under the hood.

With the pump in hand, Gordon answered, "I think I fucked up, and this isn't some little fuckup, this is huge. I'm beginning to think this might be the end or at least the beginning of the end for all of us."

"Snap out of it, get your head straight. Since I've

known you and it hasn't been forever, but the months I have known you, I've seen a man that won't quit. You're headstrong and determined."

Gordon squatted down and screwed the pump nozzle onto the tire. "This is different."

"Is it really?" John finished connecting the battery cables and stepped away from the front of the Jeep. He could see that Gordon wasn't just troubled but quite possibly dealing with a small bout of depression. Not uncommon in this world, most people had those issues, but only the strong or those who could manage it effectively survived. He couldn't have Gordon going down this path; he needed him back in the game.

"I know everyone needs some time to process shit, but I need you and your family needs you to do that once we get home. I'm not saying it's wrong to question your actions and even be upset by them, but you didn't make a wrong move. This is a war we're fighting and shit happens.

"I just wonder if I should have done something different, made a left instead of a right, you know what I mean."

The dog came running into the barn suddenly, a small groundhog in her jaws. She came over to Gordon and dropped it at his feet.

Seeing her brought a smile to his face. "Good girl."

"I'm taking her with us. My son will love her," John said.

"What are you going to name her?" Gordon asked as he pumped up the right rear tire.

"Not sure yet, I like to give a name based upon an unusual or interesting trait."

"Good idea."

"Anyway, stop stressing, we need to get this old jalopy up and running and get home."

"You know when we get back, there's a strong chance Charles and the committee will bring me up on some sort of charges and relieve me of command."

"Well, if he tries, we'll fight him too," John said.

"If you'd said that yesterday, I'd agree, but I wonder if it's worth the fight. Sometimes I just feel like throwing my hands up in the air, taking my ball and going home."

John stepped over and placed his hand on Gordon's shoulder. "That is not you, my friend. You're a fighter to the core. Yeah, you've taken some licks here, but this war is not over. We may have lost a battle, but we're a far cry from being conquered."

Gordon tested the tire and found it adequate. He removed the nozzle and stepped over to the front right tire. "John, I hear you and I know you're right, or at least my head says you are, but my heart is just fucking tired."

"It's okay to be tired, but quitting is not an option because in this world if you quit, you die."

Gordon nodded and replied, "Good point. That's true."

"Gordon, my brother, I'd say fuck it and go over to that ditch, lie down and die if you were a single guy, but you're not. You have a beautiful wife and lovely daughter waiting at home for you; they're counting on you. As a man, husband and father, you have a responsibility to them. Their lives are precious and more important than your fucking feelings. You're a man, and men honor and fulfill their responsibilities to their families. You may want to quit, but that choice was given away long ago when you said I do to Samantha. Marriages and parenthood aren't disposable or little novelties, they're sacred."

Gordon rose and looked at John. "I hear you loud and clear."

The dog walked over and licked Gordon's hand. "I hear you too," he said to the dog.

John again placed his hand on Gordon's shoulder and gripped it firmly. "Just know it's okay to have doubts or question yourself, but make a pledge to yourself to come back to the fighter you are. Know that when you have those doubts, they're nothing but an exercise, use them to become a better man, grow from them but never forget who you are and who is looking to you for leadership and protection. Always honor that man. No, he's not perfect, but he's true to his family, friends and principles."

"This is why I like you so much," Gordon said.

John smiled and joked, "Now if you're done with your pity party, let's get this piece of shit on the road and get home to our families."

Lake Cascade, Idaho, Republic of Cascadia

"Point and squeeze; apply steady and even pressure to the

trigger," Sanchez softly said while standing behind Luke.

Luke held the Beretta M-9 semiautomatic pistol in his shaking right hand. With his left eye pressed closed, he tensed up each time the wavering sights crossed the target.

"Stop, hold on," Sanchez said. "Put the pistol on safe."

Luke did as he said.

"You keep getting all tense, don't be."

"But I can't keep the sights on the bottle."

"Everyone has a natural arc of movement, it kinda flows like a figure eight. What I want you to do is relax just a bit, that doesn't mean you hold the pistol like a dead fish. Firmly grip it, not too hard, kinda like a handshake—not too soft that you look like a pussy and not so hard you're trying to crush the person's hand, just firm. Raise the pistol and just look down the barrel towards the target. Once you do that, apply the steady pressure. Yeah, the sights will move around, but keep applying the steady pressure and focus. When the pistol fires, it should surprise you."

Luke did exactly as he said. His instruction reminded him of Sebastian and the time they spent on the road from San Diego. He missed Sebastian and Annaliese and had wanted them to be his new parents, but the new world never brought guarantees. He had grown to love Samantha, Haley and Gordon in the meantime, and losing them wasn't an option. He didn't want to be alone again.

The pistol fired and the bottle shattered.

"Great shot," Sanchez said.

"I did it," Luke exclaimed with joy.

"Good, now do it again."

"Yes, sir," Luke said, raising the pistol.

"And, kid, don't call me sir, I work for a living," Sanchez joked.

With range time over, Luke felt very proud. Again he had showed he had proficiency with firearms; now he just needed to go from that to mastery.

"Can you get me my own pistol?" Luke asked Sanchez as they walked through the forest, heading back to the lodge.

"You want that one?" Sanchez asked.

"Ah, no."

"What's wrong with it?"

"The handle."

"We call it a grip, proper nomenclature, remember?"

"The grip is too big for my hand," Luke confessed.

Sanchez grabbed Luke's right hand and examined it. "Well, if you didn't have girlie hands, maybe you could handle a man's gun."

"I don't have girlie hands," Luke protested.

"I'm just busting your balls, it's something you'll have to get used to. For some odd reason us men like to do that. I can't explain why, but we do and we enjoy it."

"Where's your family?" Luke asked.

"All back in Puerto Rico."

"You're from Puerto Rico? Cool."

"Yeah, my momma, papa and two brothers are

there."

"Are they fine?"

"I'm not sure," Sanchez admitted.

"Why not go back there?"

"That's my plan, but it seems every time I think about doing it, something more fun happens."

"This is fun?" Luke asked, confused by his response.

"Look, kid, I'm young, dumb and full of..." Sanchez said but stopped short of completing the phrase. "I'm not having a party here, but I have to admit the apocalypse is kind of a thrill ride and I'm with my brothers."

"I thought you said your brothers were in Puerto Rico."

"No, my brothers in arms, the guys in my unit, they're my brothers. I've done more with them and know those guys more than I'll know anyone. We've seen so much shit, sorry, stuff together that I can't imagine not being with them. These guys get me, where my family at home doesn't."

"I don't understand, your family at home probably needs you."

"Maybe, but my dad and my brothers are some tough dudes. I'm not too concerned for them."

"But they're your family."

Sanchez stopped Luke and looked at him squarely in the eyes. "Listen, little dude, family is a versatile word. You don't have to be blood with someone to love them as much as someone who has your blood running through them. I love the guys in my unit and they love me. We're cut from the same cloth; I know how they think and they know how I think. The bond I have with them is stronger than what I had with my own flesh and blood at home. If I left to go home, I'd be leaving the only real family I've ever had to go back to a house and to people who don't truly know who I am. So I ask you to open your eyes and understand that family is a bigger word than, say, your biological parents or siblings. It's those people who will do anything for you, who are there for you and you for them. They are the ones who choose to be in your life and aren't obligated by blood."

Flurries began to fall.

Sanchez looked up and said, "Growing up in San Juan, we never had snow; in fact, the first time I ever saw it was in Big Bear when I was nineteen. I thought I'd hate it, coming from a tropical island, but I can honestly say I really love it."

Luke didn't know how to respond to Sanchez's speech on family. His mind swam with thoughts and emotions.

Sanchez finally realized Luke wasn't following him. He stopped and turned around. "Come on, let's get you back. Samantha's probably getting worried."

Luke ran up beside him.

Sanchez pulled out a Glock 27 .40 caliber, dropped the magazine and cleared the receiver. With the slide back, he handed it to Luke. "How about this size?"

Luke took the pistol and held it. The size was much better. "I like it."

"Good, now I just need to ask Samantha if you can have it."

"Um, no."

"Sorry, I need to ask her."

"I mean, don't call her that, call her my mother."

Cheyenne, Wyoming, United States

One by one cabinet members and distinguished officials took time to visit Conner privately. Some had a genuine concern for how the transition would go while others only cared about their own well-being and wanted Conner to put a good word in with Cruz.

Baxter exited Conner's office to find Schmidt sitting and waiting. He stepped over to him and with a crooked grin said, "I'm sure you're not happy about this."

"I'm a survivor. I'll be just fine," Schmidt replied as he stood up.

"Well, I thought I should tell you that we pulled a fingerprint from a piece of casing from one of those bombs. The lab is working right now to see who it belongs to. Once we have that, we'll know exactly who was behind the bombings," Baxter warned, clearly making a subtle accusation that he suspected Schmidt and his men.

Schmidt stepped closer to Baxter and said, "That's good news, it really is. Getting all the facts is so important. Now if you'll excuse me, I need to speak with the president."

Baxter stepped aside and motioned with his arm for

Schmidt to pass by.

Schmidt slowly walked past him but couldn't let Baxter's veiled threat go unanswered. "Oh, General, I didn't tell you, but my team was investigating Secretary Wilbur before her unfortunate murder and has found some curious intel on other accomplices. In fact, one of the prisoners they interrogated yesterday said she would give us all the names in exchange for immunity."

The veins in Baxter's neck flared. "You have no authority to be interrogating anyone. This is my investigation."

"Not entirely, the president wanted to ensure it was done properly, so he had me put together a special unit. I'm about to get permission now from him concerning this woman."

"Who is it?"

"Don't you fret about it, General, you'll find out soon enough," Schmidt concluded and entered Conner's office. When he closed the door, a broad and toothy grin graced his face. Of course, all of it was a lie; he didn't have a woman. He'd only wanted the general to get worked up because it was his investigation, but seeing his response made Schmidt suddenly suspicious that Baxter might somehow be involved.

"Major Schmidt, my most loyal and trustworthy of officers," Conner bellowed from across the room.

"I think I just might be that," Schmidt replied.

"What's that?"

"I think you're right, I just might be your most loyal and trustworthy," Schmidt answered, taking a seat in his usual chair in front of Conner's desk.

"Now I know my announcement came as a shock, and I'm sure you're wondering what the hell I'm doing. And you're probably concerned about your safety and so forth."

Schmidt raised his arm and said, "It was a shock, sir, but my safety no longer concerns me. I'm a dead man walking now."

"Yeah, that is a problem."

"That is reality," Schmidt said, referencing the final diagnosis that came back—he had stage four non-Hodgkin's lymphoma.

"How do you feel?"

"Pardon my language, sir, but like shit."

"I'm sorry, shall I get you set up with my doctor for some strong drugs, you know, for the pain?"

"I'll be fine, sir."

"Okay, well, I'm glad you're here. I wanted to explain what I'm doing because you might be thinking it all doesn't make sense. I could practically hear your thoughts screaming at me earlier. Like why would I have you set those bombs only to retire days later?"

"The thought did cross my mind."

"I'd be lying if I said I wasn't tired of all the bullshit and constant second-guessing from everyone. But I did mean what I said in there. I think the country has become so jaded and so polarized that I could give them exactly what they want and they'd still be pissed. For all of those on the other side, I can't do anything right. I normally would just blow it off, but when Cruz called and expressed his own personal concern, he sounded like them. I then knew that if my oldest friend was against me, my days were numbered. So I'm going to give them what they want, I'm going to let them lead this rambling wreck of a country. I'm going to give them the keys and watch them crash this thing into the ground, and when everything is smoldering, they'll be begging for me to come back and right the ship. I know you're thinking it's a big risk, but I have you and your men."

"Sir, sorry to interrupt, but General Baxter just informed me—"

"I know, he told me he has a fingerprint."

"But if it comes back positive for one of my men?"

"Then I know you'll take care of it."

"That's not a plan, sir, we need to get in front of this."

"Do you know what man it might be?"

"It could be one of two," Schmidt admitted.

"Then get rid of those two," Conner coldly said.

"Yes, sir."

"Anything from the silos?" Conner asked, just thinking about Pat.

"No, sir, it will take a while. There's a lot of ground to cover."

"Anyway, don't stress. I know I'm taking a big risk here, but I don't think I can lose. You see, I'm so tired of all this bickering and whining; it would be nice to just do nothing. I've made my mark and I personally don't care about my legacy," Conner said, although the last part was a lie he was saying more to convince himself.

"Sir, I'm here to do what you want. I have always been here to serve. I don't think I have long to go, but if you're ready to wash your hands of all of it, then so be it."

"I am, but I'm not. If this thing goes sideways, which it might, trust me, I'll come back with a vengeance. What I need you to do is clean up our tracks; make sure there's nothing that links us to the bombings or anything else we've done over the past few months."

"Yes, sir."

"Then that's it, Major, my door is always open anytime you want to come over," Conner said, then stood up with his hand outstretched.

Schmidt stood, took his hand and shook it. "Thank you for the privilege, sir."

"You know, once I go, I'd recommend you retire too. Go out on your terms."

"Are you saying they won't keep me?" Schmidt asked.

"Do I have to answer that?" Conner said.

"I suspect not," Schmidt said.

"Go tidy things up and make sure you're here tomorrow bright and early for the ceremony."

"Yes, sir," Schmidt said and left.

After each conversation, Conner felt confident about his decision. He was actually looking forward to being retired. The overall good spirits everyone seemed to be displaying, minus a few, was contagious. It showed him just how much his presence and leadership was divisive and stressful to his staff. Something in him wanted Cruz to be successful in his alternate policies, but something also didn't. If Cruz was successful, it would make his actions invalid.

Conner thought about this and began to contemplate a bold and unpredictable move that could blunt Cruz and bolster his legacy.

Grandview, Idaho, United States

The sun had just fallen behind the mountains in the west and cold air was descending from the north. Gordon could see the dark clouds to the north and said, "I think that's a storm."

"Maybe so, but one thing is for certain, it's going to be cold as hell driving this north with no top," John said, referring to the Jeep lacking a top or cover. The two worn-out bucket seats were the only things inside the old Jeep unless you counted the stick shifter. The Jeep was bare bones, small, and it promised to be a slow and cold ride in it.

"I grabbed a stack of blankets," Gordon said.

"And I found these," John said, holding up two balaclavas.

"That was a score." Gordon laughed.

"I don't think we can load more shit on this old rig," John said, looking at the stacks of food, water, fuel and boxes of assorted but critical items like toilet paper, soap, lighters, duct tape, Kleenex, aluminum foil, alcohol, condiments, candy, lotion, Ziploc bags, sunscreen, feminine products, cotton balls, salt and even condoms. Getting pregnant, while wonderful, was also more fatal without modern medicine, and bringing a new child into the world wasn't something either man wanted right now.

"Come on, girl, get in," Gordon said, then whistled.

The dog jumped into the passenger seat, slid into the back and lay on a makeshift bed that John had made.

"I hate driving at night," John said.

"Me too, but I want to get home, and if all goes well, we'll be home before the sun rises," Gordon said.

John got behind the wheel and turned the Jeep over. Its old four-cylinder engine rumbled and popped.

"High performance, huh?" Gordon joked.

"Bundle up," John said as they pulled out of the garage and headed northwest along Highway 78.

Sandy, Utah

Annaliese wasn't expecting a visitor, so when someone tapped on her bedroom door, she was surprised. She got up and opened the door to find Samuel and her mother standing there. The dour looks on their faces told her something horrible had happened.

"What's happened?" she asked.

"It's about your cousin Blake," Samuel said.

Blake was a second cousin, but nevertheless they had been close during her childhood. Blake's parents had lived in San Diego when they were younger. Being close in age, they spent most weekends and all holidays together. Annaliese had enjoyed her time with Blake, and when they moved away to Wyoming, she cried for days. The two stayed in contact through texts and social media, but it wasn't the same. Occasionally they saw each other at a random Christmas or family get-together, and when that happened, it was like they hadn't missed a day.

"He's dead, isn't he?" Annaliese asked.

Her mother replied, "Yes, the poor soul was killed the other day in Cheyenne."

"How?"

"The reports, well, you know how sketchy news is, but it seems he was shot. I guess he attended a protest and things turned ugly. There were some explosions, just craziness, and he got caught in the middle."

"Who shot him?"

"US soldiers," Samuel said.

Hearing this ripped at her. For the second time, someone she loved was shot by the very people who were supposed to protect them. She walked away from the door and sat on the bed.

Her mother rushed in and began to comfort her.

Samuel didn't know what else to say, and not being one who was good at the comforting thing, he said his goodbyes and left.

"Is it ever going to stop?" Annaliese asked.

"I don't think so, that's why we have to have faith," her mother said.

"Faith? I have faith in the knowledge that the people I love will continuously be killed. I have faith in that fact."

"I know you're angry, but things happen. We must find strength and solace in God right now."

Annaliese turned to her, a tear streaking down her face, and said, "I'm having a hard time with that. I can go out there every day and take care of people, but guess what, more will come. Why? Where is God? I've heard you say there are miracles, but healing one child isn't a miracle if you let millions of people die. I want that explained. Can you explain it to me, please?"

"You're just upset," her mother said.

"You're damn right I'm upset. I want this to end, but it won't. We have to stop it, and we're doing that now one day at a time, but let's really examine what we're doing here. We're treating the symptoms not the disease. We need to find a way to kill the disease."

"I don't know what that means, but I know everything you're doing here is God's work."

"Really? Last time I checked, I put this together with your help and Samuel's help, not God. He's nowhere to be found except when one random person needs to be saved from drowning, then voila, he provides a miracle," Annaliese said loudly.

"You're upset, and now you're saying mean and hurtful things," her mother said, getting up from the bed.

"Hurtful to God or you, Mother?"

"You're in pain. God forgives you," her mother said and left the room.

Annaliese lay back on the bed and began to sob. Memories of her and Blake came rushing towards her.

She opened her swollen eyes and declared, "God, if you do exist, do something to stop this. Give me something that I can use to put an end to the madness."

One floor below her, Hector lay listening, the entire conversation coming through the old ventilation ducts. He knew what he'd do if he had the power he once had. He added to the pledge he had silently made to her. If he ever gained the power and influence he once held, he'd give it to her so she could avenge the ones she had lost.

South of Boise, Idaho Republic of Cascadia

"Which way?" John said. They were stopped at a tee in the road. Left took them to Highway 95 and right to Highway 55. Both routes took them north to McCall, but one was shorter than the other. However, the shorter route took them through more of the city.

Gordon was impatient. They had made good time, and if the weather held, they could be home in four to five hours. He sat looking into the black either way. So strange how dark things were with no city lights or electricity, he often thought. "I just want to get home; take the 55."

"Okay," John said and turned right.

The dim headlights beamed down and a sign caught Gordon's eyes.

John also saw it. "Hey, that handmade sign has your name on it."

It was the sign Samantha had made months ago in the hopes Gordon would see it and follow. He did and it led him to Eagle's Nest and his family. His brother, Sebastian, had also followed the signs and it resulted in a homecoming for the entire family.

Gordon wondered how his old neighbors were doing. He thought about stopping, but doing so would take time, and for him that was a precious commodity. He pushed the idea out of his mind.

When a second sign appeared further down the road, his curiosity grew more. The people of Eagle's Nest were good people. He wondered how their summer went and if things had turned out for them.

John made a left and got on Highway 55.

The abandoned vehicles that had riddled the highways for months now were beginning to look weathered. Tall grasses grew out of cracks and crevices, and leaves, trash and debris covered untouched parts of the road like a blanket. Within years large parts of the road would just vanish; they would be reclaimed by nature.

John weaved in and around the old cars.

The dim headlights were inadequate and made it difficult to see far ahead. What also didn't help were the frequent turns.

Gordon was always ready for someone to jump out at them at any moment and ambush them.

An orange glow appeared in the distance just beyond the horizon.

"You see that?" John asked.

"I sure do."

"From the size of it, that must be one big fire," John commented.

"Yeah, let's stay clear of it too," Gordon said.

"I'm a risk taker not an idiot; of course I'll steer clear of it."

"Hey, pull over, I've got to take a piss," Gordon said.

John found a clear shoulder and slowed down to a full stop.

"Kill the lights and engine," Gordon ordered.

John did as he said. "Are you going?"

"Ssh, listen," Gordon replied.

Both men sat in the complete darkness and allowed their ears to adjust to the quiet. The steady wind whipping had dulled his hearing, so he wanted to acclimate.

Their ears began to pick up sounds, but the one that alarmed them was coming from the large fire in the distance. Screams and cries echoed in the night sky.

Just above a whisper, John said, "What the hell is going on?"

"I don't know, but now I'm curious," Gordon said, getting out and stepping away to go urinate.

"My jaw is, like, frozen. It's hard to talk," John said, massaging his jaw and mouth.

Gordon climbed back in and asked, "Do we have a map?"

"Nope."

"Hmm, from the looks of it, the fire is around Eagle."

"That's the town you guys lived in for a bit, right?"

"Yeah."

"Gordon, do we really want to go check this out? It may not be the best idea to veer off course," John suggested.

"I know I have a history of doing shit like that, but this is more for recon. What if that's a military unit of Conner's or some sort of rogue army marching north or a large band of marauders like the Villistas? We need to know if they're heading north, we need intel," Gordon said, making a strong case. The Villistas were a former cartel that had become the guerrilla army of Pablo and his Pan American Empire.

John sighed and said, "God, why are you so right?"

"Always a jokester."

"No, I'm serious, I want to argue against it, but we do need to see what's going on."

"Fire it up, let's go," Gordon said.

Eagle, Idaho, Republic of Cascadia

When they were within a quarter mile of the massive blaze, John pulled the car off the highway and parked it behind a large grove of trees.

The plan was to travel by foot and take positions on a large hill that overlooked the area.

The air had grown even colder.

Gordon's face and fingers were so cold it inhibited some of his motor skills.

The cries and screams were accompanied by cheers and roars of laughter.

The glow in the sky was bright, enabling John and Gordon to see each other clearly. Near the top, they finished the rest of the trip by low crawling until they crested the hill. Below was a small valley that ran long ways east to west and was surrounded by large hills on all sides. Directly in the center was a massive bonfire, it had to be the largest single blaze Gordon had ever seen. The wood, mostly full trees, was stacked twenty feet high and the circumference was over thirty feet. The heat close to the fire had to be intense because they could feel its warming effects on the top of the hill. Circling the fire were large posts with people tied to them, all facing the enormous fire. Their moans and cries carried upwards.

All Gordon could imagine was these people were being cooked alive as some form of torture.

A large crowd was to the far right of the valley. They were surrounding a small pit where two people were fighting.

John pulled out a pair of binoculars and zoomed in. "Holy shit, it's like a gladiator show."

"Fucking animals."

"Whoa," John said, followed by the loud reaction of the crowd; some cheered while others booed.

"What?"

"One guy just cut off the head of another. He's now holding it up."

"How many do you count?" Gordon asked.

"Um, a ton."

"How many?"

"Oh, fifty people cheering and watching like a pack of undisciplined voyeurs."

"How much ammo do you have?"

John put the binoculars down and looked at Gordon. "What the hell are you thinking?"

"Oh, don't worry, I don't have visions of riding in there and saving those poor victims, though I would if I had my army. I'm just making sure we'll have enough ammo if those people come after us."

"Good, because attacking them will result in us ending up in the pit," John quipped.

"Who do you suppose they are?" Gordon asked.

"I don't know and I don't want to find out. Let's just get the hell out of here before something happens."

Gordon scanned the area and got a good headcount. Whoever they were, they weren't human to him. Anyone who could enjoy watching people die like that deserved nothing but the same.

A woman screeched, drawing John and Gordon's attention to the pit.

"Please, no!" she begged as they pulled her from a corral and tossed her in the pit.

Another woman was taken from the corral and also tossed in, but she didn't go easily, she kicked and fought, but it was futile. When she hit the bottom of the pit, the other woman, who was younger, helped her up.

A man approached and tossed in two hatchets. "Pick them up and fight!" the man ordered.

"No, I will not fight my daughter!" the older woman

who had resisted declared. She kicked the hatchet away from her.

The man turned and pointed to the corral.

Several men grabbed a small child no older than twelve.

The intense scene had John and Gordon on edge.

Gordon hated watching; the urge to do something burned inside him.

The boy was brought to the edge of the pit and the man who was the ringleader put a large blade to his throat. "Fight or I kill him right here."

"Don't you hurt him. He's my grandson!" the older woman screamed.

"Motherfuckers," Gordon grumbled. The dilemma was impossible to fathom, he thought. They were having a mother and daughter fight to the end, and if they refused, they'd kill the boy who was the son and grandson to the women.

"Fight!" the man ordered.

"John, we can't just watch this shit and do nothing," Gordon said.

"I fucking knew it," John complained.

"You're telling me you can walk away after seeing this shit? That's what was wrong with our society before, too many lookers and not enough doers. We're not those type of people, we don't watch others get hurt because doing so makes you just below the bully or attacker, and in my eyes you're a scumbag."

"I'm not saying we shouldn't, but if we had just pressed north, we wouldn't know this shit was happening and we'd be that much closer to home."

"But now we know what's happening," Gordon said.

"Only because you fucking insisted," John angrily replied.

"You're pissed off at me?" Gordon asked.

"Yeah, a bit, because I'm like you, I can't watch and do nothing. You brought me here and now I have to act."

Gordon double-checked he had all of his magazines and said, "I'll start on the right, you on the left, we'll meet in the middle."

"Fine," John grumbled.

"I'm going to go right a few hundred feet so we're not on top of one another," Gordon said, then rolled back. As he was getting to his feet, a gunshot cracked not far away. Gordon listened and swore it came from the far end of the valley. He ran back up the hill and jumped down.

John's rifle then came to life.

Both the prisoners and their captors began to scream and run in all directions.

The shooter across the valley shot again and again and again.

Now Gordon knew where they were, not from the sound but from the muzzle flash.

"John, heads up, opposite hill from you, at one o'clock," Gordon informed him.

"I see, but I think they're on our side. They're tagging those assholes down there."

Gordon got behind his rifle and aimed at the target-rich environment. But while there were many to shoot, the challenge was they were all moving at a breakneck pace for cover. He found a man to the far right aiming towards John. He took aim and began to squeeze.

A gunshot cracked from the far hill.

The man he was aiming at was struck in the back and it exited his upper chest. A spray of blood followed the bullet as the man crumpled to the ground dead.

"Damn, they're a good shot," Gordon said as he looked for a new target.

John was squeezing a round off every ten seconds and hitting three out of four of his targets.

Gordon hadn't yet taken a shot. He'd wanted to shoot the ringleader, but that target was also gone, shot by the stranger. He heard the sound of a truck and looked further to his right; there he saw a group of men climbing in the bed of a pickup truck. "You're not going anywhere, motherfuckers," he said and squeezed off half a dozen rounds into the open bed, hitting the men. The truck sped off but soon veered hard to the left and crashed after the unknown shooter took out the driver.

Gordon couldn't believe how effective they were at killing these savages. By a rough count twenty were down, but there were still thirty left.

All three took one well-aimed shot after another. The captors were running but couldn't hide as their bullets rained down on them. It was like shooting fish in a barrel, Gordon mused as he changed a magazine and went back to firing. With each passing second the availability of targets grew less and less until they were all gone.

"I think that's it," Gordon said.

"I agree, oops, hold on, right…"

CRACK.

The unknown shooter fired and hit the lone survivor through the hip. The man tumbled to the ground and cried out in pain.

"He's all yours!" a woman yelled from the hill.

So the unknown shooter was a woman, very impressive, Gordon thought. But that voice, did he know her?

A group of prisoners charged the wounded man, carrying machetes, axes and knives.

He begged for mercy, but none was shown.

They began to beat, chop and slice at him.

Gordon took inventory of the kills and counted fifty-two. The prisoners were safe and not one was hit by their accurate gunfire.

John called out, "Who are you?" His voice echoed off the hills.

No reply.

"Thanks!" John yelled.

Still no reply.

"I don't think she wants to talk," John said.

"Maybe she's shy," Gordon joked. His heart was beating fast and his adrenaline was racing. He didn't want to admit it to anyone, but John would understand. "That, my friend, was…"

"Crazy?"

"I was thinking more like fun, or is that wrong?"

"Not when you're taking out scumbags. Then it's fun."

"Should we go help them down there?" John asked.

"I think we've done enough. Let's get back on the road."

They got up, dusted off, and headed towards the Jeep.

The dog began to bark then fell silent.

"I think someone's at the Jeep," Gordon said and began to sprint.

John was right behind him.

When they reached the Jeep, the dog was gone.

"Well, the Jeep is here, but the dog is gone," John said. "Come here, girl, where are you?"

Gordon whistled but nothing, no dog.

John walked around, but there wasn't a sign of the dog or anyone. "Damn. It's too dark."

"That's why we have flashlights," Gordon said, turning his on and directing the beam towards the clump of bushes and out towards the rolling hills. He then looked around just outside the Jeep for any signs of blood. He shined the beam near the right rear tire and paused. "Fuck."

"What's wrong?"

"The damn tire is flat."

John jogged up.

Gordon was a bit suspicious and put the light on the other tires but found them fine.

John knelt down and found the puncture in the side wall. "Yep, we've been sabotaged, and I'm guessing it was our little female friend."

Gordon flashed the light inside the Jeep and found

everything there except a box was open. Gordon looked inside and said, "Water is missing and so is my Chef Boyardee. She took my Chef Boyardee!"

"Just shut up, this whole thing was your idea. You're upset she took nasty canned food? The bitch took my dog."

Gordon shook his head, frustrated by the setback but also amused. His eyes caught something under the windshield wiper. It was a note. He grabbed it and began reading.

"How sweet, she left a fucking note?" John groaned.

"Ha, so funny." Gordon laughed.

"You seriously think this is fucking funny? It's not, Gordon, it's bullshit. We pull off to help people; then our vehicle is disabled and my dog is stolen!"

"It's only funny because it's so ironic, that's all. Maybe I'm tired, I tend to get a little punch-drunk when I am. Plus your dog wasn't stolen. That dog weighed like fifty pounds, she just doesn't have any loyalty, sorry to break the news to ya."

John grumbled under his breath and sat down.

The note read, *'Thanks for helping and the food. Sorry about the tire, but I don't trust anyone. And the dog is super sweet, I promise to take care of her. – Nemesis'*

"What does it say?"

"She calls herself Nemesis. What kind of name is that? She must think she's some sort of superhero. The world ends and people suddenly fashion themselves as caped crusaders…and she promises to take care of the dog."

"What a pain in the ass."

Gordon crumpled the paper and tossed it. "It sure is. Say, where's that motivational speaker guy who got me all pumped up earlier?"

"He's pissed because someone just made his life harder and took his dog."

Gordon couldn't hide that he was sort of giddy. It was a strange reaction for him, but he wasn't going to fight it. Practically speaking, they had a spare tire, so all this little adventure cost them was a bit of time, a little ammunition, water and his beloved Chef Boyardee. Killing those people wasn't necessary to him personally, but having done it filled him with pride. They had rid the world of some very bad people. Who knows, he thought, if they hadn't killed them, those people might have ended up in McCall.

John grunted and cursed as he prepared to jack the Jeep up.

Gordon took in the moment because he knew it wouldn't last, and more than likely, speaking from experience, of course, he'd be faced with something horrible and quite possibly tragic.

NOVEMBER 3, 2015

"We have to distrust each other. It is our only defense against betrayal." – Tennessee Williams

Cheyenne, Wyoming, United States

"Mr. President, the vice president has arrived," Conner's executive assistant told him, peeking her head in his office.

"Excellent, get him in here right away," Conner replied. He walked away from a box he was loading to greet his old friend.

Cruz stepped inside the room, stopped and put his hands on his hips. "No, no, no, this color will not do!" he joked.

Conner laughed and said, "Don't worry, they have a gallon of periwinkle downstairs with your name on it."

"That's perfect!" Cruz laughed.

Both men embraced.

"So good to see you, my friend, so good," Conner said, patting Cruz on the back. He stepped back and looked at Cruz. "Are they feeding you guys too much down there, or are you pregnant?"

Cruz rubbed his belly and answered, "They have the best rice pudding. I think it was made in 1980, but it's damn good." Cruz had put on some weight and his black hair with a few grays had become more grays, but his handsome baby face looked the same.

"I haven't succumb to the devils of food; in fact, the apocalypse has been good for my waistline," Conner commented, raising his arm so Cruz could see how lean he had become.

"You do look good, so you're telling me the presidency is the next best thing to Weight Watchers?"

Conner switched his tone and replied, "I wish, this job is what you make of it, and I'm thrilled to be done with it."

Cruz put his arm around Conner as both men walked to a tufted leather sofa and chair that sat next to a large bookcase off to the left of Conner's desk. "I still can't believe you're resigning. You know, I would have never pegged you as someone to just…quit."

Conner fell into the chair and said, "I don't look at it as quitting. This job isn't supposed to be permanent, and I was never elected, so I didn't have a term to fulfill. After your call the other night, I got thinking that I had become the problem. Maybe if I stepped aside, you could get some things done that I couldn't." Conner paused for a second but needed to say something so that Cruz knew he felt his time in office had been productive. "Even though the conflicts are over, you just need to handle the final details."

Cruz raised his eyebrows, curious as to what Conner was talking about. "What does that mean?"

"It means I stole a small bit from your playbook."

"And that was?"

"I was able to contact the leader of the Cascadians,

and wouldn't you know it, he was willing to strike a deal."

"You did what?" Cruz asked, sitting up in his seat.

"I have to be honest, Andrew, I wasn't sold on your way of doing things and I didn't want to leave office as the man who only crushed skulls and killed people. I wanted a legacy that said, *'I ended the wars of secession and rebellion.'* It sounds nice, doesn't it? It will look good on the entrance to my presidential library."

"Why would you go and do something like that without consulting me first, especially after your announcement yesterday?"

"You're angry?"

"I'm not angry, I just don't understand why you go and do things without getting input," Cruz protested.

"I got input from you, I believe you specifically mentioned doing exactly what I did," Conner said, defending his actions.

"I just would have liked to—"

Conner interrupted and asked, "To be the one so you could take the credit?"

"It's not that, never mind," Cruz relented.

"I think it's a win-win for us and them," Conner said.

"So what were the terms?" Cruz asked.

"Surprisingly this Charles Chenoweth was very accommodating; I think he could see the writing on the wall. After we wiped out one of his armies, he all but felt we were going to come and kill them too," Conner said and continued, "You see, Andrew, what I did against them did work and what you proposed worked. I brought them to their knees and your way brought them to submission but voluntarily."

"Good, so what were the terms?" Cruz asked again.

"They come back into the nation fully. He and some on his committee will be given pardons and be allowed to finish their short terms. They will all have to sign declarations swearing allegiance to the United States. We will send in US troops at a later date to help organize a new election that will occur in three months."

"So the governors of those states won't be given their positions back? Just like that, you kick them aside?"

"It was a compromise and one that ensures we don't have to fight or go in there killing people. Mr. Chenoweth told me in so many words that they would disappear into the mountains and begin a guerilla war that would go on forever. We both know how that can work out, so to prevent that, I gave him that one term, plus I wanted him to feel like he was winning on something."

Cruz nodded and pondered.

Conner continued, "What he also pledged to do was give us the coordinates for their last remaining force that is west of McCall. Once we have that, our air force will deal with them. He then volunteered to give up the more radical wing of their movement, the Van Zandts, and if Gordon Van Zandt is alive, we'll finally get him and bring him to justice here in Cheyenne. I recommend a public trial followed by a quick public execution."

"This guy is giving you a lot, can he deliver?"

"So he says. He will get everything set and speak with his committee to finalize those details. I'm expecting a call from him soon, like any minute, once they've voted to move forward with the surrender."

"Unbelievable, I have to say, Brad, bold and effective. Great job," Cruz said, acknowledging the deal was a good one and one he could work with. It promised less bloodshed and a reunification of those states that had been lost.

"I thought so too," Conner admitted, feeling proud of his decision.

"Did you do anything that I should know about concerning the rebels in Cheyenne?"

"Nothing is different. That, my friend, is your problem to handle."

"I will."

"Now go get yourself cleaned up and be back here in a couple hours for the ceremony," Conner said, a large grin on his face.

Cruz exited the office, both excited and nervous for the future.

Conner went back to packing his boxes. His confidence was at an all-time high. The closer he got to his last second as president, the more he had no designs on coming back or getting in the way. He had thought about it, but it just didn't make sense. He had acted contrary to his past beliefs when he reached out to Charles Chenoweth and it had worked out. The wars of secession and rebellion would soon be over, and he would be given credit for it, so he could go into retirement proud because he'd be known as the man who had saved the United States.

His phone rang.

Conner stepped over and grabbed it. "Yes."

"Mr. President, this is Major Schmidt."

"Yes, Major, how are you?" Conner asked happily.

"It's all cleaned up, the two we mentioned yesterday are gone and there is nothing that links us to the bombings because I've gone above and beyond and taken care of my team personally."

"You did?" Conner asked, shocked.

"It had to be done, sir, to guarantee no one could talk."

"Good man, thank you, Major."

"Thank you, sir, my privilege."

"I'll see you soon, then."

"Yes, sir."

Conner hung up the phone and walked to the window. The sun had just crept over the horizon, its rays making for a new day, one for him and his country.

Sandy, Utah

"Run! Get to the bunker!" Eli Bennett screamed as he ran into the center of the yard. Eli had been a real asset to the community since arriving with Annaliese months ago. His background in avionics and engineering had been beneficial in developing a windmill system for power. They hadn't yet completed its construction, but if his plan worked, they'd be able to generate enough power for much of the housing on site.

The distinct sound of a .50-caliber machine gun roared in the distance.

Samuel burst from the house, with Annaliese close behind. "What is it?"

"There are people coming. They've broken down the gates and are killing everyone!" Eli hollered with a panicked look on his face.

"Where is Robert?" Samuel asked, referring to Robert Blankenship, the head of security for the property and once deputy sheriff of Salt Lake County.

"He's dead. They're all dead, gunned down. I was up there working when they came out of nowhere. Hurry, we have to get to the bunker," Eli yelled.

"We're not just giving up yet, we need to plan a defense," Samuel said, stepping off the deck, a rifle in his right hand.

Annaliese came up behind him, walking and putting on the shoulder holster that Hector had given her.

"You can't defend against this, Sam. We gotta hide," Eli barked.

"I'm not about to cut tail and run just yet. It'll take an army to run me off," Samuel declared with bravado.

"Sam, this is an army. They've got tanks and armored vehicles."

Shock spread across Samuel's face. He thought of the two uniformed men from the other day and knew his assumptions had been correct. He turned to Annaliese and ordered, "Get your mother." Turning back to Eli, he said, "Get everyone you can find and head to the bunker."

Hector wheeled out onto the deck in his wheelchair and down the ramp. He was back in it but only for short bursts to rest while he built up his stamina. "No."

They ignored him.

Annaliese raced back into the house while Eli took off yelling for everyone to head to the bunker.

Hector pushed right up to Samuel and yelled, "No!"

"No what!" Samuel yelled back.

"Run, run, no…bunker!"

"Run? Listen, boy, you're crazy. They can't get us in the bunker," Samuel snapped and turned to walk away, dismissing Hector's suggestion.

The roar of heavy weapons again sounded in the distance.

"RUN, RUN, RUN!" Hector screamed.

Samuel kept walking away.

Hector looked towards the house then back to Samuel and the people who were now scrambling towards the bunker behind the hospital.

Annaliese came out with her mother and saw Hector heading down the driveway towards the sound of fighting.

"Hector, where are you going?" she hollered.

He heard her but kept moving.

"Hector!"

Lake Cascade, Idaho, Republic of Cascadia

"I'm heading out!" Luke yelled as he raced to the door. He had his morning training with Sanchez and it was something he didn't want to miss.

Samantha called from her room, "Please drop off Brady's pants and underwear at Joyce's."

"I don't want to be late," Luke replied.

"She's just across the hall. Give them to her; I want her to know I even washed them."

"Oh, c'mon," Luke groaned.

"Just do it, love you. Oh, I almost forgot," Samantha cried out and raced out of her bedroom and up to Luke waiting by the front door.

"What?" Luke asked, contorting his face in frustration.

Samantha grabbed the bag of clothes and handed it to him, then said, "Lance Corporal Sanchez and I spoke last night, and I think it's fine if you have that pistol."

Luke's eyes lit up with excitement. He hugged her and said, "Thank you. I promise I'll be responsible. I won't let Haley get near it, I'll keep it clean, because that's what you're supposed to do and…" Luke rambled, clearly elated by the news.

Samantha touched his face and swept his long brown bangs out of his eyes. "I know you'll be responsible with it. I need you to be a man now."

Luke stood straight and proudly declared, "I will be."

"I know you will. You'll make me and Gordon proud."

"I will."

"Now go and drop those clothes off, and please hand them to her personally."

"Okay."

Samantha gave him a kiss on the head and opened the door for him.

Luke stepped out and walked down the hall to Joyce's room. His mind raced with visions of him being grown up and defending his family with honor. He saw himself a brave soldier of the republic, fighting for the freedoms of his people. Luke approached Joyce's door and saw it cracked open. He went to knock but stopped when he heard Joyce.

"But we just got here. What about the threat in town?" Joyce complained.

"Get your shit and your boys. I have my people downstairs; we have to get you out of here now," Charles ordered.

"But why, where are you taking us?" Joyce asked.

"Do you always have to ask a thousand questions? Why can't you just do as I ask when I ask? Trust me, it's important that you come with me."

"I'm not doing anything unless you tell me why," Joyce replied defiantly.

Charles grabbed her by the arm and barked, "This whole place is going to go crazy any minute. I sent a driver over here, but your refusal is beyond contempt. The fact that you made me come over here to convince you pisses me off."

"Why is this place about to go crazy?" Joyce asked.

Charles grabbed a bag and began to stuff items into it. "You're lucky I care for you because if I didn't, I would have just left you here."

"What is going on?" Joyce asked, almost screaming.

Charles jumped over to her and snatched her by the upper arm. "Shut up! We can't have anyone hear!"

"Hear what?" Joyce asked again, refusing to go without knowing what was happening.

"I've struck a deal with President Conner and the United States. We are to surrender, and in exchange, they'll not fucking kill us. I just saved your life. Now get your shit together."

"You surrendered?"

"Yes, there was no other choice. He called me late last night and offered terms that I couldn't refuse. If I didn't, he was going to do to us what he did to Gordon and his men, so if you value your life like I do, you'll get going now."

"But why are we leaving?"

"Are you drunk?" Charles asked, leaning in to smell her breath. "You are, you're fucking drunk."

"I only had one, just an eye-opener."

"Listen, part of the terms was to arrest all those connected to the Van Zandt's, that includes quite a few in this building and around the resort. Michael Rutledge has been taken into custody already, and those loyal to us in the militia are coming this way now."

Luke recoiled when he heard Charles's admission. He turned to go warn Samantha when he dropped the bag of clothes.

Charles saw the door was cracked and opened it fully to find Luke standing there.

"You? What did you hear?"

Luke looked stunned. "Nothing."

Charles grabbed him and pulled him inside, slamming the door behind them.

Sandy, Utah

Hector pressed forward down the rocky and uneven driveway until he saw the tank coming towards him. He stopped, thought about what he should do, and decided then and there he'd take a stand, literally and figuratively.

Bracing his weight against the arms of the wheelchair, he pushed himself into a standing position. With his feet firmly planted, he stepped away from the chair and stood defiantly in the way of the rumbling tank.

Annaliese delivered her mother to the burgeoning bunker and raced back to get Hector.

Samuel saw her leave and called after her, "Anna, where are you going?"

"To get Hector."

"No, we don't have time," Samuel hollered.

"I'm not leaving him out there," she replied, running away.

"He made that decision. Now let him go!" Samuel yelled.

Annaliese didn't listen; she disappeared around the barn.

"Go get her, Samuel!" Annaliese's mother barked.

"But she's being foolish," Samuel protested.

"She's your niece. Go get her and Hector, now go!"

she yelled.

Samuel grunted and sprinted as best he could for a sixty-five-year-old, his Mini-14 rifle in his grasp.

The shooting had ceased.

Hector stood with his hands up.

The T-72 tank rumbled to within six feet and came to a full stop. The turret whined as it turned the 125-millimeter cannon to face Hector.

Hector looked into the rifled barrel and wondered if his life was about to be taken. When the hatch on the turret opened, he knew he'd bought himself some time and that was all he needed.

A man emerged from the tank and looked down at Hector. In his teeth a chewed cigar hung. He pulled it out and said, "You're a brave man."

Uniformed soldiers enveloped Hector, with their rifles at the ready.

The man climbed out of the turret and stepped onto the front of the tank. A grin stretched across his face as he cocked his head and looked at Hector. "How is it that the bravest man here is a cripple?"

Hector closed to within a foot and braced himself against the tank. He looked up and said, "Stop."

Amused, the man, an officer by the insignia on his collar, laughed and said, "I did stop."

Annaliese came running around the bend in the driveway.

The soldiers turned their rifles towards her.

Hector yelled, "No!"

Annaliese stopped and froze when she saw the men.

Samuel then appeared and did as Annaliese had when he saw the mass of men and tanks.

"Listen, cripple, there doesn't need to be any more killing. Just turn over all of your supplies and we'll let you live," the officer said.

"No, you won't," Hector said, struggling to speak.

"I won't? Maybe you're right," the man said, pulling out a sidearm and pointing it at Hector.

"Don't shoot him, please!" Annaliese begged.

"Look, boys, we'll have some fun later with that pretty one." The man laughed.

Hector leaned in and said, "Look at me."

"Huh?" the man asked.

"Look at me."

"I'm looking at you, and you're one ugly man. Now I'm bored with this. I have a hungry army to feed."

Hector swallowed hard and found the words. "My name is Pablo Ignacio Juarez Luiz and I am your emperor!"

The man chuckled.

Hector turned to the men around him and repeated, "My name is Pablo Ignacio Juarez Luiz and I am your emperor!"

All eyes turned to him; they were shocked by what this cripple was saying.

"You are not. Our emperor died," the officer said.

"I am Pablo Ignacio Juarez Luiz. I am your emperor and I am very much alive!"

"Liar!" the officer barked.

"I survived and I am here to lead you once more!"

The officer pointed the pistol but couldn't get the nerve to squeeze the trigger. After Hector had made his declaration, he could see his strength and his courage—this man could only be his emperor.

Pablo looked at the officer and said, "Come, my brother, embrace your emperor."

The man lowered his pistol; tears welled up in his eyes. He jumped off the tank and looked deep into Pablo's eyes. "It is you."

Pablo's throat was on fire, seared by an intense pain, but he couldn't stop now. "Lower your guns. These people are our friends."

The soldiers did as he said.

Annaliese and Samuel stood frozen, unsure of what they should do.

Pablo turned around on his wobbly legs and said, "Anna, I want you to meet my family."

Annaliese's jaw hung open; she had nothing to say.

Pablo slowly and painfully walked to her, his men falling in behind him like water flowing back after a break. He stopped just feet from her and said, "*Hola*."

"What is this, Hector?"

He nodded.

"I know you can talk, so talk," she demanded.

"It hurts," he said, then spit a large bloody mass onto the ground to give her a physical display.

"Talk."

"These men belong to me."

"Who are you?"

With his throat swelling, he waved for the officer to

come forward. "Answer her."

"This great man is Pablo Juarez, the emperor of the Pan-American Empire."

"I thought you were all wiped out," Samuel said, his memory recalling the nuclear blast that had destroyed Pablo's northern army but not the one he had sent to the south.

"No, sir, the emperor in his wisdom split the army. We were directed south. After the blast killed our brothers to the north and word came that our emperor died in the blast too, we halted our march east. We found refuge in the mountains west of here. Slowly as the days turned to weeks then months, men left never to return. Our army dwindled and soon ran out of food and supplies."

"So then you come and kill my people!" Samuel barked.

The officer looked sheepishly at Samuel, now knowing these people were friends of Pablo's. "Had I known the emperor was here, I never would have."

Pablo placed his right hand on the man's shoulder and said, "You're a survivor."

"*Sí.*"

"So are we, and you don't see us murdering people," Annaliese barked, challenging the excuse.

"Forgive me, forgive us," the officer said, his head bowed.

Pablo reached out and took Annaliese's hand, but she pulled away.

"I don't even know who you are," Annaliese said

angrily.

"Yes, you do," Pablo replied.

"No, I don't."

He swallowed hard and said, "You saved me more than once."

"Where do we go from here?" Samuel asked, unsure of how they'd come to a resolution.

"Water," Pablo said.

Several soldiers ran up, offering their canteens.

Pablo took one and drank. He looked at Annaliese and said, "You decide what happens."

Stunned, she didn't know how to respond.

"Think clearly, Anna," Samuel said.

"These men," Pablo said, then paused. He looked at the officer and asked, "How many?"

"Only one thousand eight hundred and seventy-nine left, sir."

Pablo was amazed by how little remained of his army. "All of these men are yours now."

"What am I suppose to do with an army?"

"Might I suggest?" Pablo asked.

"Sure."

"I listened to you that night your cousin died. I heard your prayer to the Almighty," Pablo said, he turned with his arm and finished, "I think God gave you his answer."

Southern Checkpoint, Highway 55, Five Miles south of Cascade, Idaho, Republic of Cascadia

"My face is frozen," Gordon mumbled loudly, the cold air whipping and swirling around him.

"Almost there, the south checkpoint is in view," John replied.

They slowed down and pulled into the barricaded entrance of the checkpoint. The road was narrowed to a single lane with large concrete jersey walls on either side. A hundred feet ahead the lane ended at a crossbar with a small shed erected to the left. They crept along until they reached the shed.

"Where is everyone?" John asked, shocked that no one was there.

A pickup and one Humvee were parked just behind the shed.

The door of the shed opened up and three armed men wearing civilian clothes exited. On their upper sleeves they bore a patch that had a clenched fist emblazoned over a blue, white and green circle. This was the patch of the Cascadian Workers Army, a radical and militant left-wing group that Gordon despised but the committee used as their personal security force.

Neither John nor Gordon recognized them, and they wondered why they were there.

"Papers," an older man asked, stepping up to the side of the Jeep.

John looked at Gordon and said, "What's the CWA

doing here? Why are they manning the checkpoints?" John looked back at the man and asked, "Where are the Marines?"

The man cocked his head and asked, "Who are you?"

A tingle shot up Gordon's spine as his senses were screaming that this entire situation was wrong.

John stared at the man and asked again, "Where are the Marines?"

The tension rose after John's stern question. The two other sentries gripped their rifles more firmly but hadn't yet raised them.

Gordon slowly moved his hand towards his holstered pistol.

"Who are you?" the man asked again, this time louder and with an authority he thought he had.

"I'm not answering shit until you tell me what happened to the Marines who usually man this checkpoint," John said.

The two sentries grew tenser and began to fidget.

"If you don't provide me papers or tell me who you are, I'll have to arrest you."

Gordon could see how this could go very badly for them. They were hemmed in between two barriers, and neither had their weapons out. The two sentries were just a few inches from raising their semiautomatic Kalashnikov rifles and ending their lives. There wasn't a scenario he played out that had them survive.

"Hold on, everyone chill out," Gordon said, putting his left hand up and standing up in the Jeep.

"Sit down!" the man ordered.

"Calm down, we're from the army. We survived; we're just coming back is all," Gordon said.

"Who are you?" the man once again asked.

Feeling that his name would benefit them, Gordon declared, "I'm Gordon Van Zandt, you might have heard of me."

The two sentries had and responded accordingly by leveling their muzzles at Gordon and John. The older man stepped back, pulled out his pistol and barked, "You're under arrest!"

"What the fuck, hold on!" Gordon yelled.

John went to move, but Gordon prevented him.

"Just sit tight, don't," Gordon urged.

"Get out of the vehicle and on the ground!" the old man ordered.

"On whose authority are you doing this?" Gordon asked.

"Chairman Chenoweth, now get out of the vehicle now!"

Cheyenne, Wyoming, United States

The main hall of the capital was filled to capacity, with many visitors standing to see the transfer of power from one president to another. What made this historical was it was the first of its kind in US history, and it showed the people of Cheyenne and the United States that peaceful transitions were still possible.

When the news broke in the city that Conner was

resigning, a mixture of jubilance, anger and uncertainty reverberated. Those who sided with Pat and opposed Conner took to the streets in violation of martial law and the anti-protest laws to celebrate. When Conner saw the swelling numbers, he knew how large his opposition really was. They had arrested many, but it proved that many sat in silence and objected to his leadership but were too afraid or too lazy to act. This silent majority symbolized an election loss had he ever run. He was now more than ever certain of his decision to vacate the office that had been thrust upon him. He would happily go into obscurity, but where that would be was still undecided.

The ceremony would be short, with him formally signing a document resigning the office. He wouldn't give any speeches and would slip back to allow his friend to take the spot. Time was allocated for Cruz to give his first speech after he was officially sworn in.

A single table and chair sat in the middle of the large hall. This was to be the spot it would happen.

Waiting for his cue, he stood on the sidelines. To his right several people away, Major Schmidt stood, his dress uniform on. To his left, General Baxter proudly stood, his chest broad and his head held high. He wondered if Baxter had worked against him and assumed he had, but now none of it mattered. Soon all of it would be in Cruz's lap. Thoughts again came of where he would go. He wasn't so sure he'd stay in Cheyenne, but where should a retiring former president with low approval go? An island sounded good, an island in the South Pacific sounded really good. Thoughts of it all made it all more appealing.

He was beginning to get intoxicated by the thoughts of not having to deal with the doubters, liars, backstabbers, whiners, complainers, the list could go on. He'd leave them all to go at each other while he went to go enjoy what days he had left. He recalled his conversation with Schmidt yesterday, he'd told him he'd come back if needed, but now he wasn't so sure of that. Screw it. Many of his fellow countrymen seemed to dislike him, so why bother?

A well-dressed young beautiful woman came up to Conner and said, "Mr. President, it's time."

"Is it? Good," Conner answered. He followed the woman to the table and took a seat.

In front of him was a single piece of paper and a pen.

"Just sign and it's done, right?" Conner asked the woman. He was a bit nervous. This was it, he was about to end his career.

"Yes, sir."

Conner picked up the pen and unscrewed the top. He glanced over the document. It was a boilerplate format for anyone resigning, with a few clauses concerning his security detail and the fact he'd have to remain silent and never disclose anything confidential. He hovered the pen over the place for his signature and paused.

"Murderer!" a voice boomed from the crowd.

Conner looked up and saw Pat, his eyes wide with crazed anger. He lunged from the crowd with a pistol in his hand. Conner sat and didn't respond. It was almost comical that upon his day of resignation he'd finally be assassinated by a man he used to call friend.

"You're a dictator. You murdered Bethanny!" Pat screamed as he sprinted towards Conner with the pistol out in front.

Several security officers were right behind Pat and tackled him to the ground.

Pat dropped the pistol and scrambled to pick it back up, but the security officers had him firmly in their grasp. "You're a murderer!"

"Bethanny? You mean Secretary Wilbur?" Conner asked Pat from his perched position in the chair, the pen still in his unwavering hand.

"Yes! You executed her, shot her down in an alley and left her like a piece of garbage!" Pat screamed.

Pat was emotional, but his emotions told Conner of something more. It seemed that Pat was in love with her.

Schmidt came towards Pat, his fists clenched.

Following right behind was Baxter.

"You, you're his henchman, a fucking butcher, curse you!" Pat yelled at Schmidt.

Baxter stepped around Schmidt and stood clearly in view.

Pat shifted his attention to Baxter and yelled, "And you, you—" Pat's head snapped back, the side of it exploding from a single shot. His body went limp and fell into the arms of the security officers.

The crowd screamed in fear and surprise when the gun went off.

Schmidt jumped too; he wasn't expecting to hear a gun fire with Pat being detained. He looked at Baxter and asked, "What the hell?"

Baxter lowered the semiautomatic pistol and said, "I thought he might get free. He looked like he was about to break free."

"Yeah, right," Schmidt said with a chuckle.

Cruz ran up to Conner's side and asked, "Are you okay?"

"Yeah, I am," Conner replied. He looked down at the paper, put the tip of the pen down and signed. He took a deep breath, exhaled, tossed the pen aside and stood. Motioning with his arms, he said, "This mess is all yours now."

Lake Cascade, Idaho, Republic of Cascadia

The crack of gunfire startled Samantha. She raced to the window, but her view was of the old golf course, with the gunfire coming from the opposite side of the building.

"Haley, where are you?"

"In my room, Mommy."

Another burst of gunfire sounded. This time it sounded like it was in the building.

Samantha opened a drawer and pulled out a Sig Sauer P239, Gordon's favorite 9mm and now hers. By the weight she could tell it had a full magazine, but to ensure there was one in the chamber, she press checked it. Confirmed, the pistol was loaded and ready.

"Mommy, is someone shooting?" Haley asked. She

had left her room and was standing just behind Samantha.

"Yes, go to your room and hide in that spot in your closet," Samantha ordered.

"Okay, Mommy," Haley said and ran off.

The spot Samantha was referring to was a small crawl space that led to an unimproved attic space behind the walls.

Samantha followed her and put Haley back there.

"Are you gonna hide with me?" Haley asked with fear in her eyes.

"I can't really fit in there."

"But I'm scared. Don't leave me in here alone," Haley pleaded.

Samantha hadn't seen Haley this scared in a long time. "It will be fine, no, actually it may not be. But I need you to hide while I see what's going on."

"But, Mommy—"

"Please, Haley, just do what I ask. Trust me, I don't want to leave you, but I have to. This little space will only hold you and Luke," Samantha said, then realized Luke hadn't come back from his training. Feeling hurried, she closed Haley in, leaving her a flashlight, food and water, and went to go find Luke.

She opened the front door to find several people she knew from town chattering about the gunfire that had now ceased.

"Samantha, what's going on?" a woman asked, rushing up to her.

"I don't know. Have you seen Luke?" Samantha asked.

"Sam, Sam, people are shooting. Are we under attack?" another woman about her age asked, jogging towards Samantha with her two young children in tow.

"Everyone, I don't know what's going on; I'm in the same boat as you. Has anyone seen Luke, or have they seen who might be shooting?" Samantha asked.

The first woman who approached Samantha said, "I saw some people out front. They had machine guns and approached the front. I didn't see what happened, but I heard shooting."

"What did they look like?" Samantha asked.

"Regular clothes," the woman answered.

"Not uniforms?"

"No."

A single gunshot sounded below them.

Several women screamed.

"Who has guns?" Samantha asked.

They all raised their hands.

"Go get them. I suggest you hide the little ones. Then meet me in the hall here. There's only one way up here, and it's that stairwell there," Samantha said, pointing down the hall. "No one comes in unless we know them. If we don't, then you know what I mean."

"What's going to happen?" the older woman asked.

"I know what's not going to happen and that I'm not going out without a fight," Samantha declared.

McCall, Idaho, Republic of Cascadia

"So the great Gordon Van Zandt lives," Charles said as he pulled the hood off of Gordon.

Gordon shook his head and asked, "What the fuck is going on?"

"You're my prisoner, or I should say you'll soon be the prisoner of the United States. You see, I've made a deal, and I learned from you that I should make deals where I don't need to consult with my partners. You're a great teacher, Gordon; I've learned a lot from you. I made a deal with President Conner to spare my life and the lives of us from Olympia."

"You're making a big mistake, Charles. You can't trust the president."

"I believe I can."

"You're wrong. He's just trying to divide us, nothing more," Gordon insisted, not knowing the scope of the arrangement Charles and Conner had made.

"Gordon, we've lost the war because you were a piss-poor military commander. You went south and thought you could just roll in and take territory. I knew that plan was foolhardy and it cost us our army. When I asked for more troops to be stationed in Olympia, you disregarded me again and it resulted in Olympia being left practically defenseless, and now we both know what happened there," Charles preached as he walked around Gordon, who was tied to a chair inside an empty bay inside the fire station.

Gordon looked around the empty bay. Only he and Charles were there. Outside he could hear laughter and talking from what sounded like a decent-sized crowd. The laughter was disarming because to him this was not a laughing matter.

"Where's my family?" Gordon asked, his focus turning to them.

"We're getting them right now, well, the rest of them. I brought your boy, though."

"Where's Luke?" Gordon asked.

"He's fine, we have him with the others," Charles said.

"Charles, please, what are you doing? This is foolish. The war is not lost, we just need to make a plan. They can't win if we don't quit," Gordon stressed.

"I disagree, and when I got that call from President Conner, I knew that was the deal to make."

"But why?"

"Because I don't want to die, okay. I want to live, I want to see another sunrise."

"So all this talk about freedom and having your own country was bullshit? You didn't really mean it. Yeah, you were willing to have it given to you, but when it came time to fight and die for it, you stopped short there."

"Fuck you, Gordon. The dream of Cascadia was mine from the start. I have always wanted it, but the cause is lost. It's futile to fight for something when we've clearly lost," Charles barked.

"But we haven't. Let me go and I'll detail for you how we can win. It doesn't have to be this way. Look at what you're doing now. You've fallen into a trap made by Conner. He's now divided us and we're fighting against one another. You had one chance to have a new country, but you're now ensuring that will never happen again. No one east of central Washington will listen to you if you live and want to do this again. This is your one and only chance. Let me go; we'll move past this and reorganize," Gordon pleaded, pulling out all the arguments he could think of.

Charles stopped his pacing and thought about what Gordon had said. It would be the end of the dream he'd had since being a young man, and there wouldn't be a chance to resurrect it. It would be gone forever, but one thing that was for sure was he'd be alive. "I'm sorry, but my life is now more important than being free. I choose to live under a man like Conner rather than have my own country."

"Then you have lost, but I haven't. I will keep fighting," Gordon bellowed.

"Actually, that's not going to happen either. You see, the deal requires I gather all of you up and turn you over to US authorities. They wish to try you for treason. Unfortunately, Gordon, your fate as well as your compatriots' and your family's is sealed."

Gordon's anger rose. He struggled with the bindings that held him, flexing his muscles and straining to break free.

"But what is important before you go is to have a trial here for you and the others. You are not only a traitor to the United States, but many of us from the west believe you're a traitor too. Before we turn you over, you will be tried here too."

Lake Cascade, Idaho, Republic of Cascadia

The women on the fifth floor established a defensive position by placing furniture in the hall, and barricaded themselves behind it.

Yells and screams from the lower floors created fear, but none panicked. They had everything to fight for, and the thought of allowing whoever was coming for them to get their children was not an option. The saying that a woman is the fiercest fighter when her children are threatened had been tested before and proven; now the men who were coming for them would soon have firsthand knowledge.

"Okay, ladies, when that door opens, just point, shoot and don't stop until they're dead," Samantha ordered.

Several gunshots rang out one floor below.

"They're coming," a young woman named Alice said. Her hands and lip were quivering with fear. She had never been in a fight and the thought alone of a gunfight terrified her.

Samantha looked down the line and was proud of the eight strong women who were willing to stand their ground. She didn't know the outcome but was happy to be in the company of these ladies.

Automatic gunfire erupted outside followed by yelling. This time the shooting was off the large deck that overlooked the golf course.

"I'll be right back," Samantha said and raced to see who might be fighting over there. She ran into her room and to the large window. Looking down, she saw nothing.

More automatic gunfire sounded but deeper in the building and coming from the first or second floor.

She ran back into the dimly lit hallway and alerted the women. "I think someone is here to help. I think the gunshots I just heard are our people."

"God, I hope so," Alice said.

"Screw them, I want to shoot someone. How dare they come here and mess with us," an older woman name Francine barked.

"I'm with you, Francine," Samantha said.

"Are you crazy?" Alice asked.

A volley of gunfire sounded in the lower floors; it sounded like a gun battle.

This gave Samantha hope.

Standing in a line, their weapons extended, the women waited nervously as the endless volley of gunfire mixed with screaming came from below. They knew someone would finally reach their floor; they just didn't know who it might be.

Then as quickly as it had erupted, the gunfire suddenly stopped. Cries and yelling came after, which turned into an eerie silence.

"What do you think is going on?" Alice asked.

"I think someone won. I just hope it was the good

guys," Samantha replied.

The stairwell door suddenly opened and a voice called out, "Anyone up here?"

Samantha remained silent, but Alice couldn't refrain from responding, "We have guns. We'll shoot you!"

"It's okay, we're Marines," the voice answered.

"Is that you, Lance Corporal Sanchez?" Samantha asked.

"Yes, ma'am," Sanchez replied.

"Thank God." Samantha sighed.

"Are we clear to come up? Getting shot by friendly fire isn't on my to-do list for today," he joked.

"Lower your guns, ladies," Samantha ordered.

The women did as she said, and with that their tension and fear went too.

"All clear!" Samantha yelled.

"Okay," Sanchez replied and stepped from the darkened stairwell into the hazy light. Following him were several other Marines and three local militia. He marched towards them and said, "Sorry we're late. Is everyone okay up here?"

"Just frightened is all."

"Are the kids safe?" Sanchez asked Samantha.

"Haley's fine, but Luke's not with you?"

"No, he never showed up for training, and then this all started and we were pulled away to address an attack near the cottages just south of here. We had no idea they were coming after everyone."

"Where's Luke?" Samantha asked, her voice stressed.

"I don't know," Sanchez replied.

"We have to find him. Who were these men, and what were they doing here?" she asked.

"They were CWA and they weren't here to kill but to capture you all; that's the most we've gotten so far. We have one downstairs now," Sanchez reported.

Samantha climbed over the barricade and pushed past Sanchez. "Take me to him now."

"Yes, ma'am."

Samantha stopped and looked to Francine. "Fran, go get Haley from the closet. Tell her I'll be back soon."

Francine stood tall and said, "We've got your back, Sam. Go get your boy."

Samantha raced down the darkened stairwell, occasionally stepping over bodies until they reached the first floor.

Sanchez led her through the lobby and outside through the shattered front doors.

Bullet holes, debris, blood and bodies were everywhere.

Under the porte cochere a man in civilian clothes was sitting with his arms bound behind him. His face was covered in blood and his bare arms had cuts, with a gunshot wound in his right forearm.

"That's him right there," Sanchez said, pointing to the man.

She stomped over and stood directly in front of him. Her meager five-foot-three-inch stature seemed greater due to her anger and determination. "Where have you taken everyone?"

"I've answered all I'm going to answer," the man said, coughing up a little blood and spitting it out.

"What were you doing here and why?"

"Fuck you, I'm not saying another word. I already told these goons that we were sent to arrest you all. I'm not saying another word."

"Yes, you will," Samantha barked, her hands on her hips.

He looked up and glared at her. "No, I'm not. I've got nothing to say."

"Why—"

"I told you," he interrupted.

"No, why do you think you don't have to talk? Do you think there will be some sort of settlement or that we won't torture you to get what we want because we're afraid of whoever you work for? You're wrong. I will torture you myself until you tell me every last thing I want to know."

"Ha."

Samantha grabbed him by his long greasy black hair and punched him in the face. "Tell me who sent you and where you've taken those you've captured?"

"No."

Samantha reached back and punched him again, but this time she hurt her hand.

"Ha, ha." The man laughed, spitting out more blood.

Sanchez handed her a blackjack, a small leather-covered piece of steel used as a club.

"What's this?" Samantha asked.

"My old man was a cop in San Juan. He called it the

persuader."

Samantha took it and examined the small but surprisingly heavy club. "It's lady sized."

"It might be small, but it packs a huge punch."

The man widened his eyes when he saw the weapon.

Samantha wrapped the leather strap around her hand and laid the club in her hand. The weight felt good.

"You hold it like that and…" Sanchez said in an attempt to describe the best way to use it.

Samantha reached back and came down hard on the man's boney shoulder.

"Do that," Sanchez quipped, appreciating that she didn't have trouble figuring out the best way to use it.

"Arghh!" the man cried out.

She only paused to get better footing. She'd wait to ask again, she wanted him to feel pain. She held the club over her head and came down again on his collarbone.

The man wailed in pain and bent over.

"Hold him up. I'm going to break his fucking shoulder," Samantha barked at the Marines.

The other Marines standing there looked oddly at her but didn't move.

"You heard the woman, hold him up," Sanchez said. "Don't you know who this is? It's Samantha Van Zandt."

The Marines stepped forward and grabbed the man, who was in agonizing pain from the hit to his collarbone.

"Wait, no, wait!"

Samantha didn't wait; she came back down again on his collarbone.

"Argh! No! Please! I'll talk!" the man cried out.

"No, I don't need to hear you talk. You pissed me off, I think I'm going to beat you for a bit."

"No, please. You said you're Samantha Van Zandt? We have your husband, Gordon, we have him. I know where he is."

Samantha had raised the blackjack above her head but stopped when he mentioned Gordon. "You have Gordon?"

The man was weeping. "Yeah, we have him. We arrested him this morning."

"Where are you holding him? Where are you holding everyone you've arrested?" Samantha asked.

"We have him at the firehouse. Everyone else is being housed at the ice rink."

Samantha looked at Sanchez, who replied, "Got it. We'll rally up to head that way."

"Who are you working for?" Samantha asked.

"Chairman Chenoweth, he ordered all those aligned with the Van Zandts and Rutledges to be arrested."

Samantha grabbed him by his hair and lifted his face to hers. "Why?"

"He made a deal with the United States. He's surrendered, but one condition was to turn over you all."

Disgusted by his answers, she pushed his head down and stewed on everything he said.

"Come on, boys, let's load up," Sanchez barked to a group of Marines and militia.

"Don't leave without me," Samantha ordered Sanchez.

"Roger that, ma'am. I'd say take your time, but I

don't think we have that."

"I'm almost done." She turned and glared at the man. "How dare you."

"Please don't hurt me."

"Why is it those who hurt others always beg not to be hurt themselves?" Samantha said and smacked him hard on top of his head.

The man's eyes rolled back in his head and he fell to the ground face first.

Samantha turned around, walked up to Sanchez and handed him the blackjack. "Your dad was right, it is the *persuader*."

McCall, Idaho, Republic of Cascadia

Gordon continued to struggle with his restraints, but there wasn't any chance he'd break free. The positive for him, if there was one, was he wasn't alone anymore. Charles had his CWA bring in John, Michael, Nelson, and Chief Rainey, the McCall police chief, and tied them all to chairs like Gordon. He then brought in a table and folding chairs and placed them in front of them.

Gordon watched this and couldn't help but be reminded of other times he was on trial for trumped-up things. His memory went back to his court-martial in the Marine Corps and the time Mindy, the HOA president from Rancho Valentino, had him brought before the board. All were equally stupid, but none were as potentially fatal as this one. The stakes were high, and this trial would eventually lead to Cheyenne and with no doubt his execution.

Charles called the loyal remaining members of the committee forward. They walked in and took seats behind the table.

With the committee seated, Charles ordered the two large firehouse garage doors opened up so the few townspeople who followed him along with the other prisoners could watch. His goal for doing this was to humiliate Gordon as much as he could before having him sent to the airport and picked up by the United States.

Unable to wait, Gordon spoke up. "You won't be successful. Once Top and Gunny Smith hear what you've done, they'll come for you."

Charles laughed and replied, "That's not going to happen. Soon they'll be gone too. I hate to lose them, but Conner wouldn't allow us to keep any military forces. I gave their coordinates to him, and soon they'll be destroyed."

"You're a fucking bastard!" Gordon yelled.

"Believe me when I say it pained me to do it, but there was no other choice."

Gordon shook his head in anger.

John Steele was sitting to Gordon's right. He cocked his head and said to Gordon, "Have you told him yet?"

"Huh?" Gordon shrugged, not knowing what John was talking about.

"Would the prisoners be quiet," Charles ordered.

"You haven't told him, have you?" John said, being

deliberately vague.

"Tell him what?" Gordon asked.

"Be quiet!" Charles barked. He pointed at two CWA guards, who headed towards John and Gordon.

Knowing that he was about to be silenced, John turned to Charles and said loudly, "I was just asking Gordon here if he had mentioned that we're going to fucking kill you!"

"Silence that man!" Charles barked.

"Now you did it," Gordon said.

One guard grabbed John while the other punched him in the face.

"We won't tolerate this type of behavior," Charles declared.

"Why are you holding this kangaroo court for a government that no longer exists? Are we role-playing now, huh, is that what we're doing?" Gordon said, mocking Charles and the committee.

The guards turned their attention on Gordon now and did exactly to him what they had done to John.

Gordon shook his head, the punch had hurt and made him see stars, but he wasn't about to show that to Charles. He looked at John and joked, "These little commie leftists hit like the pussies they are."

Gordon took another punch from the guard.

Again he mocked them, "Let me help you out, if you stuck to a real diet instead of your organic wheat grass and spelt bread, you'd have a bit more muscle and it might just hurt."

"Oh no, you didn't!" John laughed.

Together the men were having fun mocking Charles and his people. It came at a price, but if he and John were going out, they weren't going to go quietly.

More members of the CWA came forward and took punches and jabs at the men.

Charles allowed the punishment to go on for a minute before he called the trial to order. "Enough, leave them be. I need them alive."

A cut below Gordon's eye bled and ran down his face.

John's nose appeared to be broken and his lower lip was split.

Even though they had suffered, they weren't deterred.

"Where's your fucking beret?" Gordon asked Charles.

Charles shook his head in frustration but refused to allow the men to further disturb the trial. "Duct tape their damn mouths."

The guards did as ordered.

"Now we can begin without further delay," Charles said.

The whole time Gordon and John were causing trouble, Luke was watching from the crowd of detainees. At first hearing Gordon was alive and back filled him with hope until he saw him bound and being beaten. He slowly inched his way to the front of the group and was only twenty feet from the back of Gordon and the others. Charles hadn't hurt him, and when he delivered him to the holding facility, all they took was his backpack and neglected to search him. What they didn't know was he was carrying the Glock that Sanchez had given him. When he was first dropped off, he was tempted to pull it out so he could escape, but his fear was too great. As each minute passed, he further pushed away the idea of using it for fear of getting killed. Now he was watching the man he considered a father figure be tried with his fate eventually being death. Losing Gordon was something he couldn't bear. He had already lost his biological mother and father; then Sebastian and Annaliese were taken from him. How could he sit back and watch Gordon get taken from him too?

Charles convened the trial and swiftly read the charges. He turned to the committee members and asked them to raise their hands if they agreed to the charges and if the punishment should be deportation to the US authorities. In unison they put their arms up, signaling their support.

Just like that the trial was over. It was short and sweet. No cross-examination, just a reading of the charges with examples about each man and what they did to warrant the charges. It wasn't a trial, it was a sentencing. They were convicted before the trial began. There wouldn't be a chance to dispute the charges or request an appeal. They had been tried and sentenced to be turned over to the United States.

"Take these men to the trucks for immediate deportation," Charles ordered.

Luke began to shake. What should he do? Should he do something? He needed to act.

The guards freed Gordon and the others from the chairs.

When Gordon turned, he saw Luke. He couldn't smile because of the tape but signaled to him that he cared by winking.

Luke continued to shake. He reached under his sweater and felt the cold grip of the pistol. All he had to do was pull it out and begin shooting the guards. An internal struggle took place as his fear was telling him no but his love was telling him yes.

Gordon too was thinking of a way to combat the situation, but with his hands tied behind his back, he was limited. However, getting in the back of the truck wasn't an option. He began to run through scenarios and where he was; right there and then was most likely the best place to resist. Once he was on the truck, he could possibly be restrained to it, and once he was in the hands of the US forces, he'd be screwed.

The truck was backed up to the open door.

He was now fifteen feet from the truck and needed to come up with a solution. He couldn't allow himself to get on that truck. Fourteen feet, thirteen, twelve, eleven, he was getting closer. He counted the number of armed guards to equal seven. Should he just make a run for it? If he acted, would the others follow? Ten feet, nine, eight.

"Fuck it," Gordon said and turned.

As if choreographed and perfectly executed, a gun fired, hitting the guard that he himself was about to kick.

The bullet ripped through the guard's throat. Blood squirted all over Gordon and splattered on the floor. He grabbed at the wound and fell to the floor, gagging.

Shocked by the surprise shooting, Gordon paused for a second, but suddenly realized this was his moment and there was no better time than now. He charged at the next guard he saw and kicked him in the crotch, dropping the man to his knees. Once there, Gordon planted his size twelve boot in his face. The guard fell backwards, dropping his gun.

Three more shots rang out.

John, Nelson and Rainey sprang into action as well. They each went after guards.

Rainey knocked one to the ground, but when the guard hit the ground, he leveled his rifle and shot the police chief in the gut.

Gordon grabbed a knife from the dead guard and cut his restraints. With his hands free, he picked up the man's rifle, turned and shot the guard he had knocked to the ground. He swiftly targeted the next guard he saw and shot him. He turned when he heard gunfire behind him. His eyes widened when he saw the shooter was Luke.

Single-handedly, Luke had shot three men and had advanced on the hapless committee, who sat frozen in fear.

The last guard turned his rifle on Luke, but Gordon shot him first.

Luke approached the table and one by one shot the committee members.

Gordon watched Luke's rampage with shock. He never would have imagined this boy was capable of such ruthless efficiency.

With precision Luke finished the committee members. Blood was splattered and pooled across the table and floor.

Gordon then noticed that Charles was missing. He looked for the man who had now become his archenemy, but he was nowhere to be found.

The truck and the crowd of Charles's supporters were gone, fled for their own protection.

The detainees, feeling the timing was right because it was safer, came forward to help.

"Where is he?" Gordon hollered.

The floor was covered in blood and bodies.

Michael freed himself then attended to Nelson and John. When they saw Rainey was down, they went to his side and found him dead.

A rumble of vehicles turned their attention outside.

Sanchez's Humvee led the way. He pulled up, and before it stopped, Samantha jumped out, her trusty Sig in her hand. She spotted Gordon right away and ran to him.

The two embraced.

"Where's Haley?" Gordon asked.

"Safe, she's safe," Samantha replied, happy to be in Gordon's arms. "God, I've missed you. I was so worried."

"Me too," Gordon admitted.

Luke stood, with the Glock still firmly in his grip. He watched the blood drip from the table onto the floor. He had acted decisively; he had saved Gordon.

Sanchez rushed in and went directly to Luke. "Hey, little man, you good?"

"Ahh, yeah, I think so," Luke answered, his body rigid.

"Did you do that?" Sanchez asked, nodding towards the table.

"Um, yeah, and that and that and him too," Luke said, pointing to all the people he had killed.

Sanchez placed his hand on his shoulder and said, "You're a natural."

Luke shrugged his hand off and said, "Don't touch me."

"It's cool, I understand. If you ever want to talk about it, you know where to find me."

Gordon watched Luke interact with Sanchez. He could see the boy was shell-shocked, what child his age wouldn't be? "He saved me," Gordon told Samantha.

"He did?"

"Yeah, if it wasn't for him…he showed great courage."

"He's becoming a man."

"But I know he doesn't feel that way. He's confused," Gordon said.

"We got him, we got him!" a militia member shouted, running into the station. Right behind him a Marine and another member of the McCall militia escorted Charles in.

The Marine held up a satellite phone and said, "He was on this calling someone when we found him."

"Oh shit, that reminds me, Sanchez, get on the horn, contact Master Sergeant Simpson. Tell him to disperse, hide, take cover, just be on the alert. US aircraft are headed their way."

"Roger that, sir," Sanchez said and ran to the Humvee.

Gordon walked over to Charles and stood smiling. He took the phone and hit the redial button. The phone clicked and seconds later a loud tone sounded. He put it to his ear and waited for an answer.

"President Cruz's office," a woman answered. It was Heather, the presidential executive assistant.

"President Cruz?" Gordon asked, not expecting to hear that name.

"Can I help you, sir?"

"Yes, can I speak with the president?"

"The president is busy, but I can take a message. Can I ask who's calling?"

"Yeah, tell him that it's Gordon Van Zandt," Gordon said, leveling his pistol at Charles.

Charles flinched and began to weep loudly.

"Is that it, sir?"

"No, tell him the deal is off. We'll never surrender," Gordon finished, then squeezed the trigger.

Cheyenne, Wyoming, United States

"I don't know yet. I've narrowed it down to two people," Cruz said, replying to a question from Baxter concerning a new vice president.

"What kind of vetting shall I do?"

"Vetting? Oh, I'm not too concerned about these people. I just need to speak with them then sleep on it."

"Have you given thought to the former governor of Texas? Having her could form a much stronger alliance."

"I'll consider her too, but…"

A knock on the door forced Cruz to pause.

"Yes!" Cruz hollered.

The door opened and Heather stepped in and said in a congenial tone, "I know you didn't want to be disturbed, but you've had two strange calls."

"Fine, come in," Cruz said, waving her in.

Heather looked at her notepad and read what she had written. "The first call was from a Charles Chenoweth. He said he needed an emergency evacuation and that things had gone wrong. He was about to tell me where he was before something happened, I heard some commotion, then the phone went dead. He sounded scared, like he was in trouble."

Cruz lowered his head and sighed. "And the second call."

"Another man then called minutes later, same line, he said his name was Gordon—"

"Van Zandt," Baxter blurted out.

"Yes, Gordon Van Zandt," Heather confirmed.

"And what did he say?" Cruz asked.

"He said that the deal was off and that they weren't surrendering," Heather read.

"Shit!" Cruz said.

"We've got aircraft headed there now," Baxter informed Cruz.

"I know, I know."

"Um, sir, I thought I should tell you that before Mr. Van Zandt hung up, I heard what sounded like a gunshot."

"Okay, thank you, Heather, is that all?" Cruz asked.

"Yes, that's it."

"Oh, and if Mr. Van Zandt calls back, ever, please patch it through."

"Yes, sir," Heather replied and left.

"What now?" Baxter asked.

"Recall the jets and the teams that were sent to pick them up. I need to think about this," Cruz ordered.

"Yes, sir," Baxter said, picking up the desk phone and calling out.

Cruz spun around and looked out the window. How was he going to deal with Gordon and his Cascadians? He thought Conner's plan was perfect, but he should have known that nothing goes as planned. He promised himself and the people of the United States that he would lead differently than Conner and would tackle things in a more comprehensive manner. He stood up and walked to the window. Staring out, he saw the people of Cheyenne moving about, living their lives unaware and probably unconcerned of the events in Idaho. A name etched in the wooden windowsill caught his attention. He looked more closely and saw it read Julia. Hmm, apparently Conner spent a lot of time in the same spot looking out and pondering the next steps he would make. He promised that he'd be different than his predecessor on policy, but when it came to the arduous task of being a leader, they had a bond, and for the first time he found himself feeling sorry for Conner and the burden he had carried.

Warren Air Force Base, Wyoming, United States

Schmidt exited his quarters, and with two large duffels, a rifle and tactical gear slung over his shoulder, he walked to the convoy of vehicles that were parked at the curb.

He didn't know exactly why he had been asked to go, but he didn't have anything else to do now. He was a man without purpose and a man with little time left.

He opened the rear right door and peered in. "Mr. President?"

"Yes, c'mon, toss your gear in the back," Conner said.

Schmidt did as he said and threw all of his stuff in the back of the Humvee. He got in and closed the door. "Sir, I just have to say thank you for thinking of me. It's an honor that you'd—"

"Schmidt, just shut up, enough of the pomp and bullshit, we're both civilians now," Conner said, handing Schmidt a flask.

"What is it?"

"Does it really matter? Drink up."

Schmidt hesitated.

"It's not like you have to worry about getting cirrhosis or something, drink up," Conner insisted and pushed the flask into his hand.

Schmidt took it and drank. "Whiskey."

"Yes, and the good stuff, a great rye whiskey from back east."

Liking the smooth taste, he tipped the flask again.

"There you go," Conner said excitedly.

Schmidt handed the flask back and asked, "Why did you ask me to go with you?"

"Two reasons, or maybe three. I like you, yes, can you believe someone would like a big knucklehead like you? Well, I do. Two, you're loyal, finally someone who thinks like me that I can trust, and three, I don't have any friends but you. Yeah, Andrew is a friend, but he's a bit tied up for a while."

"I like you too, sir."

"I order you not to say sir ever again."

"Yes…okay."

"I hope you packed for a long trip," Conner said.

"Where are we going?"

"Houston, we're headed to Houston."

"Texas, hmm, it will be interesting to see how they're doing," Schmidt said.

"And there, we'll catch a ship."

"To where?"

"Where would you like to go? Ever had a place you always wanted to visit, a place on the bucket list?"

"I never much thought of it. I've always been a military man and it was my life."

Conner patted Schmidt on the leg and laughed. "Well, those days are over."

"I know."

"So once we hit Houston, where do you want to go?"

"You secured a ship?"

"Yep."

"I guess I'd want to go where it's not been affected, South America maybe or Australia."

"Fuck those Aussies, damn arrogant bunch now with all their demands. You know I was thinking of Buenos Aires. I hear it's beautiful and the women are gorgeous. Maybe we can go to Santiago, Chile, from there."

"Sounds good, wherever."

"Let's go, airman, drive us to the plane."

"Yes, sir." The driver put the Humvee in gear and sped off.

Conner took the flask, took a swig and smiled. "South America is a good choice for men like us."

"Why's that?"

"They like dictators there."

NOVEMBER 9, 2015

"A plan without a backup plan and without a backup of the backup plan is not a plan at all." – G. Michael Hopf

McCall, Idaho, Republic of Cascadia

Days after Charles's uprising, Gordon had received a call from Cruz offering a plan similar to what had been offered before, but Gordon refused. Surrendering was not the answer for him and the people of Cascadia. Rumors began to spread that Cruz was only negotiating from a place of weakness. Gordon knew that wasn't the case. He had met Cruz and saw him as a reasonable man. At any moment he could send in jets and destroy them, but he didn't, but that wasn't to say it wasn't part of a contingency if he couldn't convince Gordon into some settlement.

The republic was a mess. They still had an army, but it was much smaller. Olympia was still occupied, and the bad blood between the two factions made it impossible to talk or make a cohesive plan.

Gordon was confused and disliked the new role of chairman that had been thrust upon him. First, he disliked the name, which he promptly discarded and replaced with president, and he was offended by the instant political maneuvering that took place the second he took the position. His place was on the battlefield, but that wasn't where he was needed.

He needed a plan B, he needed an alternative to the status quo. The stalemate between him and Cruz would only last so long. Eventually, Cruz would have his hand forced and they'd take action. This put Gordon in the unfortunate position to make the first move, a move that could backfire like before. Like a coach that needed a miracle play to win the game, he needed that one thing that could change everything, he needed a game changer. But where would that come from? What could that be?

Vexed, he spent days pacing the back deck of his house.

Samantha, Michael, John and Nelson all gave counsel, but no one had the answer he needed. All eyes and hopes were on him. He had never felt more alone than now, a man adrift with the dreams of a nation on his shoulders. Many times he found doubt enter his mind. Should he just give in? Should he settle and hope that Cruz would honor his word? His past experiences told him no, they weren't trustworthy. Shouldn't he lean on his experiences for guidance? Of course, he thought.

The sliding door opened and Samantha stepped out. "Are you hungry?"

"No."

She hurried over and gave him a hug. "Oh my God, come inside, it's so cold."

"No, I like it out here," Gordon said.

The cool crisp midday air felt good. He especially loved how it smelled. Yes, it did smell different; all the seasons did in Idaho.

"You're so stressed, I can feel it," Samantha said, squeezing him.

"That's not stress, I think I'm frozen," Gordon joked.

She kissed him on the cheek and said, "Please come in and take a break. Your family misses you."

"I'll be in soon."

Someone tapped on the glass behind them.

Gordon turned to see Haley standing with a book in her hands. She pointed at it and mouthed, 'Read this to me.'

"You keep doing what you're doing. I'll go read to her," Samantha said, walking away.

Gordon watched Samantha take Haley by the hand.

Haley pulled away and pointed to Gordon.

Seeing this made his heart hurt. Haley needed him. He had been gone for so long, and even though he was home now, he was still not present.

Samantha tugged and pulled her away.

The scene upset him. He loved his family and longed to spend the time with them he knew was critical, but how could one lead a nation and a war and still be that family guy? He had come a long way from the website designer in San Diego. In eleven months he was now the leader of a fledgling new country. The irony of it all was he was skilled at designing websites, not at leading a country. Everyone talked about what they would do if they were in charge, but theorizing and doing were two different things. He had a taste of it as a military leader;

now he had to set the course for the entire country.

Gordon didn't pray often. He liked to say that he and God had a falling out after Hunter's death. But an urge came over him, he looked up, closed his eyes and prayed out loud, "God, I don't talk to you much, but of course you know that already, you're God, right? Um, I need help, I'm lost and I don't know what I should do next. Everyone is counting on me to pull this off, but more importantly, my family is looking to me to keep them safe. How do I do that? What should I do? Please, help me. I'm sure you've been busy these days with everyone's prayers, but you're God, so you can handle it." Gordon paused. "This is so stupid," he continued, then paused again. "No, sorry, it's not stupid, I apologize. Um, God, I need help, my family and my country need help. Please give me a sign, show me something that will give me the answer." He opened his eyes and looked towards the majestic mountains. The beauty of the land was sometimes breathtaking; only human beings had the means of tainting such a pristine thing, he thought. After waiting several minutes with no *signs*, he turned to go inside when his phone rang. He picked it up and looked at the number calling but didn't know it. He then wondered if this was his sign. He hit the talk button, put the phone to his ear and said, "Hello."

EPILOGUE

October 19, 2066

McCall, Idaho, Republic of Cascadia

Hunter was on the edge of his seat. "Who was it?"

"It was…" Gordon said, but a loud knock at the door interrupted him. "Ahh, the steaks."

"What, huh?" Hunter asked.

"Yes, dinner," Sebastian cheered, jumping up and going to the door. He unlocked it and threw the door open. There in front of him stood an elderly man, about the same age as Gordon.

"Dinner is served," the man said, stepping in with a box in his arms.

"There you are," Gordon said, getting to his feet slowly.

"Granddad, aren't you going to tell me who was on the phone?" Hunter complained.

"After dinner, come, I want you to meet someone near and dear to me," Gordon said, waving Hunter over.

Haley and Hunter followed Gordon.

Gordon gave the man a big hug and said, "Good to see you, I hope you brought enough for you too?"

"Oh, I can't, I need to get home."

The man was tall, slightly shorter than Gordon. He had short well-groomed gray hair that was styled conservatively. He had a presence about him that could only be described as confident.

Haley stepped past Gordon and gave the man a hug. "So good to see you, it's been so long."

"Too long," the man said.

"Hunter, Sebastian, come here. I want you to meet a dear friend of mine. Without him I wouldn't even be here. He helped me more than I can say…"

"Hold on, you're being way too generous."

"No, I'm not," Gordon insisted.

"Yes, you are," the man said to Gordon then turned to Hunter and Sebastian and said, "He thought so highly of me that he didn't let me serve with him when he was president."

"You served but not in an official manner, I couldn't risk it. I needed you to be separate. You're not being fair. I needed you by my side, and you were there through everything. Hell, the fake assassination was your idea."

"Only because I really wanted to take you out but decided to just have it as make-believe."

"Pfft," Gordon hissed. "Boys, I owe my life to this man. I'm honored to introduce you to the one and only John Steele."

"Holy shit!" Hunter exclaimed. "You're *the* John Steele; I read so much about you."

"I hope it wasn't in the gossip columns," John joked.

"No, all the stuff you did after independence. You helped revolutionize our banking and judicial systems."

"I helped."

"That's not true, we're taught about how—"

"Nice to meet you, sir," Sebastian said, extending his

hand.

"Same," John said. "Anyway, I was just dropping these off. Let me know if you need anything else."

"Stay for a drink, I opened that last bottle of scotch," Gordon insisted.

John looked at his watch and said, "Fine, twist my arm."

"Go put the steaks on," Gordon ordered Sebastian, who went to task immediately.

Gordon poured John a drink. They tapped glasses and cheered each other. "So, are you enjoying this old man's tales?"

"Thoroughly," Hunter said.

"Did he tell you about Nemesis?"

"Yes," Hunter replied.

"Which time?"

"There were more?" Hunter asked.

"Two more times," John answered.

"Tell me, please," Hunter pleaded.

Gordon raised his hand and objected, "Let me tell the stories. I like to keep things in context; otherwise people will get confused."

"So where did he leave off?" John teased.

"With a mysterious phone call, who was it?" Hunter asked.

John raised the glass and took a large sip. "You know, I'll let him finish that one. It's a great one, and that one call would lead to what he called *the game changer*."

"Because it was," Gordon said confidently.

"You're killing me by leaving me with a cliff-hanger,"

Hunter protested.

Haley came over to Hunter's side and said, "Stop complaining so much, a part of life is anticipation."

"Mom, you know I'm not patient."

John tipped the glass back and finished the drink. "Thanks for the scotch, and nice meeting you all."

They all exchanged farewells, but John couldn't just leave without tossing out a nugget of information that would lead to hours of conversation. "Oh, I know he won't want to talk about it, but he should."

Gordon shook his head and said, "Don't say it."

"I won't say it, but you need to take credit for that. No one knows just how he turned the tables that day in Salt Lake City; it's one of those little nuggets of history that doesn't even get the respect of being a damn trivia question."

"I actually did plan on telling them, don't you worry," Gordon said. "Now get out of here, you've overstayed your welcome."

"By everyone," John said and left.

"Let's go eat," Gordon said, getting back up and heading towards the kitchen.

Hunter grabbed Haley and asked, "Mom, why are we here?"

"He wanted to finally meet you," she replied.

"Why now? Timing is everything, and after listening to these stories, he's a master strategist. This isn't a grand homecoming, this is something more."

"You'll have to ask him that."

"You know something, don't you?" Hunter asked.

"I'll say this; he's not doing well, health wise."

"That's not it. This isn't some sweet, long farewell."

Haley patted him on the face and said, "You do have some brains up there."

"What is it?"

"I'll leave that for him to explain, but I'll give you a clue. In order for someone to rise to their rightful place, they have to know who they really are and where they come from. You see, your grandfather didn't believe in it before but became a devout believer in destiny, and he knows that this country's days are still ahead of it."

"What does that mean?"

"I'm hungry, chew on that while I chew on some steak," Haley said and walked away.

Hunter watched Haley join the others in the kitchen. He felt so blessed to have this experience even though he didn't know exactly what that experience truly was, but he was ready for the journey.

Gordon caught Hunter's eye and gave him a nod.

Hunter returned the nod.

"Grab the bottle and come in here," Gordon called out.

Hunter did as he asked and joined the group.

Gordon poured fresh glasses of scotch. Raising his glass, he said, "Let's toast."

"To steaks," Sebastian said.

Hunter said, "To legacy."

"Good one." Haley laughed.

"What shall it be, Granddad?" Hunter asked.

"This toast will come as a surprise especially after

torturing you all with longwinded stories of the past, but without the past we can't conquer the future. The past is our great teacher, but we must listen to her. So raise your glass and toast to the future."

They clanged their glasses together and in unison said, "The future."

READ AN EXCERPT OF THE NEW G. MICHAEL HOPF BOOK AVAILABLE NOW

NEMESIS: INCEPTION

February 22, 2015

"The two most important days in your life are the day you are born and the day you find out why." – Mark Twain

Crescent, Oregon

"Lexi…Lexi…WAKE UP!" the reoccurring voice from her dreams shouted.

She sat up quickly, her heart racing as a cold sweat clung to her skin. She wiped the sweat with her shaking hands and blinked in an effort to clear her eyes, but it did no good in the pitch-black space. Fumbling, she found a glow stick, cracked it and shook vigorously. Soon a yellow glow lit the dark crevasses of the room. Her vision adjusted, but the room offered nothing for her champagne-colored eyes to feast upon. The walls were lined with boxes, and at her feet, a large metal shelf held cans and bottles. The smell of the room at first was off-putting, but she soon didn't notice the mix of dust, cardboard and stale beer. The damp back storeroom of The Mohawk Bar and Grill wasn't luxury accommodations, but having a relatively safe place to rest your head from the winter cold and dangers of the road came pretty close. At first she had refused the offer for shelter, only accepting it when she realized the place was full of provisions and an older single man who she sized up as beatable in a fight. After surviving for two months in the new world, her situational awareness was always on. She chalked it up as one of the primary reasons she was still alive.

Lexi rubbed her eyes and grunted in frustration when the nightly dream that prevented her from getting the rest she needed popped in her mind. She had grown weary from her inability to sleep soundly. Before the collapse, sleeping had been one of her best friends. Not a weekend morning went by where she'd be awake by eleven, and her weekday mornings were a struggle to rise, each morning a repeat of the last as she hit the snooze button a dozen times. Now her sleep, if one could call it that, was punctuated with night terrors and restlessness.

A knock at the door startled her. She reached under the pillow and grabbed her pistol, a Glock 17 9mm semiautomatic.

"Lexi? Are you all right? I heard you scream," the voice said from behind the door.

She looked and saw a dark shadow blocking the dim light from underneath the door. She didn't know John, much less completely trust him. She had only met him a week before.

After her narrow escape from a small band of marauders, she had crashed the motorcycle she had stolen along the highway south of town. A small detachment of Marines had found her and offered assistance.

Not having a place to call home, the Marines took her to the Mohawk. The Marines had created a relationship with John not long after arriving in town. Crescent was a small town, and with no other business operating besides the Mohawk, it provided a place for what remained of the community to gather. John had no family and nothing else, so keeping his only love, the Mohawk, open was a natural decision for him. He quickly ran out of perishable foods, but his supply of alcohol was abundant and part of his plan was to use it as currency. John was a large burly man, his black hair now streaked with silver. His wife had left him years ago and, with no children, the townspeople were family.

During her stay, she had spent her time working out and training out back with her long sheath knives. Then she would find an excuse, any would do, to find adequate time to drink.

John found himself watching her and was impressed with her skills. In fact, he was curious who he had staying in his back room. Today he made it a point to find out.

"Lexi, you in there?" he asked again, this time trying the knob. The door was locked.

Lexi looked at the door; her instincts born out of the chaos of the new world told her not to open it. Not truly knowing John and with her numerous negative experiences, she remained hesitant to trust anyone. Then her reasonable and pragmatic side won out. She didn't have a place to go and he had supplies she could use on her hunt for Rahab.

"I'm fine!" she called out. She walked to the door, unlocked it and quickly stepped back.

John opened the door slowly and gently poked his head in. The light from his lantern cast a yellowish glow across the storeroom.

"I heard screaming. I was worried," John said, looking around the space.

Lexi had taken a seat back on the floor again, her pistol tucked in her lap. "It's all right."

"I'll let you get back to sleep, then," John said with a smile.

As the door was closing, Lexi called out, "Hold on!"

John craned his head back in. "Yeah."

"Ah, what time is it?"

"Oh, um, it's around five in the morning."

"Okay, thanks."

"You hungry? I can whip up something?"

"Actually, I'm thirsty."

"There's some water over in the corner, help yourself," John answered. He now half stood in the room. He pointed to a stack of bottled water.

"I was thinking of something a bit harder," Lexi said, a smile now stretching across her face.

A big drinker himself, John thought for a moment then opened the door fully. "It's noon somewhere, right?"

Lexi took the shot glass in her hand. The sides of it were slick from the over pour. One thing that hadn't changed since the lights went out was her love of partying and drinking alcohol. Before, hard alcohol wasn't her forte, but without ice and mixers, her favorites were no longer available. Determined to get the effect alcohol generously gave, she took to drinking whatever she could get her hands on. She looked at the bottle of Grey Goose and chuckled to herself. Before arriving in Crescent, she'd come upon a family. They had been welcoming even to the point of sharing their home-distilled spirits. The taste was repulsive, but she drank it anyway. She had never drunk paint remover before but only imagined that was what it tasted like.

She held it up and said, "What are we toasting to now?"

"Gosh, I don't know, what haven't we toasted to yet?" John asked, referring to the half-dozen shots they had already taken.

"I got one!" she said as she held her glass higher. "Death to all scumbags! May they die a slow and painful death!"

John raised his eyebrows in astonishment. He wasn't prudish, but Lexi's crude mouth and seemingly ruthless belief system did shock him.

She put the glass to her lips and with one gulp drank the vodka. "Ahh, that was good!" she said with excitement as she slammed the glass onto the bar.

John hesitated but soon followed and swallowed his

shot of vodka.

"Hit me up, bartender," Lexi stated, sliding her glass towards John.

Ignoring her, he finally asked her an intimate and personal question, "Lexi, what happened to you?"

She leered at him and didn't answer.

"Why are you…so angry?"

"Is that a serious question? Really? Look the fuck around. Who wouldn't be angry?"

"I'm not."

"Then you're an idiot!" she snapped at him.

"Ha, I think you're cut off," John said, taking her glass.

"Wait, wait, wait, I'm sorry. That came off too…"

"Too angry," John quipped.

John walked away with the glass and placed it along with the bottle of vodka at the back of the bar.

"You're right, I'm sorry. You're not an idiot, I am. I just don't want to talk about…this," she said, motioning with her arms referencing the surroundings.

"You're going to sit at my bar, sleep under my roof, eat my food, drink my booze and not tell me who you are? You've been here a week and all I know is you drink a lot, work out and play with your knives."

Lexi thought about what John said for a moment and came to the conclusion he had a point. "You're right and I'm a bitch. I, um, I just don't like to talk about stuff, because doing so makes it seem real. Just sitting here like we've been doing for the past two or so hours talking about nothing but old movies, food, cocktails etcetera allows me to escape the fucked-up world we live in. It allows me to…forget."

John walked back and stood directly across from her.

"I've seen a lot of bad shit out there. I've seen what people are capable of. It's disgusting and revolting and I fucking hate it," she said.

"I can't say I've seen what you've seen out there because I decided to stay right here. Never saw the need to venture out beyond the town limits."

"Don't. Stay right here. It's a hot mess out there."

John grabbed the bottle and her glass and placed it in front of her.

She reached for it, but he slid it back just a few inches, indicating he wasn't quite ready to give it up.

The faint sound of John's rooster could be heard outside.

Lexi craned her head and looked at the nearest window; there she saw the morning's first light beaming through the thin metal blinds.

She turned back to John and said, "What do you want from me?"

"Nothing really, but if you're going to stay here, I'd like to know who you are, at least. I don't need to know the gory details. I'm just an old man who likes to know who I'm talking to. I look at it this way, before I lived my life not concerned about other people. I was one of those people who never listened to anyone. In a conversation, I took the time the other used to talk to think about what I was going to say. I never truly listened," John said, and then paused to think. "You know, that's probably why my marriage failed. I never listened; all I did was talk and talk."

"Like now?" Lexi joked.

John smiled and said, "Yes, like now. I'll just finish with this. After everything happened, I decided to listen. I finally told myself that life is fragile and all this can end at anytime, so why not take the time to get to know people. Everyone has a story."

Lexi sat staring at John as a feeling of sadness came over her. Not one to show her emotions anymore, she decided to respond in a gentler way than her typical crass self. "Fine, sounds like a fair deal. You're feeding and sheltering me, the least I could do is tell you who I am. The thing is, it's not exciting. In fact, it's downright boring, and the other shit that happened after was just plain horrid. But if telling you my boring story gets me another drink or two, I can do that," she said. A smile broke her stoic face.

John too smiled and looked at the young woman who sat in front of him. If he had to guess, he'd say she was in her late twenties. Her choppy and unevenly cut hair looked like it had been blonde once, but her dark brown roots had grown out so long that what remained of the blonde was now just on the tips. Her body was not skinny but slender with lean muscle. Her eyes were a light brown and her skin was a golden tan from the sun. Across her face, hands and arms he could see signs of cuts and bruising, she had definitely been fighting her way from wherever she came.

He slid the glass back to her, pulled the cork on the

Grey Goose and poured her another shot.

She grabbed the glass quickly and was about to slam it down when he interrupted her.

"Hold on, sweetheart. What are we toasting to this time?"

Lexi again smiled and her answer came quickly. "Let's drink to getting to know one another."

"I like that."

They tapped glasses and drank.

Like before, she slammed the shot glass down and wiped her face. She could feel the effects from the vodka. "You have anything to snack on?"

"I can make some breakfast."

"I'm not a high-maintenance person, just a bag of chips or something will do."

"I wish, I ran out of…wait a minute, hold on," John said and quickly went into the back.

Lexi took the time of his absence to look around the bar. Her previous self would never have gone into a place like this, it would have been too 'redneck' or 'white trash' for her. Her past life was filled with nightclubs or trendy hip places. She never was one for dive bars and or family-type bar and grilles, like the Mohawk. She spun on the stool till it faced a jukebox; without walking to see the playlist, she had a good guess the type of music that it held.

John returned almost giddy with excitement. "I almost forgot I had these," he said, holding up a large family-sized bag of Cool Ranch Doritos.

"No wayyyy!" She squealed like a kid.

"Yes, way."

"They're, like, my favorite."

"Mine too." He laughed.

"You, my friend, are definitely not a fucking idiot, you're the man!" she said loudly, barely able to restrain her excitement.

"And if you don't like that flavor, I also have…" He pulled a bag of regular nacho from behind his back.

"I'm not even high and I think I can eat a whole bag myself," Lexi excitedly said.

"Help yourself," John said as he opened both bags and placed them on the bar.

Lexi dove right into the chips. The texture and crispiness of the chips was still there. She only imagined they were past due, but she couldn't tell if the quality was inferior. Maybe it was because she hadn't had one in so long or she had forgotten how they tasted before.

"If you pull a Twinkie or HoHo out of your ass, I think I might have sex with you," Lexi joked.

"As a matter of fact…"

"No shit?" she muttered, pieces of chips falling out of her open mouth.

John turned to leave, stopped, turned back around and said, "Joking."

"I was joking too. I wouldn't have sex with you, sorry. You're just a bit too old for me," Lexi said, stuffing a handful of chips into her mouth.

"Ha, sorry, sweetie, I look at you as the daughter type."

"Since you want to talk about who we are, you go

first," Lexi urged.

"Nope, you go; I'm providing the feast and refreshments."

Filling her mouth with a few more chips, she began.

"I was born and raised in a not-so-shitty little town called La Jolla to a bitch of a mother who cared more about her next dinner party or socialite function than taking care of me or my sister. I have to laugh now; we were more like props for her. We were raised by a series of nannies over the years."

John just watched Lexi talk and all he could think was how someone could not love their children. He didn't have the experience, but he felt deep down that if he and his ex had had children, he would have loved them so deeply and given them everything.

"My mom was such a bitch she drove my dad away when I was six; my sister was a baby. He couldn't take her shit anymore."

"I'm sorry."

"I am too, I loved my dad. He won custody of us, but was killed in a small plane crash not two weeks later." She hesitated as she dreamt about the life she could have had. "Who dies in plane crashes? I mean, the odds are so slim that it was like fate said I was fucked from birth. God wasn't about to let me and Carey have a normal life."

"I don't think God—"

Lexi interrupted him, "No preaching, okay. I don't care if you believe in God, but any God that would allow children to be mistreated and this shit to happen can't be the nicest guy."

John cracked a grin and said, "Fair enough."

"Pour me another shot."

John obliged and listened through two more shots as she described her school days. He just looked at her and thought that deep down was a little girl who had been hurt tremendously throughout life. She had grown up relatively wealthy, but a child didn't really care about those things. A child values time and attention above all else. There she lived a life of poverty, one void of the love and nurturing a child needs from a parent. From what he gathered, she and her sister, Carey, had a very close relationship. Not wanting to leave her sister, she went to college locally. Then as if following a script of disappointment, her sister graduated high school and moved away to go to college. This deeply disappointed Lexi, but like a parent, she accepted it and decided that Carey was now old enough to take care of herself.

After her sister left, Lexi's life fell into a shallow and rhythmic repetition of work and partying with *friends*. With no goals or aspirations, all she had to look forward to was the next party. The relationship with her mother was estranged, they'd see each other for holidays, but Lexi couldn't wait to get to the bar and forget her life. Intimate relationships were nonexistent for her, with men coming in and out of her life quickly. When a man would show any sincere interest in her, she'd get rid of him. It wasn't that she didn't trust them, she didn't trust fate. Putting faith in love meant that she'd have to be vulnerable, and like other things in life, what happiness she'd experience would be wiped out by the pain of when that person would leave or disappoint her. Lacking any real connection other than Carey, she'd count the days until Carey would come into town.

John just listened. After first making a brief comment and seeing Lexi's irritated response, he just sat and didn't say another word. He filled her glass every now and then, but after a couple more, she slowed her drinking as she lost herself in telling her own story.

Her long diatribe stopped when she mentioned her sister's last visit. Shortly after that, the lights went out and the world changed forever. She sat, looked at her glass and drank it down swiftly.

John went to pour another, but she said, "I'll be right back." She abruptly stood, steadied herself from the alcohol-induced vertigo and marched towards the bathroom.

Lexi couldn't get to the bathroom quick enough; it was if she was having an anxiety attack. She hadn't told anyone so much. Opening up and being honest about who she was and where she came from was not a strong suit for her. She never had friends who took that type of interest. In fact, she liked them for that very reason. She had discovered it was easier to keep people at a distance because if she got to truly know someone, she would find herself not liking them.

When she walked back into the bar, John wasn't there. She looked around but couldn't find him. A loud clanging from the kitchen drew her attention; there she found him cracking eggs into a large skillet.

"Hey, you took a while in there."

She leaned up against the wall and joked, "Must have been those Doritos."

"You like fried eggs? I thought you could use some protein," he said as he looked over the eggs cooking.

"Love eggs, thanks. So, what's your story?"

"Not much to tell. Born just a few miles away, went to the local high school, married my high school sweetheart, got a job working for a lumber company but always wanted a place like this. My wife had other plans for her life; living in a small town became too much for her. She left me years ago, and instead of remarrying, I got this place. This here and all the loyal patrons have been my family since then."

"No kids?"

"Nope, never was lucky enough."

"Count your blessings. Believe me, we're pains in the asses."

"Oh, I don't believe that," he said as he gently slid a couple eggs on a plate.

She took the plate from him and smiled when she saw they were perfectly cooked sunny-side up.

He walked back and was cracking a couple more eggs for himself when she said, "Thanks, John."

"You're welcome, sweetie."

Lexi watched him work diligently. His large wrinkled hands firmly holding the spatula and the stained white apron tied around his waist made him look like a professional short-order cook, which in many ways he was, being the owner of a bar and grill.

"Anyone work for you?"

"Yeah, but I haven't seen them for weeks now. I heard they went to Portland."

With so much horror and cruelty in the world, here was a man who was gentle, sweet and generous. It was refreshing to meet someone like him.

Her journey since the EMP attack had destroyed the power grid and brought society to its knees had shown her extreme examples of good and bad. It was as if when the rule of law and the blanket of legal consequences were ripped away, those who were deeply flawed or evil people exposed themselves. They were always there, but without the threat of arrest, they took to the streets. This also played out on the opposite side as well, with many good people willing to risk and sacrifice. Even though she had experienced both, Lexi kept her guard up.

She looked down at the eggs again. The special attention and consideration to not just make eggs for her but to make them sunny-side up said a lot about John. She liked him.

"You better go eat those before they get cold. Utensils are just to the left of the cash register."

Lexi left the kitchen, grabbed a fork and sat down. She went to poke the yolks but again looked at them. Never could she remember her mother doing this for her, but early memories of her father popped into her head. Her father was a busy man and was typically gone by the time she woke during the week, but her weekends were always special occasions. Not a Saturday would go by where she didn't have something special cooked for her;

pancakes, French toast or sunny-side up eggs was the typical fare on the menu. When her father moved out, she still got to experience this but less, as he only had her and Carey every other weekend. She resented her mother for driving her father away then denying him full access. It wasn't that she cared, it was done more out of spite and so she could get more money. However, her father was clever and, of course, had a great attorney. He eventually won full custody, but then life showed up and he was lost forever. When the thought of her father dying came to mind, she dashed it while simultaneously slashing the yolks with the fork.

John came out from the kitchen and said, "Good?"

"Yeah, they're great, thanks," she said, grabbing the bottle and pouring another shot.

"You're quite the drinker. How old are you?"

"Just turned twenty-nine, but I feel like I've lived three lives."

"Tell me about it," John said, tossing the apron on the bar and walking around to the front of the bar and taking a seat on a stool next to her.

She liked him, but when he sat not two feet from her, she reacted by scooting down a few inches.

John noticed and said, "Sorry."

Brushing off his apology, she asked, "So that's it for you, this place?"

"Ha, well, don't put it like that! That sounds so negative."

"Sorry, that didn't come off the way I was intending."

"So you meet anyone as great as me on your journey?" he jokingly asked.

"No one as *great* as you, John! You're one of a kind."

"I wouldn't think so," he said, winking at her.

"You're a good guy and I have met other good people too, but they come and go."

"People just passing or you just passing through?"

"Both, but some just die. I'm fucking cursed, I think. I've been lucky. Had some good people help me and Carey, but shit just happens out there. You know, I can't believe shit hasn't gone down here."

"We've had some troubles but probably nothing to compare to what you've seen."

Lexi only nodded and continued to eat her eggs.

"Can I ask you something?"

"Oh shit, here it comes."

"Where's your sister? You talked so highly of her and mentioned she was with you before the attack."

Lexi turned and looked at him hard. "Some motherfucker murdered her. He thrust a knife deep into her chest."

John choked down his food and felt awkward about asking. "I, ah…"

"You asked and that's what happened. So you want to know why I'm here, sitting at your bar, eating your eggs and drinking your booze? This is a pit stop on my way to go kill that piece of shit."

"Is he nearby?"

"He's somewhere in Oregon, I know that."

"What's his name?"

"I doubt you know him, but his name is Rahab. He's the leader of a cult that Carey and I ran into in the California desert."

John thought for a moment to see if that name rang a bell, but it didn't.

"What happened?" John asked, knowing the question would elicit a charged response, but now he was curious as to what happened to this young woman.

"My sister had always been, I hate to say it, but the dumb one in the family. She always looked at life through rose-tinted glasses and went around without a damn care. It's so strange to think that we both came from the same DNA. She was always hurting herself. You know that person, the one that shit always happens to, not bad, but she was the one who always spilled her drink or made a mess. That was her."

John went back to listening as he slowly ate his eggs.

"She was always the one bringing lost dogs home, shit like that. But something changed in her after we were taken by Rahab and his people. She, for once, didn't just let things happen to her without thought. She decided then to take a stand, but that wasn't the time," Lexi said, pausing. She looked off in thought. "Her timing was always the worst." This comment was more of a thought expressed out loud. Her mind now swam with thoughts of her little sister. "Do you know that type of person, the one that shit always happens to?"

John nodded.

"She managed to get two weeks off for Thanksgiving. Of course, her luggage gets lost the moment she arrives and other assorted BS happens when she's in town. I have to laugh now, but I wasn't laughing then," she said, looking down, her mind going over the situations that frustrated her then. She longed for those moments, no matter how difficult or annoying they were. "You know, I'd do anything to have my sister and all her klutziness. I miss her, a lot."

John poured her another shot and slid it over.

Lexi grabbed it but stopped short of tossing it back. "For all her faults, my sister had a good heart and occasionally gave good advice." Lexi drank the shot and pushed the glass away from her.

"I know it doesn't mean much, but I'm sorry for your loss."

Lexi cocked her head and said, "I am too, but I have purpose now."

"Oh yeah, what's that?"

"Finding Rahab and his people and stopping them."

"Any other family?" John asked, shifting the conversation to something he hoped was less emotional.

Lexi paused and grunted. "Nope, some cousins sprinkled here and there, but I was never close with them."

"Friends?"

"Nope…well, I wouldn't call them friends, but they helped me escape from Rahab. They even invited me to go to Idaho; apparently they have a safe haven up there."

"Why not go?"

"Maybe, they were really nice people. Who knows, one day, we'll see," Lexi said, putting her head in her hands and slowly running her fingers through her hair. "Timing really is everything in life."

"I guess so."

"No, it is. Timing put me on the road outside of town so those Marines could help me. It also put me on the road headed to Vegas when we encountered Rahab's people. It's everything in life. Just take a minute away here or there and it changes the outcome."

John nodded as he thought about it.

"Carey was supposed to fly back on the fourth, but she stayed because of me. She still might be alive if it wasn't for me."

"Or not," John said.

"Or might still be," Lexi countered sternly, not wanting John to deviate from the *story* she had told herself.

"You can't blame yourself."

"Of course I can and I always will. I was such an idiot then," Lexi said, slurring.

"Why did she stay?" John asked.

"She stayed to celebrate or at least that's what I called it," Lexi said. She gave John a look and grinned. "I know it might be hard to believe, but I used to be a big partier."

John raised his eyebrows and chuckled. "You don't say."

"I have a reason to drink now, it helps me forget, but back then I drank to just have fun."

He knew that wasn't true one bit.

"Are you sure you want me to continue my sad

story?"

"It can't be all sad."

"Trust me, it is. This isn't directed at you per se, but why do men think they can take advantage of women?"

"What do you mean?"

"Just that men think women are objects to be fondled, fucked and discarded. It sickens me, and you know what, it was a man, a sick, depraved and perverted fuck that started this roller coaster for me. In fact, this man set me and Carey on the path that led to me sitting right here."

"Rahab was his name, right?"

"No, no, this was before Rahab. The piece of shit I'm referring to was my old boss."

John poured her another drink and pushed it towards her.

Lexi only looked at the glistening shot glass. The clear liquid looked inviting, but she withheld the temptation to drink. "You look at me and think you might know me, but I was a different woman not long ago. I was the typical Southern California blonde party girl with no real ambition or goals unless it led me to a rave, bar or house party. Looking back now, I wish I had prepared more. My life before was pointless and a massive waste of time. Anytime I encountered someone talking about being prepared, I gave them the standard eye roll. How could I have ever thought this whole fucking world would fall apart? Who knows this shit?"

"A few did."

Lexi shook her head and lamented, "I really wish I

was more prepared, maybe I could have saved Carey. And I made so many stupid mistakes and then there's the bad luck," she said, holding her head low. She pressed her eyes closed and exhaled heavily.

John felt sorry for her. He hadn't lost anyone and his knowledge of the outside world was limited.

She lifted her head, grabbed the shot and poured it down her throat. Holding the glass in her left hand, she pointed it at John and said, "I can tell you this, I will never ever allow anyone, man or woman, to take advantage of me or any other innocent again."

"That's honorable."

She shot John a look and snapped, "Honor has nothing to do with it."

"So this former boss, what happened? What did he do?"

Lexi slid the glass back and said, "Fill it up and I'll tell you."

READ AN EXCERPT OF THE NEW G. MICHAEL HOPF BOOK AVAILABLE NOW

EXIT: THE VAN ZANDT CHRONICLES

JANUARY 22, 2015

"The hardest thing to learn in life is which bridge to cross and which to burn." – David Russell

Outside Bishop, CA

"Hunter! Hunter! No!" Gordon cried out as he tossed and turned in his sleep. His sweat soaked shirt clung tightly to his lean muscular torso and the white bandage that covered the slash on his face absorbed the building sweat from his brow.

Every night since witnessing the brutal murder of Hunter he had the same nightmare. Like a horror movie that replayed only it's most grisly scenes his subconscious mind subjected him nightly to the same shocking and grotesque moments from that day.

The first time Gordon had his nightmare, Brittany tried to wake him. It took her that one shove to realize it was best to allow him to process his demons and that called for leaving him alone. She didn't know what haunted him but she had a good idea. He had only shared tidbits of his past. She knew he came from San Diego, had been a Marine once and that Idaho was their destination. Having lost her husband to the barbarism of the new world she could understand why someone wouldn't openly share the loss of loved ones because doing so brought back the memories of their passing. She didn't want to relive it so didn't press him on his past. The gold band on his ring told her he was married and the name Hunter made it clear he must have had a family. The fact that he was alone gave her the impression they were dead.

Gordon roughly turned and mumbled out loud, "Don't do this! Don't do this!"

She looked at him and frowned with sorrow because the pain he was experiencing was painful to watch.

"Don't do this!" Gordon whimpered, tears streamed down his face.

Brittany reached out to touch him, but stopped short when her son, Tyler said, "Don't, Mom, remember what happened last night?"

"Your right, I just feel so sorry for him."

His dreams were tormenting him and when he began to shed tears a natural urge to embrace him came over her. She didn't know him well, but her brief time told her he was a good man.

They had been together for four days and he only showed caring and compassion. Never once did he make a sexual advance and the way he was with, Tyler was great.

He took time to engage him and showed a true desire to help.

Tyler was like Gordon. He had witnessed the murder of his father and it ate away at the young boy causing him also to have a tough time sleeping.

"Mom, is he okay?" Tyler asked from the soft but worn sofa that he called his bed.

"I think he just saw some bad stuff," Brittany replied.

Gordon thought this best to keep everyone close as a precaution, so all three were sleeping in the same room of an abandoned house they had found the day before.

Not one to need a break he had to find a place to rest. The large cut on his face had become incredibly painful, to the point of making it difficult for him to do much. He tried to suck it up but couldn't.

Brittany was supportive of the decision to stop as she could see Gordon was suffering and she felt his wound had become infected.

"No, no, no!" Gordon cried out.

Tyler got up from the old sofa he called his bed and came over to Brittany who was laying on a mattress tossed on the floor.

"Close your eyes!" Gordon cried out.

Tyler snuggled closer to Brittany who brought him in closer. Their eyes were fixated on Gordon as he shifted and twitched, his facial muscles contorting and his eyes rolling around behind his eyelids.

"He scares me a bit."

She sighed and said, "I think he's fine, he's just been through a lot."

"If he has dreams like this every night, we'll never get any sleep."

"You should try to sleep sweetheart," Brittany said looking at her watch. "Honey, close your eyes, it's five in the morning."

"I can't."

"How about I rub your head, you loved that as a little one?"

"I'm not a baby anymore, Mom."

"You'll always be my baby; I don't care how old you get."

Tyler lifted his head and asked, "Why don't you have dreams like that?"

She petted his head and replied, "Oh, I have nightmares too honey, we can't judge him. Something very bad must have happened to him."

"I feel sorry for him," Tyler softly said.

"I do too," Brittany said.

Deep in Gordon's mind the images flashed of Rahab holding the knife high above his gentle and sweet boy. He could see his son's beautiful face, his deep blue eyes and light brown, wispy hair.

"No, please, God, no," Gordon whimpered just before the final image of his nightmare came. Gordon's breathing increased as did his movements. His legs moved up and down along with his arms. "No!" he screamed out as he once again witnessed Rahab driving the blade deep into Hunter's chest. Like an electrical shock to the system, he woke. His exhaled heavily and sat up. Sweat streamed down his face and he looked around the room. His eyes were wide as he scanned the dimly lit space and not only adjusting his vision but reacquainting himself to the present.

Tyler clung to Brittany tight but neglected to bury his face into her side for fear he needed to keep an eye on Gordon. Unlike his mother, he was weary of Gordon and after his experiences with the other men couldn't come to trust a stranger, especially one who seemed troubled.

"You okay?" Brittany asked Gordon.

"Ahh, yeah, I'm fine, bad dream," Gordon replied looking slightly embarrassed to find they were watching him when he woke. The yellow glow from a propane lantern bounced their shadows off the walls.

Brittany smiled.

Gordon wiped his brow and tried to return with a grin but his face was racked with pain. He grimaced and clenched his fist in anger.

Brittany noticed this subtle move and asked, "You sure you're okay?"

"It's just my face, it hurts really bad. I've had one injury after another. I can't catch a damn…" he paused then continued, "Darn break."

Tussling Tyler's hair, Brittany laughed, "He's heard those words before. Unfortunately my husband liked to curse. He'd spend so much time alone and speaking only to guys that when he'd return from long runs it would take him a day to adjust to family life. So, Tyler here would get an earful of f-bombs, d-bombs and s-bombs."

"Men can have real potty mouths, that's for sure," Gordon said grinning out of one side of his mouth.

"Where's your family?" Tyler asked abruptly.

The question hit Gordon between the eyes. He recoiled and decided not to go there.

Brittany squeezed Tyler and admonished him, "Hey."

"Sorry, it's just that…" Tyler said.

"If he wants to share anything, let him," Brittany scolded.

Gordon gave them an awkward look and shifted off the question by asking another, "You have some Advil, don't you?"

Brittany got up and walked over to a small bag. She opened it and pulled out a bottle of Advil capsules. "Here," she said tossing it at him.

"Thanks," Gordon replied catching it and quickly opening it. He poured six into his hand and swallowed them with a large drink of water. He reached up and gently touched his face.

Brittany walked over and squatted in front of him.

He pulled back but she leaned in further. "Just hold still, I want to look at your wound."

"It's fine."

"No, it's not, your entire cheek, heck, the entire side of your face is swollen," she said and reached towards the bandage.

He pulled back again.

She cocked her head, smiled and softly said, "It's okay, Gordon, I won't bite. I'm here to help you."

Gordon looked into her blue eyes and could see truth there. He had already spent two days with them but after each nightmare, it would take him a bit of time to become trustworthy again. It was his choice to save them and their brief time together had only shown them to be nothing but nice people. Relenting to her request, he leaned towards her.

Using her fingernails, she pulled up the edges of the tape and began to pull it away from his face.

Days of sweat and grime made the adhesive gooey. As she pulled it pulled his swollen cheek with it.

Gordon grunted in pain but held steadfast so she could remove the soiled bandage.

It took her one quick glance at the first exposed stitching to see if was infected and badly.

The stitches were stretched taunt on the swollen skin.

When she removed it completely she bit her lip and flatly said, "As I thought, it's infected."

Gordon took notice of the lip biting and now knew it was some sort of unconscious habit she'd do when focusing on something intently. "Do we have anything?" he asked.

"Yeah, one second," she said and went for her bag. She dug through and pulled out a small first aid kit.

"What are you going to do?" he asked.

"I have to remove these stitches, clean the wound, and stitch it back up," she answered.

Tyler grew curious about the small medical procedure and sat up. He scooted a few feet closer.

Gordon understood the boy's curiosity and if he was going to learn the ways of the new world, he'd have to see just how to do what she was proposing. The question for him was she able to do what she proposed?

"Ah, have you done this sort of stuff before?"

She pulled out the suture kit and opened it. Wanting to display confidence she stopped what she was doing, looked at him squarely and replied, "Yes, I've done this before. Not a wound the size of that, but I stitched up my husband's leg before on a hiking trip."

"So, just that one time?" Gordon asked.

"Yep, that's it, I'm not an expert but it needs to be done."

Resigned to the fact she was right and that he could feel the swelling and the intense pain caused from the infection he gave in and stopped asking questions. "Do what you need to do."

"Do you want anything for the pain besides the ibuprofen?"

"A whiskey would work," Gordon cracked.

"Sorry."

"Just do it, I'll suck it up."

She prepped the wound and talked as she went. "If it gives any consolation, I do sew and know how to croquet. Oh, and I'm fast, within reason and did I mention considerate."

"Just get it over with."

Taking a pair of scissors and tweezers she went for the knot at the bottom of the cut. Stopping just before clipping the tip she hesitated, "Now you're not going to punch me or anything if this hurts?"

"No."

"I'm not joking by the way, I've seen you thrashing and after trying to wake you before I don't want to be on the receiving end of one of your punches."

"I don't hit women."

She winked at him and joked, "Never said you did, but sometimes people react differently to pain than others."

A bit irritated, Gordon said, "Can you please just get this over with. My face hurts and I need this cleaned up."

"Okie dokie, here I go and it's best you don't talk anymore," Brittany suggested.

He nodded with his eyes.

Tyler crept over until he was an arm's length away.

Out of the corner of his eye, Gordon watched him look at his mother remove the old scab crusted stitches. When one would tug at the skin or thick scab he'd flinch or blink heavily, but for the most part he took it all in like a first year med student.

With precision and care, she removed the old stitches, cleaned the festering wound, applied antibacterial ointments and sewed it back up.

Gordon closed his eyes shortly after she began and drifted into a meditative state with the hopes of finding comfort from the physical pain. It worked for the most part, but his mind quickly replayed the images of Hunter. For him there was no escape from the emotional pain of losing Hunter, but the anger sat just below it and it too festered. The hatred and anger ate away at him and when he was awake and able to control his thoughts, he'd consciously push Hunter's face away and bring Rahab's forward. He could not allow himself to forget Rahab. He needed to remember each detail until he found him and then only after he destroyed him could he move past and forget.

"All done," Brittany said, a smile etched across her freckled face. She was proud of herself for taking care of Gordon. She had done one small stitch years ago but this was different. Someone needed her for their possible survival and she had been there for them.

After losing her husband she feared she may not survive but that all changed when they ran into Gordon and he handed her that pistol. Right then her destiny changed. She used that simple weapon to make herself equal with someone who was much bigger and stronger. She had leveled the playing field a little that day and now she was mending large wounds. Not getting to cocky but she was beginning to feel like a survivor.

Tyler didn't look away the entire time and even asked questions. He wanted to learn and for Brittany that was important. Gone for him were the days of innocence, birthday parties and video games. He'd be forced to grow up fast and if he was to survive he needed skills.

She cleaned the scissors, tweezers and needle as well as her hands then put everything back in the precise spot of the suture kit and put it back in the bag.

"Well, how do you feel?"

"Better, but I still feel like crap," Gordon replied honestly. He raised his hand and touched the fresh white bandage. His cheek was still swollen but it did feel better than before she cleaned it.

"Lay back, get some rest," Brittany said.

He looked outside and saw the morning sun was making its appearance. Ignoring what she said he made his way towards the back of the house. He hadn't relieved himself yet and the urge was strong. On his way he caught his reflection on a hall mirror. He stopped and looked at himself. The circles under his eyes were deep and dark. His face looked lean and the skin not covered by the bandage looked tanned and weathered. His face was covered with thick brown and gray stubble, with the gray more prominent than ever before. When his cut finally healed it would complement the other scars that graced his face. In fact his body was becoming a showcase of scars. It seemed the second he would heal, he'd get injured again. He wondered how much his body could take before it would finally break. Before the lights went out he would joke with Samantha that he felt old because his joints creaked and cracked just simply walking down the stairwell of their two story house. Now his body was in a permanent state of pain or injury, but his will to survive was strong. The only thing stronger was his will to avenge Hunter.

Back inside, Gordon strode into the room and said, "We should hit the road." He then noticed they both were sleeping and deeply by the heavy sounds of their breath.

Brittany was lying on her side cradling Tyler in her arms.

Gordon at first wanted to wake them but stopped short of doing so. There wasn't any doubt that his restless sleep was impacting them and if they were going to be good traveling companions he needed them tan, rested and ready as he used to say in the Marine Corps. Resigned to the fact he wasn't leaving just then, he grabbed his rifle and took up a position near a large window that overlooked the front yard.

Looking out his thoughts drifted to Samantha and Haley. He wondered where they were and prayed Nelson was keeping them safe. Regret about his decision to leave swept over him but he pushed it away. It wasn't that he believed they would be okay without him; he knew the risk but still did it. He stubbornly left his family in the hands of another man so he could go out and avenge another part of his family. Was it an easy decision? No, but one that had to be made he convinced himself. He knew how persuasive Samantha was, she was the master at communication and without any doubt she could talk him into doing most things. If he had returned he'd never be able to leave and the regret of leaving Rahab alive would haunt him forever. It had to be done the way he did it he thought. There was no time to wait. If he was going to catch Rahab before he vanished into the tapestry of the new world, he needed to go for him now. Each time his pragmatic side deemed his mission righteous his sentimental side would counter with one question, would his family be there when he returned? It was that simple question that struck him every time like a dagger to his heart.

ABOUT THE AUTHOR

G. Michael Hopf is the best-selling author of THE NEW WORLD series and three others books. He spent two decades living a life of adventure before he settled down and became a novelist full time. He is a combat veteran of the Marine Corps and former executive protection agent.
He lives with his family in San Diego, CA
Please feel free to contact him at geoff@gmichaelhopf.com with any questions or comments.
www.gmichaelhopf.com
www.facebook.com/gmichaelhopf

Books by G. MICHAEL HOPF

THE NEW WORLD SERIES

THE END
THE LONG ROAD
SANCTUARY
THE LINE OF DEPARTURE
BLOOD, SWEAT & TEARS

NEMESIS TRILOGY

NEMESIS: INCEPTION

DETACHMENT TRILOGY

DETACHMENT: BOOK ONE

THE VAN ZANDT CHRONICLES

EXIT

G. MICHAEL HOPF

Made in the USA
San Bernardino, CA
01 May 2016